JUNICHIRO TANIZAKI

The Key AND
Diary of a Mad Old Man

Junichiro Tanizaki was born in Tokyo in 1886 and lived there until the earthquake of 1923, when he moved to the Kyoto-Osaka region, the scene of *The Makioka Sisters*. By 1930 he had gained such renown that an edition of his complete works was published. Author of more than twelve novels, he was awarded Japan's Imperial Prize in Literature in 1949. Tanizaki died in 1965.

INTERNATIONAL

BOOKS BY
JUNICHIRO TANIZAKI

FICTION

Quicksand

The Reed Cutter and
Captain Shigemoto's Mother

Naomi

*The Secret History of the Lord
of Musashi* and *Arrowroot*

Diary of a Mad Old Man

Seven Japanese Tales

The Key

The Makioka Sisters

Some Prefer Nettles

NONFICTION

In Praise of Shadows

❀

The Key

AND

Diary of a Mad Old Man

❀

JUNICHIRO TANIZAKI

❀

The Key

AND

Diary of a Mad Old Man

❀

TRANSLATED FROM THE JAPANESE
BY HOWARD HIBBETT

Vintage International
VINTAGE BOOKS
A DIVISION OF RANDOM HOUSE, INC.
NEW YORK

CONTENTS

The Key

New Year's Day

❁

This year I intend to begin writing freely about a topic which, in the past, I have hesitated even to mention here. I have always avoided commenting on my sexual relations with Ikuko, for fear that she might surreptitiously read my diary and be offended. I dare say she knows exactly where to find it. But I have decided not to worry about that any more. Of course, her old-fashioned Kyoto upbringing has left her with a good deal of antiquated morality; indeed, she rather prides herself on it. It seems unlikely that she would dip into her husband's private writings. However, that is not altogether out of the question. If now, for the first time, my diary becomes chiefly concerned with our sexual life, will she be able to resist the temptation? By nature she is furtive, fond of secrets, constantly holding back and pretending ignorance; worst of all, she regards that as feminine modesty. Even though I have several hiding places for the key to the locked drawer where I keep this book, such a woman may well have searched out all of them. For that matter, you could easily buy a duplicate of the key.

I have just said I've decided not to worry, but perhaps I really stopped worrying long ago. Secretly, I may have accepted, even hoped, that she was reading it. Then why do I lock the drawer and hide the key? Possibly to satisfy her weakness for spying. Besides, if I leave it where she is likely to see it, she may think: "This was written for my benefit," and not be willing to trust what I say. She may even think: "His real diary is somewhere else."

Ikuko, my beloved wife! I don't know whether or not you will read this. There is no use asking, since you would surely say that you don't do such things. But if you *should*, please believe that this is no fabrication, that every word of it is sincere. I won't insist any further—that would seem all the more suspicious. The diary itself will bear witness to its own truth.

Naturally I won't confine myself to things she would like to hear. I must not avoid matters that she will find unpleasant, even painful. The reason why I have felt

obliged to write about these things is her extreme reticence—her "refinement," her "femininity," the so-called
modesty that makes her ashamed to discuss anything of
an intimate nature with me, or to listen on the rare occa-
sions when I try to tell a risqué story. Even now, after
more than twenty years of marriage, with a daughter herself old enough to marry, she refuses to do more than perform the act in silence. Never to whisper a few soft,
loving words as we lie in each other's arms—is that a real
marriage? I am writing out of frustration at never having
a chance to talk to her about our sexual problems. From
now on, whether she reads this or not, I shall assume that
she does, and that I am talking to her indirectly.

Above all, I want to say that I love her. I have said this
often enough before, and it is true, as I think she realizes.
Only, my physical stamina is no match for hers. This year
I will be fifty-five (she must be forty-four), not a particularly decrepit age, yet somehow I find myself easily fatigued
by love-making. Once a week—once in ten days—is about
right for me. Being outspoken on a subject like this is
what she most dislikes; but the fact is, in spite of her weak
heart and rather frail health she is abnormally vigorous
in bed.

This is the one thing that is too much for me, that has
me quite at a loss. I know that I am inadequate as a husband, and yet—suppose she became involved with another
man. (She will be shocked at the very suggestion, and

accuse me of calling her immoral. But I am only saying "suppose.") That would be more than I could bear. It makes me jealous even to imagine such a thing. But really, out of consideration for her own health, shouldn't she make some attempt to curb her excessive appetites?

What bothers me most is that my energy is steadily declining. Lately, sexual intercourse leaves me exhausted. All the rest of the day I am too worn out to think. . . . Still, if I were asked whether I dislike it, I would have to say no, quite the opposite. My response to her is by no means reluctant; I never have to whip up my desire out of a sense of duty. For better or worse, I am passionately in love with her. And here I must make a disclosure that she will find abhorrent. I must tell her that she possesses a certain natural gift, of which she is completely unaware. Had I lacked experience with many other women I might have failed to recognize it. But I have been accustomed to such pleasure since my youth, and I know that her physical endowment for it is equaled by very few women. If she had been sold to one of those elegant brothels in the old Shimabara quarter, she would have been a sensation, a great celebrity; all the rakes in town would have clustered around her. (Perhaps I shouldn't mention this. At the very least, it may put me at a disadvantage. But will knowing about it please her, or make her feel ashamed, or perhaps insulted? Isn't she likely to feign anger, while secretly feeling proud?) The mere thought of that gift of hers arouses my jealousy. If by any chance another man knew of it, and knew that I am an unworthy partner, what would happen?

Thoughts of that kind disturb me, increase my sense of guilt toward her, till the feeling of self-reproach becomes intolerable. Then I do all I can to be more ardent. I ask her to kiss my eyelids, for example, since I am peculiarly sensitive to stimulation there. For my part, I do anything she seems to like—kiss her under the arms, or whatever—in order to stimulate her, and thus excite myself even more. But she doesn't respond. She stubbornly resists these "unnatural games," as if they had no place in conventional love-making. Although I try to explain that there is nothing wrong with this sort of foreplay, she clings to her "feminine modesty" and refuses to yield.

Moreover, she knows that I am something of a foot-fetishist, and that I admire her extraordinarily shapely feet—one can hardly think of them as belonging to a middle-aged woman. Still—or therefore—she seldom lets me see them. Even in the heat of summer she won't leave them bare. If I want to kiss her instep, she says "How filthy!" or "You shouldn't touch a place like that!" All in all, I find it harder then ever to deal with her.

To start off the New Year by recording my grievances seems rather petty of me, but I think it is best to put these things in writing. Tomorrow will be the "First Auspicious Night." Doubtless she will want us to be orthodox, to follow the time-honored custom. She will insist on a solemn observance of the annual rite.

January 4

❀

Today an odd thing happened. I've been neglecting my husband's study lately, and went to clean it this afternoon while he was out for a walk. And there on the floor, just in front of the bookshelf where I'd put a vase of daffodils, lay the key. Maybe it was only an accident. Yet I can't believe he dropped it out of sheer carelessness. That would be very unlike him. In all his years of keeping a diary he's never done anything of the kind.

Of course I've known about his diary for a long time. He locks it in the drawer of the writing table and hides the key somewhere among the books or under the carpet. But that's all I know, I don't care to know any more than that. I'd never dream of touching it. What hurts me, though, is that he's so suspicious. Apparently he doesn't feel safe unless he takes the trouble to lock it away and hide the key.

But then, why should he have dropped the key in a place like that? Has he changed his mind and decided he wants me to read it? Perhaps he realizes I'd refuse if he asked me to, so he's telling me: "You can read it in private—here's the key." Does that mean he thinks I haven't found it? No, isn't he saying, rather: "From now on I acknowledge that you're reading it, but I'll keep on pretending you're not"?

Well, never mind. Whatever he thinks, I shall never read it. I haven't the faintest desire to penetrate his psychology, beyond the limits I've set for myself. I don't like to let others know what is in my own mind, and I don't care to pry into theirs. Besides, if he wants to show it to me I can hardly believe what it says. I don't suppose reading it would be entirely pleasant for me, either.

My husband may write and think what he pleases, and I'll do the same. This year I'm beginning a diary of my own. Someone like me, someone who doesn't open her heart to others, needs to talk to herself, at least. But I won't make the mistake of letting him suspect what I'm up to. I've decided to wait until he goes out before I write, and to hide the book in a certain place that he'll never think of. In fact, one reason why keeping a diary appeals to me is that although I know exactly where to find his, he won't even realize I have one. That gives me a delicious sense of superiority.

Night before last we observed the old New Year's custom—but how shameful to put such a thing in writing! "Be true to your conscience," my father used to say. How he would grieve at the way I've been corrupted, if he only knew! . . . As usual, my husband seemed to have reached an ecstatic climax; as usual, I was left unsatisfied. I felt miserable afterward. He's always apologizing for his inadequacy, yet attacks me for being cold. What he means by cold is that, to put it his way, I'm far too "conventional," too "inhibited"—in short, too dull. At the same time, I'm "splendidly oversexed," he says, quite abnormally so; it's the one thing I'm not passive and reserved about. But he complains that for twenty years I've never been willing to deviate from the same method, the same position. And yet my unspoken advances never escape him; he's sensitive to the slightest hint, and knows immediately what I want. Maybe it's because he's afraid of my too-frequent demands.

He thinks I'm matter-of-fact and unromantic. "You don't love me half as much as I love you," he says. "You consider me a necessity, a defective one at that. If you really love me you ought to be more passionate. You ought to agree to anything I ask." According to him, it's partly my fault that he's not able to satisfy me fully. If I'd try to stir him up a bit he wouldn't be so inadequate. He says I won't make the slightest effort to co-operate with him—as hungry as I am, all I do is sit back calmly and wait to be served. He calls me a cold-blooded, spiteful female.

I suppose it's not unreasonable of him to think of me in that way. But my parents brought me up to believe that a woman ought to be quiet and demure, certainly never aggressive toward a man. It's not that I lack passion; in a woman of my temperament the passion lies deep within, too deep to erupt. The instant I try to force it out, it begins to fade. My husband can't seem to understand that mine is a pale, secret flame, not one that flares up brilliantly.

I've begun to think our marriage was a dreadful mistake. There must have been a better partner for me, and for him too; we simply can't agree in our sexual tastes. I married him because my parents wanted me to, and for all these years I've thought marriage was supposed to be like this. But now I have the feeling that I accepted a man who is utterly wrong for me. Of course I have to put up with him, since he's my lawful husband. Sometimes, though, the very sight of him makes me queasy. Yes, and that feeling isn't new. I had it the first night of our marriage, that long-ago honeymoon night when I first went to bed with him. I still remember how I winced when I saw his face after he'd taken off those thick-lensed glasses of his. People who wear glasses always look a little strange without them, but my husband's face seemed suddenly ashen, like a dead man's. Then he leaned down close, and I felt his eyes boring into me. I couldn't help staring back, blinking, and the moment I saw that smooth, slippery, waxy skin I winced again. Though I hadn't noticed it in the daytime, I could see a faint growth of beard under his nose and around his lips—he's inclined to be hairy—and that too made me feel vaguely ill.

Maybe it was because I'd never seen a man's face at such close range before, but even now I can't look at him that way for long without feeling the same revulsion. I turn off the bed lamp to avoid seeing him, but that's precisely when he wants it on. And then he wants to pore over my body, as minutely as possible. (I try to refuse him, but he's so persistent about my feet, in particular, that I have to let him look at them.) I've never been intimate with another man—I wonder if they all have such disgusting habits. Are those gross, sticky, nasty caresses what you have to expect from *all* men?

January 7

Today Kimura paid us a New Year's call. I had just started reading Faulkner's *Sanctuary*, and went back up to my study as soon as we had exchanged our greetings. He talked with my wife and Toshiko in the sitting room for a while, then, around three o'clock, took them out to the movies. He came back with them at six, stayed for dinner, and left after chatting till about nine.

At mealtime everyone except Toshiko had some brandy. Ikuko seems to be drinking a little more these days. I'm the one who initiated her, but from the first she has had a taste for it. If you urge her, she will drink a fair amount. It's true that she feels the effects of it, but in a sly, secret way, not letting it show. She suppresses her reaction so well that people often don't realize how much she's had. Tonight Kimura gave her several sherry glasses full. She turned a little pale, but didn't seem intoxicated. It was Kimura and I who became flushed. He doesn't hold his liquor very well—not as well as Ikuko, in fact. But wasn't tonight the first time she let another man persuade her to have a drink? He had offered one to Toshiko, who refused and said: "Give it to Mama."

For some time I have felt that Toshiko keeps aloof from Kimura. Is it because she thinks he is too attentive to her mother? That notion had also occurred to me; but I decided that I was being jealous, and tried to dismiss it. Perhaps I was right after all. Though my wife is usually cool toward guests, especially men, she is friendly enough to Kimura. None of us has mentioned it, but he rather resembles a certain American film actor—who seems to be her favorite. (I've noticed that she makes a point of seeing all his films.)

Of course I've had Kimura visit us often, because I consider him a possible match for Toshiko; and I've asked my wife to see how they get along together. However, Toshiko doesn't seem at all interested in him. She does her best to avoid being alone with him; whenever he comes to see her, even when they go out to the movies, she invariably asks her mother to join them.

"You spoil everything by trailing along," I tell Ikuko. "Let them go alone." But she disagrees, and says that as a mother it's her responsibility to accompany them. When I reply that her way of thinking is outmoded, that she ought to trust them, she admits I'm right—but says that Toshiko wants her along. Supposing she does, isn't it because she knows her mother likes him? Somehow I cannot help feeling that they have a tacit agreement about this. Although Ikuko may be unaware of it—may believe that she is merely acting as a chaperone—I think she finds Kimura extremely attractive.

January 8

❖

Last night I was a little intoxicated, but my husband was worse. He kept after me to kiss his eyes, something he hasn't insisted on lately. And I'd had just enough brandy to do it. That would have been all right, except that I happened to look at the one thing I can't bear—his gray, lifeless face after he's taken off those glasses. When I kiss him I close my eyes, but last night I opened them before I finished. His waxy skin loomed up before me like a wide-screen close-up. I winced. I felt my own face go pale. Luckily, he soon put his glasses back on, as usual to begin poring over me. I said nothing, and turned off the bed lamp. He stretched out his hand, trying to find the switch, but I pushed the lamp away. "Wait a minute!" he begged. "Let me have another look. Please . . . " He groped in the dark, but couldn't find the lamp, and at last gave up. . . . An unusually long embrace.

I violently dislike my husband, and just as violently love him. No matter how much he disgusts me I shall never give myself to another man. I couldn't possibly abandon my principles of right and wrong. Although I'm driven to my wit's end by his unhealthy, repulsive way of love-making, I can see he's still infatuated with me, and I feel that somehow I have to return his love.

If only he had more of his old vigor . . . Why has his vitality drained away? To listen to him, it's all my fault: I'm too demanding. Women can tolerate it, he says, but not men who work with their intellect: that kind of excess soon tells on them. He embarrasses me with such talk, but surely he knows I'm not to blame for my bodily needs. If he really loves me he ought to learn how to sat-isfy me. Yet I do hope he'll remember that I can't stand those revolting habits of his. Far from stimulating me, they spoil my mood. It's my nature to cling forever to the old customs, to want to perform the act blindly, in silence, buried beneath thick quilts in a dark, secluded bedroom. It's a terrible misfortune for a married couple's tastes to conflict so bitterly on this point. Is there no way we can come to an understanding?

January 13

❀

Kimura came over at about half-past four today, to bring us some mullet roe that his parents in Nagasaki had sent him. After chatting with Toshiko and Ikuko for an hour or so, he got up to leave. At that point I came down from my study and asked him to stay for dinner. He accepted at once, saying he would be delighted, and settled down comfortably. I went back upstairs while Toshiko prepared the meal. My wife remained in the sitting room with him.

We had nothing special to offer, except his mullet roe and some carp *sushi* that Ikuko bought at the Nishiki market yesterday. Soon we were having these tidbits as an appetizer, with brandy. Ikuko is fond of salty things, particularly carp *sushi*. I don't care for it, nor does Toshiko. Even Kimura, who likes such things, found it a little too strong for him.

Kimura has never brought us a present before today;

he seems to have been angling for an invitation to dinner. I wonder what he's after. Which one attracts him, Ikuko or Toshiko? If I were he, and had to say which of the two I found more attractive, I have no doubt that, despite her age, I would choose the mother. But I can't tell about him. Perhaps his real aim is to win Toshiko. Since she seems unenthusiastic, he may be trying to improve his chances by ingratiating himself with Ikuko. . . .

But what am I after, for that matter? Why did I have Kimura stay for dinner again this evening? I must admit that my own attitude has been rather strange. About a week ago, on the seventh, I already had a slight—perhaps not so slight—feeling of jealousy toward him. (Indeed, I think it began several weeks ago, before the end of the year.) Yet isn't it true that I secretly enjoyed it? Such feelings have always given me an erotic stimulus; in a sense, they're both necessary and pleasurable to me. That night, stimulated by jealousy, I succeeded in satisfying Ikuko. I realize that Kimura is becoming indispensable to our sexual life. However, I'd like to warn her, though I need scarcely say it, that she mustn't go too far with him. Not that there shouldn't be an element of danger—the more the better, in fact. I want her to make me insanely jealous. It's all right if she makes me suspicious that she *has* gone too far. I want her to do that.

Even so, she ought to realize that what I ask of her—as difficult, as outrageous as it may seem—is for the sake of her own happiness.

January 17

Kimura hasn't been back, but Ikuko and I drink brandy every evening now. With a little urging, she consumes a surprising amount of it. I like to watch her struggling to stay sober, looking cold and pale; there is something indescribably seductive about her at such times.

Of course my object is to get her drunk and go to bed with her; but why doesn't she yield gracefully? She becomes more and more perverse, won't let me touch her feet. But what she herself wants, she exacts.

January 20

❖

Today my head ached all day long. It wasn't quite a hang-over, though I must have had a little too much last night.

Mr. Kimura seems worried about my drinking. He doesn't like to see me take more than two glasses of brandy. "Don't you think you've had enough?" he asks, trying to discourage me. My husband, on the other hand, keeps offering me more. Apparently he knows my weakness for it, and means to give me all I want. But I've about reached my limit. So far I've managed to go on drinking without letting them see how intoxicated I've become; but I suffer from the aftereffects. I must be more cautious.

January 28

❀

Tonight Ikuko fainted. We were sitting around the dinner table with Kimura, when she suddenly got up and left the room. She didn't return, and Kimura asked if she might be ill. Knowing that she sometimes goes to hide in the lavatory when she's had too much to drink, I told him I thought she would be back soon. But she was gone so long that he became concerned, and went to look for her.

A moment later he called to Toshiko from the hallway, and asked her to come out. (Again tonight she had hurried through dinner and promptly retired to her room.) "I'm afraid something is wrong," he said. "I can't find your mother anywhere."

But Toshiko found her—found her lying in the deep wooden bathtub, soaking. She was clinging with both hands to the edge of the tub, her head resting on her hands, her eyes closed. Even when Toshiko tried to rouse her, she didn't stir.

Kimura rushed back to tell me. I went to see what was

wrong with her. The first thing I did was to take her pulse: it was feeble, beating at only about forty a minute. I undressed, got into the tub myself, picked her up, and carried her out to the adjoining dressing room, where I laid her down on the floor. Toshiko wrapped her in a large bath towel, and said: "I'll see that the bed is ready." Kimura was at a loss to know what to do; he kept fidgeting, darting in and out of the dressing room. When I asked him to help me, he seemed relieved.

"She'll catch cold if we don't dry her off quickly," I said. "Would you mind giving me a hand?" We dried her with fresh towels. (I hadn't forgotten to "use" Kimura. He did the upper half of her body, and I the lower. I was careful to wipe her thoroughly between her toes, and I told Kimura to do the same between her fingers. All the while I kept a sharp watch on him.)

Toshiko brought in a nightgown, but, when she saw Kimura helping, left at once "to get the hot-water bottle." We put Ikuko into the nightgown and carried her to the bedroom.

"It might be cerebral anemia," Kimura said. "Maybe we'd better not give her a hot-water bottle." The three of us discussed whether or not to call a doctor. I was willing to have Dr. Kodama, though I didn't like even him to see my wife in such a disgraceful state. However, because she has a weak heart, I finally asked him to come.

Dr. Kodama confirmed that her trouble was cerebral

anemia, but added: "There's no reason to worry." Then he gave her an injection of Vita-camphor. By the time he left, it was two a.m.

January 29

❀

I can remember everything that happened last night until the time when I began to feel sick and left the room. I can even dimly recall going for a bath, and fainting in the tub. I'm not sure what happened after that. When I woke up at dawn and looked around I found myself lying in bed. Someone must have carried me here. All day long my head has been so heavy I haven't felt like getting up. I've dozed on and on, waking for a moment and then drifting off into another dream. It's evening, and since I'm feeling a little better, I'm able to write this much. Now I'm going back to sleep.

January 29

❁

My wife hasn't been up since last night's incident. It was about midnight when Kimura and I carried her to the bedroom, half-past twelve when I called Dr. Kodama, and two o'clock when he left. I went to the door with him, and saw that it was a clear, starlit night, but extremely cold. Our bedroom stove usually keeps us comfortable till morning on a single scoopful of coal, which I throw in before I go to bed; last night, however, at Kimura's own suggestion, I had him fire it up enough to make the room quite warm.

"I'll be leaving, then, if there's nothing else I can do," he said.

I couldn't send him home at that hour. "Why not stay overnight?" I asked. "I can find somewhere for you to sleep."

"Please don't bother, sir," he said. "I haven't far to go." After helping me carry Ikuko in, he had stood waiting uneasily between our beds (I was sitting in the only chair). It occurs to me that Toshiko disappeared just as he came into the bedroom.

He insisted on going home, and left, as I had hoped he would. A certain plan had been taking shape in my mind for a long time, and I needed privacy to carry it out. Once I was sure he had gone, and that Toshiko wouldn't come in again, I went over and took Ikuko's pulse. It was normal: the Vita-camphor seemed to have worked. As far as I could tell, she was in a deep slumber. Of course she may have been only shamming. But that needn't hinder me, I thought.

I began by firing the stove up even hotter, till it was roaring. Then I slowly drew off the black cloth that I had draped over the shade of the floor lamp. Stealthily I moved the lamp to my wife's bedside, placing it so that she was lying within its circle of light. I felt my heart pound. I was excited to think that what I had so long dreamed of was about to be realized.

Next, I quietly went upstairs to get the fluorescent lamp from my study, brought it back, and put it on the night table. This was by no means a sudden whim. Last fall I replaced my old desk lamp with a fluorescent one, because I foresaw that I might sooner or later have a chance like this. Toshiko and my wife were opposed to it at the time, saying it would affect the radio; but I told them that my eyesight was weakening and the old lamp was hard to read by—which was quite true. However, my real reason was a desire to see Ikuko's naked body in that white radiance. That had been my fantasy ever since I had first heard of fluorescent lighting.

Everything went as I had hoped. I took away her covers, carefully slipped her thin nightgown off, and turned her on her back. She lay there completely naked, exposed to the daylight brilliance of the two lamps. Then I began to study her in detail, as if I were studying a map. For a while, as I gazed on that beautiful, milk-white body, I felt bewildered. It was the first time I had ever had an unimpeded view of her in the nude.

I suppose the average husband is familiar with all the details of his wife's body, down to the very wrinkles on the soles of her feet. But Ikuko has never let me examine her that way. Of course in love-making I have had certain opportunities—but never below the waist, never more than she had to let me see. Only by touch have I been able to picture to myself the beauty of her body, which is why I wanted so desperately to look at her under that brilliant light. And what I saw far exceeded my expectations.

For the first time I was able to enjoy a full view of her, able to explore all her long-hidden secrets. Ikuko, who was born in 1911, doesn't have the tall, Western kind of figure so common among the young girls of today. Having been an expert swimmer and tennis player, she is well proportioned for a Japanese woman of her age; still, she is not particularly full-bosomed, nor sizable in the buttocks, either. Moreover, her legs, as long and graceful as they are, can hardly be called straight. They bulge out at the calves, and her ankles are not quite trim. But, rather than slim, foreign-looking legs, I have always liked the slightly bowed ones of the old-fashioned Japanese woman, such as my mother and my aunt. Those slender, pipestem legs are uninteresting. And instead of overdeveloped breasts and buttocks, I prefer the gently swelling lines of the Bodhisattva in the Chuguji Temple. I had supposed that my wife's body must be shaped like that, and it turned out that I was right.

What surpassed anything I had imagined was the utter purity of her skin. Most people have at least a minor flaw, some kind of dark spot, a birthmark, mole, or the like; but although I searched her body with the most scrupulous care, I could find no blemish. I turned her face down, and even peered into the hollow where the white flesh of her buttocks swelled up on either side. . . . How extraordinary for a woman to have reached the age of forty-four, and to have experienced childbirth, without suffering the slightest injury to her skin! Never before had I been allowed to gaze at this superb body, but perhaps that is just as well. To be startled, after more than twenty years together, by a first awareness of the physical beauty of one's own wife—that, surely, is to begin a new marriage. We have long since passed the stage of disillusionment, and now I can love her with twice the passion I used to have.

I turned her on her back once again. For a while I stood there, devouring her with my eyes. Suddenly it appeared to me that she was only pretending to be asleep. She had been asleep at first, but had awakened; then, shocked and horrified at what was going on, she had tried to conceal her embarrassment by shamming. . . . Perhaps it was merely my own fantasy, but I wanted to believe it. I was captivated by the idea that this exquisite, fair-skinned body, which I could manipulate as boldly as if it were lifeless, was very much alive, was conscious of everything I did. But suppose that she really *was* asleep—isn't it dangerous for me to write about how I indulged myself with her? I can scarcely doubt that she reads this diary, in which case my revelations may make her decide to stop drinking. . . . No, I don't think so; stopping would confirm that she *does* read it. Otherwise she wouldn't have known what went on while she was unconscious.

For over an hour, beginning at three o'clock, I steeped myself in the pleasure of looking at her. Of course that wasn't all I did. I wanted to find out how far she would let me go, if she were only pretending to be asleep. And I wanted to embarrass her to the point that she would have to continue her pretense to the very end. One by one I tried all the sexual vagaries that she so much loathes—all the tricks that she calls annoying, disgusting, shameful. At last I fulfilled my desire to lavish caresses with my tongue, as freely as I liked, on those beautiful feet. I tried everything I could imagine—things, to use her words, "too shameful to mention."

Once, curious to see how she would respond, I bent over to kiss an especially sensitive place—and happened to drop my glasses on her stomach. Her eyelids fluttered open for a moment, as if she had been startled awake. I was startled too, and hastily switched off the fluorescent lamp. Then I poured some drinking water into a cup, added hot water from the kettle on the stove till it was lukewarm, chewed up a tablet of Luminal and a half a tablet of Quadronox in a mouthful of it, and transferred the mixture directly from my mouth to hers. She swallowed it as if in a dream. Sometimes a dose of that size doesn't work; but I knew it would give her an excuse for pretending to be asleep.

As soon as I could see that she was sleeping (or at least shamming), I set out to accomplish my final purpose. Since I had already aroused myself to a state of intense excitement by the most thorough, unhampered preliminaries, I succeeded in performing the act with a vigor that quite astonished me. I was no longer my usual spineless, timid self, but a man powerful enough to subdue her lustfulness. From now on, I thought, I would have to get her drunk as often as possible.

And yet, in spite of the fact that she had had several orgasms, she still seemed to be only half awake. Occasionally she opened her eyes a little, but she would be looking off in another direction. Her hands were moving slowly, languidly, with the dreamlike movements of a somnambulist. Soon, what had never happened before, she began groping as if to explore my chest, arms, cheeks, neck, legs. . . . Up till now she had never touched or looked at any part of me that she could avoid.

It was then that Kimura's name escaped her lips. She said it in a kind of delirious murmur—faintly, very faintly indeed—but she certainly said it. I'm not sure whether she was really delirious or whether that was only a subterfuge. Was she dreaming of making love with Kimura, or was she telling me how much she longed to? Perhaps she was warning me never to humiliate her like this again.

Kimura telephoned around eight this evening to ask about Ikuko. "I should have stopped in to see how she was," he said.

"There's nothing to worry about," I told him. "I've given her a sedative, and she's still asleep."

January 30

❀

It's nine o'clock in the morning, and I haven't been out of bed since the night before last. This is Monday; my husband left the house about half an hour ago. Before leaving he tiptoed into the bedroom, but I pretended to be asleep. He listened to my breathing for a moment, kissed my feet again, and went out. Baya came to see how I was feeling. I had her bring me a hot towel. After washing my face briefly, I ordered some milk and a soft-boiled egg. When I asked about Toshiko I was told she was in her room. She didn't make an appearance, though.

I suppose I'm well enough to get up, but I've decided to stay here quietly and write in my diary instead. It's a good chance to think over what has happened. First of all, why on earth did I get so drunk Saturday night? I suppose my physical condition had something to do with it. Then, too, the brandy wasn't our usual Three Stars. My husband had brought home a new kind, a bottle of Courvoisier, "the Brandy of Napoleon." It was so delicious that I soon found I'd had too much. Since I don't like to be seen when I'm intoxicated, I've got into the habit of shutting myself up in the lavatory as soon as I begin to feel unsteady—and I had to again that evening. I must have stayed there twenty or thirty minutes. No, wasn't it closer to an hour, or even two? I didn't feel at all sick. Actually, I felt elated.

My mind was hazy, but it wasn't a complete blank; I remember a few things here and there. I can recall that my back and legs were so tired from squatting over the toilet that before I knew it I was leaning forward on both hands. My head sank down until it touched the floor. Then, feeling saturated with the smell of the lavatory, I got up and left. Maybe I meant to wash off the odor; maybe I simply didn't want to join the others while I was still unsteady. In any case, I seem to have gone directly to the bath and taken off my clothes. I say "seem" because it lingers in my mind like the events of an old dream; but I have no idea what happened after that. (I wonder if they called Dr. Kodama. There's adhesive tape on my upper right arm, so I must have had an injection.)

When I came to, I was in my bed, and early-morning sunlight was filtering into the room. It must have been around six o'clock, but I can't say I was fully conscious from then on. All day yesterday I had a splitting headache and felt my whole body sinking heavily, deeply down. Time after time I woke up and then dropped off to sleep again—no, I was never really awake or asleep; all day long I drifted between the two. My head was throbbing, but I kept finding myself in a strange world that made me forget the pain.

Surely *that* was a dream; but could a dream have been quite so vivid, so lifelike? At first I was amazed to feel myself reaching the climax of an excruciatingly keen pleasure, a kind of sensual fulfillment beyond anything I could expect from my husband. Soon, though, I knew that the man with whom I was in bed was not my husband. It was Kimura-san. Had he stayed overnight to help take care of me? Where had my husband gone? Was it all right for me to behave so immorally?

But the pleasure was too intense to let me dwell on such things. Never in more than twenty years of marriage had my husband given me an experience like that. How dull and monotonous it had always been—dreary, stale, leaving a disagreeable aftertaste. I realized that never before—not until that moment—had I known true sexual intercourse. Kimura-san had taught me. . . . Yet I realized, too, that I was partly dreaming. Somehow I was aware that the man embracing me only seemed to be Kimura-san, that he was actually my husband.

I suppose he carried me here from the bath that night, put me to bed, and then, since I was still unconscious, amused himself with me in all sorts of ways. Once, when he was kissing me roughly under my arms, I was startled awake. He had dropped his glasses on me; my eyes opened the instant I felt their chilly touch. All my clothes had been stripped off, and I was lying on my back, stark naked, exposed to a hideous glare of light. There were two lamps: the floor lamp and another—a fluorescent one—on the bedside table. (Possibly the brightness awakened me.) I lay there vacantly. He picked up his glasses and put them on; then, leaving my arms, he began kissing me further down, below my waist. I remember shrinking away instinctively as I groped for a blanket. He noticed I'd begun to stir, and pulled some covers over me. Then he turned off the fluorescent lamp and draped something over the other one.

We don't keep a fluorescent lamp in the bedroom: he had to bring it from his study. I feel myself blush to think how he must have enjoyed exploring my body under that glaring light. He must have seen places that even I have never looked at so closely. I'm sure I was left naked for hours; he'd fired the stove up till the room was suffocatingly warm so that I wouldn't catch cold—and wouldn't awaken. It makes me angry and ashamed to think what he did with me, though at the time what bothered me most was the throbbing ache in my head. He chewed up some tablets (probably sleeping pills) in a sip of water, and gave them to me mouth to mouth. I swallowed obediently, to get rid of the pain. Soon I began losing consciousness again, drifting off into a half-sleep.

And then I had the illusion of holding Kimura-san in my arms. But is "illusion" the right word for it? Doesn't that suggest something nebulous floating in the air, ready to fade out of sight at any moment? What I saw and felt was not so intangible, not just an illusion of holding him in my arms. Even now that sensation lingers in the flesh of my arms and thighs. It's entirely unlike the feel of my husband's embrace. With these arms I grasped Kimura-san's strong young arms as he pressed me tight against his firm, resilient body. I remember that his skin seemed dazzlingly fair, not the usual dark skin of a Japanese.

And I thought—I'm ashamed to confess it, though I'm sure my husband doesn't even know about this diary, much less read it—if only *he* could make me feel this way! Why can't he be like this? . . . Yet, oddly enough, I somehow knew all along that I was dreaming, or mingling dream and reality. I knew I was in my husband's arms, and that he only reminded me of Kimura-san. But the amazing thing is that I kept on having that feeling of pressure, of completion, a feeling I can't associate with him.

If it's the Courvoisier that brought me that illusion, I'd like to have it often. I'm grateful to my husband for the experience. Still, I wonder how much truth there was in my dream of Kimura-san. Why should he have appeared to me that way, since I've never seen him except when he's fully dressed? Is the real Kimura-san different from the one I've imagined? Sometime—not just in my imagination—I'd like to find out what he's *really* like.

January 30

❀

Kimura telephoned me at school today, shortly past noon, and asked how my wife was getting along. I told him that she was still asleep when I left the house, but that she seemed to be all right. And I suggested he come over for a drink this evening.

"For a drink!" he exclaimed. "Not after what happened the other night. If you'll excuse me for saying so, I think you and your wife ought to be a little more abstemious, sir. But I'll stop in to see how she is."

He arrived at four o'clock. Ikuko was up by then, and came to the sitting room. He said that he couldn't stay, but I insisted. "Let's have a drink to make up for last time," I told him. "You needn't be in such a hurry."

Ikuko was smiling too. Certainly she didn't show any disapproval. In fact, Kimura himself seemed to want to stay. I'm sure he didn't realize what had gone on in our bedroom after he left that night (I had even returned the fluorescent lamp to my study by the next morning); nor could he possibly have known that he had invaded my wife's fantasies, and had enraptured her. Yet why did he give the impression of being eager to have her drink again? He seemed to know what she wanted. If he *did* know, was it by intuition, or had she actually given him a hint? Only Toshiko looked displeased when the three of us began drinking. She finished her dinner quickly and went out.

Again tonight Ikuko left the room, hid in the lavatory, and then went to take a bath and collapsed in the tub. We usually heat the bath every other day, but she has told Baya that we would like it daily, for the present. Since Baya lives out, she fills the tub before going home, and one of us lights the gas under it. Tonight Ikuko lit it, just in time.

Everything happened exactly as it did the other night. Dr. Kodama came and gave her an injection of camphor; Toshiko slipped off somewhere; Kimura helped me with her, and then left. My own later actions were the same, too. Strangest of all, she murmured Kimura's name again—was she having that same dream, that same delusion, just as she had had before? Should I, perhaps, interpret it as a kind of ridicule?

February 9

❀

Today Toshiko asked if she could live away from home. She said she's been wanting a quiet place to study, and that a convenient one has just turned up. It was suggested to her by Madame Okada, an old Frenchwoman who used to be her teacher at Doshisha and who still gives her private lessons. Madame Okada's Japanese husband is bedridden with paralysis; she supports him by teaching French. Since his illness, though, she hasn't done much tutoring: Toshiko is the only student who comes to her home. The house isn't a large one, but they have no children, and they don't need the garden cottage that used to be her husband's study. If Toshiko cares to take it, Madame Okada will feel safer whenever she has to be away.

Nothing would please them more, it seems, than to have Toshiko as a tenant. They'll give her a telephone; she's to bring her piano if she likes (the floor beams can be strengthened by laying bricks); a passageway can even be added, quite easily, so that she'll have direct access to the lavatory and the bath, without having to go through the rest of the house. People seldom telephone them while Madame Okada is out. In any case, Toshiko is to pay no attention to such things; they'll see that she isn't bothered.

Besides all this, the rent will be very cheap. Toshiko has said she'd like to try it for a while.

Maybe she's disgusted because Kimura-san has been coming over to drink with us every three or four days (we've already emptied another bottle of Courvoisier), and because I've fainted in the bathtub every time. I'm sure she's noticed—and been curious about it—that her parents' room often blazes with light in the early-morning hours. But I can't tell if that's really why she wants to move or if she has some other reason, which she's hiding.

"Go ask Papa yourself, and see what he says," I told her. "If Papa says it's all right, I won't object."

February 14

❁

Today Kimura said something unexpected to me while Ikuko was in the kitchen. He asked if I had ever heard of a "Polaroid camera." It seems to be an American invention—a camera that develops and prints its own photographs. They use it to make the still pictures they show on television at the end of *sumo* wrestling bouts, to help explain the fine points of the winning hold. According to him, the camera is very easy to operate—as easy as an ordinary one—and easy to carry, too. If you can use a Strobe flash, you can take pictures without a tripod.

Polaroid cameras are still quite rare in Japan, Kimura told me; even the film itself (printing-paper superimposed on negative) has to be specially imported. However, a friend of his happens to have one, with plenty of film. "If you'd care to use it, I can borrow it for you," he said.

As he spoke, an idea came to me. But how did he guess that I would be pleased to learn about such a camera? That puzzles me. He does seem remarkably well acquainted with what goes on at our house.

February 16

❊

A disturbing thing happened a little while ago, about four o'clock this afternoon. I hide my diary in a drawer of the cabinet here in the sitting room (a drawer no one else uses), stuffed in under layers of old papers—personal documents, letters from my parents, and so on. I don't like to take it out while my husband is at home, but occasionally I want to jot something down before I forget it, or I simply have an urge to write. And so I steal a few minutes when he's shut up in his study, without waiting for him to leave the house. The study is over this room; I can't hear him, but somehow I feel aware of what he's doing—of whether he's reading, writing in his own diary, or perhaps just sitting there lost in thought. I suppose he feels the same way about me. The study is always deathly quiet, but now and then—or so I imagine—a peculiar hush falls; he seems to be holding his breath and concentrating on the room below. Such moments are apt to occur when I'm writing. I don't think that is only my imagination.

In order not to make any noise I use a writing-brush instead of a pen, and I've folded sheets of delicate rice paper into a small Japanese-style notebook. But this afternoon I became so absorbed in my diary that I momentarily relaxed my guard—something I've never done before. Just then, on purpose or not, my husband came silently down the stairs. He passed the sitting room without stopping in, went to the lavatory, and returned immediately to his study. I say "silently" because that was my impression. Maybe he didn't try to soften his footsteps; maybe I'd have noticed them if I hadn't been so preoccupied. Anyway, I didn't hear him until he reached the bottom of the stairs. I was leaning over the table, writing, but I hastily put the diary and brush case out of sight. (I don't use an ink-stone. The brush case—an antique Chinese one my father gave me—holds ink too.) So I escaped being caught in the act.

But in thrusting the notebook under a cushion, I crumpled a few of its thin leaves. I wonder if he heard that slight rustle, so characteristic of rice paper. I'm sure he did. If he heard it he must have recognized the sound, in which case he may have guessed what I'm using that sort of paper for. I shall have to be more careful. Supposing he's already guessed I keep a diary: what can I do about it? Even if I change the hiding place, there's nowhere really safe in this little room. I'll just have to try not to leave the house while he's here. For days now my head has been feeling so heavy that I haven't gone out as often as usual; I've left most of the shopping to Toshiko or Baya. But Kimura-san has asked if I'd like to go see *Le Rouge et le Noir* at the Asahi Theater. I *would* like to go. In the meantime I'll have to think of a plan.

February 18

❁

Last night makes the fourth time that I have heard my wife call out Kimura's name. By now it's obvious that she is shamming. Why should she do such a thing? Perhaps she means to inform me that she is not really asleep—but how should I interpret *that?* Is it: "I want to think my partner is Kimura-san so that I can become really passionate. After all, it's to your benefit"? Or is it: "I'm simply trying to stimulate you by arousing your jealousy. No matter what happens, I am an unwaveringly faithful wife"?

Today Toshiko finally moved to the cottage at Madame Okada's house. The telephone isn't in yet, but the work of reinforcing the floor and building a passageway has been nearly finished. Because this was supposed to be an unlucky day, Ikuko had asked her to wait till the twenty-first, a propitious one. Toshiko refused.

The piano will be moved early next week. With Kimura's help, Toshiko has already taken most of her other things. (By the time Ikuko got up—after last night's party—there was hardly anything left to do.) It seems that Madame

Okada lives in the Sekidencho district, a few blocks west of Kyoto University, about five minutes' walk from here. Since Kimura has a room near Hyakumamben, he is a good deal nearer Sekidencho than we are.

As soon as he arrived today he called from the stairs to ask if he could see me for a moment, and then came up to my study. "I've brought what I promised," he said, handing me the Polaroid camera.

February 19

❀

I cannot imagine what is in Toshiko's mind. She seems to love her mother, and yet hate her. But there's no doubt that she hates her father. Apparently she misunderstands our marital relations, and thinks it's he, not I, who has a lustful nature. She seems to think he forces me to satisfy his sexual demands, though I'm really too weak for it, and that he's addicted to coarse, perverted pleasures, which I'm dragged into against my will. (I must admit I've tried to give her that impression.) Yesterday when she came to pick up the last of her things she stopped in my bedroom to warn me.

"You're going to let Papa kill you!" she said abruptly, and left.

That was extraordinary for a girl like her, who's as reticent as I am. She *does* seem to worry that my chest trouble may be aggravated, and to hate her father on that account. Yet the way she uttered that warning made it sound oddly scornful, full of spite and malice. I can't believe she was saying it out of the warm feeling of a daughter anxious about her mother. Isn't she inwardly resentful of the fact that although she's twenty years younger she's not as attractive as I am in face or figure? From the very first she said she disliked Mr. Kimura; maybe that was because he reminded her of an actor I'm fond of. She may have deliberately hidden her real feelings, and pretended to dislike him. I wonder if she isn't secretly hostile to me.

Although I try not to leave the house, sooner or later I may have to—and my husband may come home one day when he's supposed to be teaching. I've been racking my brains about what to do with this diary. If it's useless to hide it, at least I'd like to know if he's reading it on the sly. And so I've decided to use a telltale mark of some kind. Maybe it would be all the better if it's one that only I know about, one he won't recognize; but maybe he'll stop spying if he realizes that his wife knows what he's up to. (I'm afraid that's very doubtful, though.) Even so, it's not easy to hit on the right kind of mark. I may succeed once, but I can scarcely repeat it safely. For instance, I can stick a toothpick between the pages somewhere so that it will fall out when the book is opened. The first time may go smoothly enough, but after that he'll note which pages it lies between, and put it back the same way. He's quite clever about such things. Yet I can't invent a new method every time.

After a good deal of thought, I decided to cut a length of No. 600 Scotch tape, measure it, and use it to seal together the two covers of the notebook. (I'll measure its distance from the top and bottom of the book too. Next time I'll make a slight change in its length and in the place where I apply it.) He'll have to peel it off to look inside. Of course it's not impossible for him to cut a new tape of the same size and replace the old one, exactly as it was. But that would be an awfully delicate task; I really don't see how he could do it. Besides, when he removes the tape, no matter how carefully, he's sure to mar the cover a little. Luckily, it's thick, white-glazed Hosho paper, which is easily damaged. A few millimeters of the surface will come off with the tape here and there. I don't think he'll be able to read my diary without leaving some trace.

February 24

❀

Kimura has had no ostensible reason to visit us since Toshiko moved out, but he still comes over quite regularly, every three or four days. I often telephone him myself. Toshiko stops in almost daily, but doesn't stay.

I have already used the Polaroid camera twice. I've taken full front and back views of Ikuko's body, as well as detailed shots of every part of it, from the most alluring angles: I have pictures of her bending, stretching, twisting, pictures of her with her arms and legs contorted into all manner of poses.

As to why I take such photographs: first of all, I enjoy taking them. I derive great pleasure from creating these poses, freely manipulating her while she sleeps (or pretends to). My second reason is to paste them in my diary so that she will see them. Then, certainly, she will discover—and be amazed at—the unsuspected beauty of her own body. A third reason is to show her why I am so desperately eager to look at her in the nude. I want her to understand me—perhaps even be sympathetic. (I dare say it is unheard of for a man of fifty-five to be so fascinated by his forty-four-year-old wife. She would do well to think of that.) Finally, I want to humiliate her in the extreme, to see how long she will go on playing innocent.

Unfortunately, this camera has a rather slow lens, and no range finder; since I'm not very good at estimating distances, my pictures are often out of focus. I understand that there is a new, highly sensitive Polaroid film, but it's hard to get. The kind Kimura brought is old, past its expiration date. You can't expect good results from it. Furthermore, it's bothersome to have to use a flash.

Since I can hardly fulfill my second and third purposes with this camera, I won't paste the photographs in, for the time being.

February 27

❀

It's Sunday. Kimura-san came over at nine-thirty this morning and asked if I wouldn't like to see *Le Rouge et le Noir* today. Sundays are best for him just now, he says; during the week he's busy helping students get ready for their college entrance examinations. In March things will be more leisurely, but this month he often has to stay late at school and give extra lessons. Even after he goes home he's sometimes visited by outside students who want him to tutor them. He's said to be sharp-witted, an expert at spotting questions. I think I can understand why they say that. I don't know how much of a scholar he is, but for sheer perception my husband is no match for him.

Since my husband stays home on Sunday, it's not convenient for me to go out. But Kimura-san had spoken to Toshiko on his way over. Soon she arrived, and asked me to join them. She looked as if she was thinking: "I don't want to go, but it might be awkward for the two of you, so I'll sacrifice myself for your sake and come along."

"You have to be early on Sunday," said Kimura-san, "or you won't get a seat, you know."

My husband urged me, too. "I'll be home all day," he said. "Go on: I'll look after the house. You said you wanted to see it, didn't you?"

I knew why he was encouraging me, but I was prepared for the situation, and I agreed to go. We got to the theater at half-past ten, and came out a little after one. I asked Toshiko and Kimura-san to stop in for lunch, but they refused. Although my husband had said he'd be home all day, he went out for a walk about three o'clock and stayed away the rest of the afternoon. As soon as he was gone I took out my diary and examined it. The Scotch tape didn't seem any different, nor, at first glance, did the cover. But when I looked through a magnifying glass I found two or three faint blemishes—the tape had been peeled off expertly—which couldn't be hidden. I'd made doubly sure by leaving a toothpick inside, counting the leaves to know where I'd inserted it. Now it was in a different place.

There is no longer the slightest doubt that my husband has read this diary. Should I give it up, then? I began it solely for the purpose of talking to myself, since I don't like to open my heart to another person. Now that it's obviously being read by someone else, I suppose I ought to abandon it. Yet the "someone" is my own husband, and we have an unspoken agreement to behave as if we weren't aware of each other's secrets. So perhaps I shall go on with it after all. I'll use it to talk to him indirectly, to say things I couldn't possibly tell him to his face. But even if he *is* reading it, I do hope he'll keep that to himself. Of course he's not the sort to admit it, anyway.

No matter what he does, I want him to know that I am definitely not reading *his* diary. He ought to realize that I'm very old-fashioned, a woman who's been carefully brought up, who wouldn't dream of infringing on anyone's privacy. I know where my husband's diary is; sometimes I have touched it; once in a great while I may even have opened it and looked inside. But I have never read a word of it. That is the simple truth.

February 27

❀

I was right after all! Ikuko has been keeping a diary. I haven't mentioned this before, but the fact is, I got an inkling of it several days ago. The other afternoon as I was on my way to the lavatory I glanced into the sitting room, and saw her leaning awkwardly over the table. A moment before, I had heard a rustling sound, as if rice paper were being crumpled. Not just a sheet or two—it sounded as if a substantial packet of it, a bound volume, perhaps, had been hastily shoved out of sight under a cushion. We seldom use rice paper at our house: it wasn't hard to imagine what she would be doing with that soft, discreet paper.

However, I had no chance to investigate until today. While she was at the movies I searched the sitting room, and easily found it. What astonished me, though, was that she had evidently expected me to go looking for it, and had sealed it with Scotch tape. A ridiculous thing for her to do! The degree of that woman's suspiciousness is really shocking. She ought to know that even though it's my own wife's diary I'm not such a sneak as to read it without permission. Yet I couldn't help feeling annoyed, and wondering if it might be possible to peel the tape off so skillfully that she would never detect it. I wanted to say: "Your tape is useless! That won't keep your diary safe—you'll have to think of a better way!"

But I failed. As I might have imagined, she was too much for me. Although I tried to peel the tape off with the most scrupulous care, it left a slight blemish on the cover. I realized then how foolish I had been. No doubt she had even measured the tape, but I had thoughtlessly rolled it into a ball. I sealed the diary up again with a piece that seemed to be about the same length. It's not likely to deceive her.

Still, I can assure her that although I unsealed her diary—even opened it and looked inside—I didn't read a single word of it. It's hard for a near-sighted person like myself to read such a tiny script, anyway. I hope she will believe me. Of course, with her, the more I deny it, the more she will think I'm guilty. Perhaps, if I am to be blamed in any case, I might just as well have read it. But I didn't. In fact, I am afraid to know what she may have said about her true feelings toward Kimura. Ikuko, I beg of you, don't confess! Even though I'll not see it, don't make such a confession! Lie, if you must, but say that you're only using him for my sake, that he means nothing more to you.

Kimura came to take Ikuko to the movies this morning, because I had asked him to. Some time ago I told him

I'd noticed that she scarcely leaves the house. "Lately she has Baya do all the errands," I said. "It's not like her—I wish you'd take her out somewhere for a few hours."

As usual, Toshiko went along. I don't suppose that she had any special reason for joining them, though it's difficult to interpret her actions. Toshiko is even more complicated than her mother, in some respects. I wonder if she is resentful because, unlike most fathers, I seem to be less devoted to her than I am to her mother. If that is what she thinks, she's wrong; I love them equally. Only, I love them in different ways—no father could feel quite *that* way about his daughter. I'll have to see that she understands this.

Tonight, for the first time since Toshiko moved out, the four of us sat around the dinner table together. Toshiko left early; Ikuko had her usual reaction to brandy. Later, when Kimura was leaving, I gave the Polaroid camera back to him.

"It's quite an advantage not having to worry about developing the negatives," I said. "But I don't like using a flash—maybe I'd be better off with an ordinary camera. I think I'll try our Zeiss Ikon."

"Will you send the film out?" he asked.

I had already given that a good deal of thought. "Do you suppose you could develop it for me?" I said.

He looked a little embarrassed, and asked if I couldn't do it here. I told him that I believed he knew what kind of photographs I was taking. He said he wasn't sure.

"They're not the sort I'd care to let anyone else see," I went on, "but I can't very well develop them at home. I want some enlargements, too—and we don't have a good place for a darkroom. Couldn't you make one at your house? I'd rather not let a stranger handle them."

"We may have a place for one, somewhere," he answered. "I'll speak to my landlord about it."

February 28

Kimura came over at eight this morning, while Ikuko was still fast asleep. He said he was stopping in on his way to school. I had been in bed too, but when I heard his voice I got up and came to the sitting room.

"It's all right!" he announced. I wondered what was all right; it turned out to be the darkroom. Since their laundry room is not in use just now, he can have it whenever he wants. It will make an excellent darkroom, with running water.

I told him to get it ready immediately.

March 3

❀

Kimura says he is busy with examinations, but he is more conscientious than I am. . . . Last night I took out the Zeiss Ikon for the first time in years, and shot an entire roll of film—thirty-six exposures. He stopped in again today, as nonchalant as ever. "May I see you a moment?" he asked, then came into my study and looked at me inquiringly.

As a matter of fact, I still hadn't made up my mind to entrust the developing to him. He was clearly the one person for the job, since by now seeing Ikuko in the nude was scarcely a novelty for him. Yet even he had only caught fleeting glimpses of her naked body; he had never seen it in all those varied, seductive poses. Wouldn't the photographs be likely to excite him? That was no concern of mine, to be sure; but mightn't it lead to something more? If it did, I would have only myself to blame.

Besides, I had to consider the possibility that he might show her the photographs. She would certainly be indignant (or pretend to be), not only because I had taken them, and without her knowledge, but because I had had someone else develop them. She might even reason that, having already been exposed to Kimura in such a shameful state by her own husband, she had tacit permission to commit adultery with him.

I had let my imagination go so far that I was beginning to feel agonizingly jealous, a feeling so intense, so voluptuous, that it made me eager to accept the risk. I gave Kimura the film, and told him I wanted him to do it all himself. "Be sure no one else sees them," I said. "When you finish, I'll pick out the ones I'd like to have you enlarge."

He must have been brimming over with excitement, but he didn't betray it. "I'll take care of everything," he agreed, and left at once.

March 7

❧

Today—for the second time this year—the key was lying by the bookshelf in my husband's study. The first time was on the fourth of January; I'd gone in to clean, and found it in front of the vase of daffodils. This morning, noticing that the Chinese plum blossoms had withered, I went in to replace them with white camellias, and saw the key lying in the very same place. Something is up, I thought; but when I opened the drawer and took out his diary I was startled to find it sealed with tape, just as I had sealed mine. That was his way of saying: "Be sure to open it!"

My husband keeps his diary in an ordinary student's notebook with a smooth, hard cover, not so easily marred as mine. Curious to see if I could peel off the tape—merely out of curiosity—I tried it. As careful as I was, I left some faint scratches after all. Even on that hard surface I couldn't help it. It wouldn't have mattered along the edge of the tape, but little flaws spread all around; there was no way to conceal them. I stuck a new tape on; of course he'll notice that, and be convinced I've read what is inside. But, as I've said over and over again, I swear I've never read a word of it. I suppose what he really wants is to tell me those indecent things that he knows I don't like to hear. And that's why I'm all the more loath to read it.

I hurriedly opened his diary and looked to see how much he had written. Of course that was out of curiosity too. I leafed through the pages filled with his delicate, nervous scrawl—as if the lines were so many ant tracks. But today I found that he had pasted in some obscene photographs. I shut my eyes, and quickly turned the page. Where on earth had he got such pictures, and why had he put them in? Did he want me to see them? I wondered who the woman could be.

Just then an extremely repugnant thought occurred to me. Lately, in the middle of the night, I've dreamed of an occasional blinding flash lighting up the whole room for an instant, as if by a flash bulb. Someone—my husband or Kimura-san—seemed to be photographing me. Maybe it wasn't a dream. Maybe my husband—surely it couldn't have been Kimura-san—was actually taking pictures. I remember that he once said: "You don't know how superb your own body is. I'd like to photograph it and show you." Yes, I'm sure those were pictures of *me*.

Often when I'm in that dazed sleep I have the feeling that I've been stripped naked. Until now I've thought it might be another of my fantasies, but if those are photographs of me it must really happen. Yet I don't even object to his picture-taking, so long as I'm not aware of it. I couldn't possibly allow such a thing while I'm awake; still, since he finds such pleasure in seeing me in the nude, I suppose that as a dutiful wife I ought to let him enjoy himself. In the old days a virtuous woman simply obeyed her husband's wishes, no matter how indecent or how disgusting. She did as she was told, there was no question about it. And I have all the more reason to indulge him if it's true he can't satisfy me unless he's stimulated by crazy pranks like that. It's not just a matter of fulfilling my duty. In return for being a virtuous, submissive wife, I'm able to gratify my own strong sexual appetite.

Even so, why isn't he content with looking at me? I don't see why he should want to take photographs of me in that state and then paste them in his notebook, where I can find them. He ought to know perfectly well that I'm the kind of person in whose heart lustfulness and shyness exist side by side. And I wonder who developed them for him. Did he have to let another man look at them? Was that just a nasty trick on me, or does it mean something? He's always jeering at my "refinement"—is he trying, now, to break me of that tiresome attitude?

March 10

I don't know whether I ought to mention this in my diary, or what it may lead to if Ikuko reads it. But I must confess to a feeling that I have been bringing on a serious mental or physical disorder of some kind. I call it "a feeling" because I suppose that my trouble may be nothing more than a minor neurosis.

Looking back, I think it is fair to say that I haven't always been deficient in sexual vigor. Since middle age, however, my vitality has been sapped by my wife's inordinate demands on it; my desire has become feeble. No, the desire is there, but the strength to back it up has waned.

And so I struggle to cope with my oversexed wife, whetting my appetite by all sorts of violent, unnatural methods. Sometimes it frightens me, and I wonder how long this can go on. For about ten years I was a spineless husband, overwhelmed by my wife's energy, but now all that has changed. Now, thanks to the discovery that brandy and Kimura are sovereign remedies, I am impelled by a lust so powerful that it seems almost miraculous, even to me. Moreover, I replenish my vitality by taking male hormones once a month, as prescribed by Dr. Noma at my request. And to make sure of being sufficiently potent—I do this without his knowledge, administering it myself—I also have injections of five hundred units of anterior pituitary hormones every four or five days.

Still, I suspect that my extraordinary new vigor is not so much due to drugs as to mental stimulation. The fermenting passion that comes from jealousy, the sexual impulses quickened by feasting my eyes on her nakedness—these things are driving me beyond all self-control, driving me to madness. Now I am the insatiable one. Night after night I immerse myself in undreamed-of ecstasies. I cannot help being grateful for my happiness; at the same time, I have a premonition that it will end, that someday I must pay for it, that moment by moment I am whittling away my life.

Indeed, I have already more than once had certain symptoms, mental as well as physical, which seem to foreshadow that retribution. Last Monday morning—the morning Kimura stopped in on his way to school—a strange thing happened. I had just got out of bed, and was about to go to the sitting room, when I noticed a faint doubling of the outlines of the stove chimney, the sliding doors and screens, the transom, the pillars—of everything around me. I rubbed my eyes, wondering if they were blurred with age. But that wasn't it. Evidently some abnormal change in my vision had taken place. In recent summers I have had mild attacks of dizziness from cerebral anemia, but this was obviously not the same. Unlike those attacks, which only lasted a few minutes, my double vision has been persistent. All lines—even the ribs of the sliding screens and the interstices of the tiles in the bath— seem doubled, and slightly bent. The doubling and the distortion are very slight, not enough to hamper movement or make me attract attention by any clumsiness; and so I have tried to disregard them. But even now the condition remains.

It is true that I haven't suffered any inconvenience or pain; yet I can't deny feeling uneasy. I have thought of going to be examined at the eye clinic, but that rather frightens me; I feel that it's not just something wrong with my eyes—the real disease lies in a more vital place. Besides, although this is probably caused by nervousness, I sometimes totter and almost lose my balance. I seem to be on the verge of falling. I don't know where the nerves that control the sense of equilibrium run, but it always feels as if there is a cavity in the back of my head, directly above the spine, a kind of pivot from which my body swings to one side or the other.

Yesterday I noticed another symptom, though I suppose that it too may be only a neurotic one. Around three in the afternoon, when I wanted to call up Kimura, I couldn't remember the telephone number of his school, a number I call nearly every day. Of course I have had lapses of memory before, but this wasn't ordinary forgetfulness: it was closer to amnesia. I couldn't even remember the exchange. I was startled and disconcerted. Tentatively, I tried to think of the name of the school, but that was no use either. What surprised me most was that I had forgotten Kimura's first name. Even our housekeeper's name was beyond me. To be sure, I hadn't forgotten "Ikuko" and "Toshiko," but the names of Ikuko's father and mother eluded me. As for the woman from whom Toshiko is renting a cottage, I remembered that she was French, that she had a Japanese husband, and that she taught at Doshisha University—but her name wouldn't come to me. Worse yet, I couldn't recall the name of our own street. All I knew was that we lived in the Sakyo ward of Kyoto.

A terrible anxiety gripped me. If this went on, gradually becoming more severe, I would soon be disqualified from my professorship. Not only that, I might become an invalid, house-bound, cut off from society. For the time being, however, my loss of memory has affected chiefly the names of people and places; I haven't forgotten the circumstances concerning them. I couldn't think of the Frenchwoman's name, but I realized that there was such a person, and that Toshiko was renting a cottage from her. In short, only the nerves that transmit names were paralyzed; it wasn't a paralysis of the entire system controlling perception and communication. Fortunately, too, the paralysis lasted only about half an hour. Before long the blocked nerve channels were reopened, my lost memory returned, and, except for my vision, I was back to normal.

In spite of my anxiety at not knowing how long it might last, I had managed to survive it without telling anyone, without even letting it be noticed. And now, although I have had no trouble since, I am still haunted by the fear that at any moment I may have another attack—the fear that this one may last, not for half an hour, but for a day, a year, perhaps for the rest of my life.

But what if Ikuko reads this, what will she be likely to do? Will she worry about me, and try to control her sexual instinct? I hardly think so. Even if her reason demanded it, her insatiable body would refuse to comply. Short of my collapse, she will never stop insisting on gratification.

Doubtless she will ask herself why I am writing this. "He seemed to be doing so well lately," she will think; "but he's been forced to give in, hasn't he? I suppose he means to frighten me, so that I'll be less demanding."

No, I too have lost all self-restraint. By nature I am a coward about illness, not the sort of person to take risks. Yet now, at fifty-five, I feel that I have at last found something to live for. In some respects I have become even bolder than she.

March 14

❖

Toshiko came over this morning while my husband was out. "I have something to discuss with you," she declared, looking serious. When I asked her what it was, she stared right into my eyes and said: "Yesterday I saw those pictures at Mr. Kimura's."

I didn't understand, and asked her to explain. "Mama, I'm on your side, no matter what," she said. "I wish you'd tell me the truth."

It seems Kimura-san promised to lend her a certain French book; yesterday, happening to pass his house, she stopped to get it. He wasn't there, but she went in anyway, and took the book from the shelf. When she opened it she found a number of photographs.

"Mama, what does it all mean?" she asked. I told her I didn't know what she was talking about, and she accused me of trying to deceive her. I gathered that the photographs were the same as those disgraceful ones I saw in my husband's diary the other day—and, just as I guessed, that they were photographs of me. But I couldn't think of a quick explanation. I suppose Toshiko imagined that a real scandal, something far worse than what had actually happened, was at the bottom of it. No doubt those pictures looked like evidence of illicit relations between Kimura-san and myself. For his sake, as well as for my husband's and my own, I should have tried to clear it up at once. But even if I'd been completely frank with her I don't think she'd have believed me.

I hesitated a moment, and said: "It may be hard to believe, but until you told me just now, I didn't really know there *were* any such photographs of me. If there are, Papa took them while I was in a stupor, and all Mr. Kimura did was develop them for him. There's absolutely nothing else between us. I leave it to your imagination why Papa should get me into a state like that, why he should take such pictures and have Mr. Kimura develop them instead of doing it himself. I've already told you as much as I can bear to, even if you are my own daughter. Please don't ask anything more. And please believe that I was only obeying your father. I do whatever he wants, even against my will, because I consider it my duty. It may be hard for you to understand, but to a person like myself, brought up on the old morality, there's no choice in the matter. If he's so eager to have nude photographs of me, I'm willing to swallow my shame and expose myself to the camera—especially if he's the one who operates it."

Toshiko was shocked. "Do you really mean that?" she asked. I said of course I did. "Mama, you're contemptible!" she burst out. I began to suspect I'd enjoyed offending her, and had somewhat exaggerated my true feelings.

"You think you're a model wife," she went on, with a cold, derisive smile. "Is that it?" Apparently she couldn't understand her father's motives, either. Having another man develop the films seemed utterly incomprehensible to her. She said he had humiliated me and tormented Mr. Kimura without any reason, and she kept on denouncing him till I interrupted her.

"I won't have you meddling in this!" I told her. "You say Papa humiliated me, but are you really so sure he did? I don't feel that way about it. Even now he's passionately in love with me—I suppose he had to convince himself that I look young and beautiful for my age. That may seem abnormal, but I can understand it." Because I felt a need to defend him I was able to say things I ordinarily couldn't have. And I did it rather skillfully, I think. Maybe it's just as well for him to read this, and have some appreciation of how I've tried to shield him.

"I wonder if that was all," said Toshiko. "Papa was certainly being sadistic, knowing how Mr. Kimura feels about you."

I didn't answer that. She said she couldn't believe those photographs had been left in the book out of sheer carelessness—"since it was Mr. Kimura who did it." She thought it meant something: maybe he wanted her to perform some function. And she told me some other things she'd observed about him, things it might be better not to repeat here.

March 18

❁

It was after ten o'clock when I got home tonight, because of the party for Sasaki. It seems that Ikuko had been out all evening. I thought she was at the movies, and went upstairs to work. At eleven she still hadn't returned.

Finally, at eleven thirty, Toshiko phoned. She told me she was calling from Sekidencho, and asked me to come over for a moment.

"Where is Mama?" I asked.

"She's here," Toshiko said.

"It's getting late," I said. "Tell your mother to come home. Baya's already left."

She lowered her voice. "Mama's fainted in the bath. Shall we call Dr. Kodama?" I asked who was there, and she said: "The three of us." Then she added: "I'll explain later. Anyway, I think Mama needs an injection. If you can't come, I'll get Dr. Kodama."

"Don't bother calling him," I said. "I'll be over to take care of it."

These days I make sure to keep the Vita-camphor solution on hand. I took some and left at once. Suddenly a wave of fear passed over me. Suppose my memory failed again!

I knew where to find the house, but this was the first time I had ever visited it. When I arrived, Toshiko was waiting for me inside the gate. She led me through the garden to the cottage, then excused herself and left.

Kimura greeted me apologetically. I didn't ask him for an explanation—nor did he volunteer one. It was an awkward moment for both of us, and I hurriedly set about preparing to give the injection. Bedding had been spread out on the floormats in front of the piano, and Ikuko lay there asleep. The tea table beside her was littered with plates and glasses. Her kimono and sash were hanging on the wall nearby, dangling from the ribbon-bedecked hangers that Toshiko uses for Western-style clothes; she was sleeping in her thin silk underrobe. Ikuko has rather showy tastes for her age, but that underrobe seemed especially gaudy. Perhaps I was struck by it because of the unusual time and place.

Her pulse was about as I had expected under the circumstances. All Kimura said was: "Your daughter and I carried her here together." Evidently she had been more or less wiped dry, too, although her underrobe was clinging to her body. The waist cord was untied. It surprised me to see how disheveled her hair was—it streamed down over her shoulders, and the neckband of her robe was soaking wet. When she had fainted before, at our house, her hair had always been tied up in a knot, never loose and flowing like this. I wondered if her appearance reflected Kimura's tastes.

He seemed to be quite at home, and had no trouble bringing me what I needed—washbowl, boiling water, and the rest. . . .

"We can't very well let her sleep here," I said, about an hour later.

"They go to bed early in the main house," he told me. "Madame Okada probably doesn't know what's happened."

But Ikuko's pulse was a good deal better, and I decided to take her home. I had Kimura call a taxi.

"I'll carry her out," he offered, stooping down so that I could lift her onto his back. I got her in position, still undressed, and then draped her kimono over her. We crossed the garden to the taxi; together we put her into it. The taxi was a very small one, and Kimura sat in front. All my wife's clothing reeked of brandy; the air inside was stifling. I sat holding her across my lap, and buried my face in her damp, chilly hair; then I bent over to kiss and caress her feet. I don't think Kimura could see what was going on, but he may have suspected it.

After we had carried her to the bedroom, he said he hoped I wouldn't be suspicious about what happened tonight. "Your daughter knows everything," he added, and then asked if I needed him any longer. I said I didn't.

As soon as he was gone I remembered that Toshiko had come over ahead of us, and I went to look for her. But she was gone too. Earlier, when we carried Ikuko in from the taxi, she had seemed to be waiting restlessly in the entrance hall. Presumably she left without a word, just after we arrived.

I came up to my study, and have quickly jotted down all of the night's events—all that has happened so far, that is. In the midst of writing, I have savored the thought of the pleasures which are to follow.

March 19

✾

It was dawn before I fell asleep. Trying to decide the meaning of what happened last night has been an acute but frightening joy. I have yet to hear a word of explanation, whether from Kimura, Toshiko, or my wife. To be sure, I haven't had a chance to ask—but I haven't wanted to, quite so soon. I have found a kind of pleasure in thinking it over by myself, before hearing about it from anyone else. I allow my imagination to roam freely over all sorts of possibilities—discarding one for another, and then another—until, in the tightening grip of jealousy and rage, I feel myself quiver with a savage, irresistible lust. When the truth finally comes out, that pleasure will disappear.

Toward daybreak my wife began calling Kimura's name, in her usual delirious way. But this morning she repeated it over and over again, at intervals, now strongly and now weakly. At last, as her voice was rising once again, I took her.

In an instant my jealous rage had vanished. I no longer cared whether she was asleep or awake, shamming or not; I didn't even want to distinguish myself from Kimura. At that moment I felt I had burst into another world, soared up to some towering height, to the very zenith of ecstasy. This was reality, the past was only illusion. We were alone together, embracing. . . . Perhaps it would kill me, but the moment would last forever.

March 19

❀

I want to write down all I remember about last night. I knew my husband would be out, and I'd told him I might go along with Toshiko and Mr. Kimura to a movie. At half past four Kimura-san arrived, but Toshiko didn't come until nearly five o'clock.

"Aren't you a little late?" I asked her.

"I'm afraid so," she said. "How about having dinner first? Mama, come and be my guest at Sekidencho. You haven't paid me a real visit yet, you know. And tonight I've got a pound of boned chicken!" She was carrying an armful of vegetables, too. As she shepherded us out she picked up the bottle of Courvoisier, which was still quite full, and said: "I'll let you donate this!" When I told her we shouldn't drink it in Papa's absence, she replied that her dinner wouldn't be complete without it.

"I don't want a full-course dinner," I said. "Let's keep it simple, since we're going to the movies afterward."

But she insisted that nothing was simpler than sukiyaki.

We put two little tables together in front of the piano, borrowed a gas burner from the main house, and started cooking at once. I was surprised to see that Toshiko had bought so much food, and in such variety. Not only the usual ingredients—onions, vermicelli, fresh bean curd—but Chinese cabbage, wheat-gluten cake, toasted bean curd, lily bulbs, and such. Instead of bringing them all out together, she added them little by little, one after another, as the supply diminished. There seemed to be more than a pound of chicken, too. Naturally, we didn't get around to the rice, but kept on drinking brandy.

"It's quite a novelty for your daughter to be acting as

bartender, isn't it?" Kimura-san remarked. He seemed to be drinking more than usual.

After waiting until it was too late, Toshiko said: "I'm afraid we've missed the last show." But I no longer cared. I didn't think I was becoming really intoxicated, though. It's always that way with me—I suppress the effects of liquor perfectly well, up to a certain point. Then all of a sudden I lose control. Last night I intended to be cautious, thinking Toshiko might want to get me drunk. Yet I can't deny that at the same time I felt a kind of anticipation—or hope. Maybe the two of them planned it all in advance. But they wouldn't have been likely to admit it, so I didn't ask.

Once, though, Kimura-san said: "Do you think you ought to drink this much when your husband isn't here?" But he's getting to be a much better drinker himself, and he kept up with me glass for glass. I suppose we had the same thing in mind. As for me, I felt that I was only doing what my husband would have wished, since making him jealous seems to make him happy. I'm not saying my sole object was to please him, only that the thought of it gave me such a feeling of reassurance that I found myself drinking on and on.

There's something else I want to set down plainly today. I won't go so far as to say I love Kimura-san, but the truth is, I find him very attractive. I think I could even love him, if I tried. Of course that's because I've almost let myself be seduced, in order to make my husband jealous—but I'm sure I wouldn't have done it if I hadn't liked him. Up till now I've drawn a line, and I've been careful not to go beyond it. Now, though, I have a feeling that it's quite possible I might make a false step. I hope my husband won't put *too* much confidence in my faithfulness. I've endured everything for his sake, at his desire, but I'm beginning to lose confidence in myself. I don't know what will come of all this.

Still, I must admit I was curious to see Kimura-san in the nude. I wanted to see for myself, without any interference from my husband, that naked body I'd always dreamed of—was it really Kimura-san's? Suddenly I began to feel tipsy, and went to hide in the lavatory. Toshiko called to me through the door: "Mama, the bath is ready. Why don't you go in?"

Somewhere in my hazy mind I knew I would faint, knew that the person to come for me would be Kimura-san. I can recall hearing Toshiko urge me once or twice more. Before long I made my way to the bath, opened the glass door, and went in and took off my clothes. I don't remember anything after that.

March 24

❀

Again last night my wife fainted at the Sekidencho house. She had gone out with Toshiko and Kimura after dinner, presumably to the movies; when they weren't back by eleven, I began to feel suspicious. I thought of telephoning, but that seemed absurd—I knew I would hear from them before long. As I waited, I became more and more impatient. I was trembling with annoyance—and with excitement.

A little past midnight Toshiko appeared, alone. She left her taxi waiting while she came in to tell me what had happened. After the movie—according to her story—Kimura insisted on seeing both of them home. They went first to Sekidencho, and stopped in for tea. Noticing that there was still a good deal of brandy left, Toshiko added a spoonful of it to each of the cups. Soon Kimura and her mother were having a bit more; they finally emptied the bottle. Once again, the bath happened to be ready. One thing led to another just as it had a few nights before—so Toshiko said. It hardly amounted to an explanation.

"Did you leave them there alone?" I asked.

She nodded. "The phone isn't in yet, and I didn't like to call from the main house. Besides," she went on, "I knew you'd need a cab yourself, so I found one and came." She was looking hard at me, in her malicious way. "We were lucky the other night—it isn't easy to get a cab at this hour. I waited in front of the house for a while, but there just weren't any. Finally I walked over to the cab stand by the river, and found one of the drivers asleep there. I woke him up and had him bring me." Then she added, as if to herself: "I must have left the cottage about half an hour ago."

I guessed what was in her mind, but I merely thanked her for coming and asked her to look after the house. I collected everything I needed, and went to the taxi. Of course I didn't know how far the three of them had planned this together; still, I could easily imagine that Toshiko had instigated it. No doubt she had purposely left her mother alone with Kimura for the half-hour— had it been, perhaps, an hour?—that she managed to spend in coming after me. I tried not to think about what might have gone on during that interval.

When I arrived, I found Ikuko lying there in her underrobe, just as she was the other night. Again her clothes were hanging along the wall. Kimura brought hot water and a washbowl. She seemed to be unconscious, even drunker than the time before. However, I could see through her pretense. It was obvious that she was only acting. Her pulse was fairly strong, too. Since it would have been pointless to give her a camphor injection, I decided to simulate it, and give her vitamins instead. Kimura noticed what I was doing, and asked me, in a low voice, if vitamins would be enough.

"Yes, I think so," I said calmly. "She doesn't seem so bad tonight." And I proceeded with the injection.

Later, Ikuko called Kimura's name over and over again. Her voice had a new and ardent tone—not the somewhat delirious one I was used to, but a strong, piercing, imploring quality. As she approached a climax her cries became still more intense. Suddenly I felt the tip of my tongue being bitten—then the lobe of my ear. She had never been like this before.

When I think that it was Kimura who, overnight, turned her into such a bold, aggressive woman, I feel violently jealous, and at the same time grateful. Perhaps I should also be grateful to Toshiko. Ironically enough, she seems to be quite unaware of my curious state of mind. She doesn't know that by trying to hurt me she actually gives me pleasure.

Early this morning, after intercourse, I felt an awful giddiness. Ikuko's face, neck, shoulders, arms—the entire outline of her figure seemed double. It looked as if another and identical body overlapped her own. I must have fallen asleep shortly after that, but even in my dreams that double image persisted. At first her whole body was doubled; soon the various parts were scattered in space. Two pairs of eyes and two noses in a single row, two pairs of lips above them, and so on, all in the most vivid colors. The surrounding space was sky blue, the hair black, the lips crimson, the noses pure white—and that black, that red, that white were far more brilliant than her actual coloring. They were as poisonously garish as a movie billboard.

In my dream, it occurred to me that seeing such vivid colors must be evidence of serious neurasthenia. Yet I kept on dreaming. Two pairs of feet—their skin was exquisitely fair—seemed to be floating under water. Unmistakably, they were *her* feet. Their soles floated separately, alongside. Just then a large white mass loomed up before me, like a bank of clouds; it was a shape I had once photographed—her buttocks, turned full toward me.

Hours later I had a different dream. Kimura was standing before me, naked; sometimes his head was transformed into mine, sometimes both our heads grew from a single body. The entire image was doubled.

March 26

❉

For the third time now I've seen Kimura-san without my husband. Last night there was a new bottle of Courvoisier, still unopened, sitting in the alcove. "Did you bring this?" I asked Toshiko; but she denied it, saying she had no idea where it came from.

"The bottle was there when I got home yesterday," she went on. "I thought Mr. Kimura might have brought it."

"I don't know anything about it either," Kimura-san said. "It must have been your husband. I'm sure that's the answer. He's playing an elaborate joke on us."

"If it's Papa, he's being awfully sarcastic, isn't he?"

That's the way they talked about it. It does seem likely that he put the bottle there, but I really don't know what to think. I can't be sure Toshiko or Kimura-san didn't bring it.

On Wednesdays and Fridays Madame Okada goes to Osaka to teach and doesn't come home till eleven. The other night, after we began drinking, Toshiko slipped off to the main house. (It's the first time I've mentioned this.

I've been afraid my husband would misunderstand, but there doesn't seem to be any further need to withhold the truth.) Again last night she disappeared early; even when Madame Okada came home she stayed on talking with her for quite a long while. And again I fainted. Still, no matter what my condition was, I think I managed to hold that last line of resistance. I haven't yet had the courage to cross it, and I believe Kimura-san feels the same.

"I'm the one who lent your husband the Polaroid camera," he told me. "I did because I knew he liked to get you drunk and look at you in the nude. But he couldn't be satisfied with the Polaroid, so he finally began taking pictures with a Zeiss Ikon. I suppose he wanted to search out every detail of your body—but more than that, I think he wanted to make me suffer. I think he likes having *me* develop the films; he likes exciting me, and making me fight a terrible temptation. And he relishes the thought that my own feelings are reflected in you, till you're as tormented as I am. It's cruel of him to do this to us, but I still don't want to betray him. I see how you are suffering, and I want to suffer with you—I want to suffer more and more deeply."

"Toshiko found those photographs in the French book she borrowed from you," I told him. "She said there must be some reason for it—they couldn't have been put there accidentally. What did you mean by that?"

"I hoped she might take some action if I showed them to her," he answered. "I've never suggested anything in particular. It's just that, knowing there's a touch of Iago in her, I rather expected what happened on the night of the eighteenth—and the night of the twenty-third, and this evening too. Your daughter always took the initiative. I only kept quiet and followed her lead."

"This is the first time I've talked about our relationship," I said. "I've never discussed it before, not even with my husband. He seems to avoid asking about you. Maybe he's afraid to, and still tries to believe I've been faithful to him. I'd like to think so too, but I wonder if I really have been. You're the only person who can tell me that."

"Yes, of course you have," Kimura-san said. "There's one part of your body I've never touched. He wanted me a paper-thin distance from you, and so I've obeyed his wish. I've come as close as I could without violating that rule."

"Oh, I'm so glad to hear that!" I exclaimed. "You can't imagine how grateful I am!"

Kimura-san tells me I hate my husband, but the truth is, though I *do* hate him, I love him too. The more I hate him, the more passionate my love becomes. He puts someone like you, Kimura-san, between us, and if he didn't torture you his own passion wouldn't flare up—yet when I think that his aim, after all, is to give me pleasure, I simply can't turn against him. But couldn't you look at it as I do? He is identified with you, you are part of him, the two of you really one.

March 28

✿

I have had a retinal examination at the university eye clinic. I didn't want to, but Dr. Noma was so insistent that I finally took his advice.

They say that my dizziness comes from hardening of the cerebral arteries. The brain is congested, which causes dizziness, double vision, perhaps a partial blacking-out of consciousness. In severe cases there may be complete unconsciousness. I was asked if I didn't feel especially dizzy when I have to get up in the middle of the night, when I make a hasty movement or a sudden turn; and I had to admit that I did. They say that losing one's sense of equilibrium—feeling as if one were about to fall, or sink into the ground—results from an impairment of circulation in the inner ear.

Dr. Noma examined me, too, at the internal-medicine department. Today, besides taking my blood pressure, he made an electrocardiagram and a kidney examination.

"I'm surprised that your blood pressure is so high," Dr. Noma told me. "You'll have to be careful." I asked him how high it was, but he seemed reluctant to answer. "Both readings are around two hundred," he said at last. "The worst thing is that there's such a small difference between them. Instead of dosing yourself with hormones and stimulants, you ought to take something to lower your blood pressure. I'm afraid you'll have to abstain from sexual activity, and give up alcohol too. Stay away from salty foods and stimulants of any kind." Then he prescribed various drugs—Rutin C, Serpasil, Kallikrein—and said that I should be sure to have my blood pressure checked frequently from now on.

I am writing all this in my diary, with complete frankness, in order to see what effect it will have on Ikuko. For the present I intend to ignore the doctor's warning. If there is to be any change in our behavior, the first move will have to come from her. But I expect her to pretend that she hasn't read this, and to go on being as lustful as ever. That is her nature, she can hardly help it. By now I myself am no longer able to turn back. Now too, after the other night, she has suddenly become aggressive in searching for new and varied pleasures. It is her force that drives us on. As usual, though, she never utters a word during the act. Silently, by her movements, she expresses all her erotic feelings. Since she invariably pretends to be half asleep, there is no need to dim the light. I am captivated by her drunken, sleepy, yet deliciously shamefaced manner.

At first I kept my wife at a considerable distance from Kimura. However, as the stimulation gradually wore off I began to reduce that distance. The more I reduced it, the more jealous I became—and the more pleasure I derived. My plan was a great success. But, because Ikuko and I both want the same thing, we haven't known where to stop. It is almost three months since the New Year, and I cannot help marveling that I have dared to struggle so long to cope with her. Now indeed she must realize how much I love her. But what lies ahead? How can I continue to whip up my passion? At this rate the stimulation will soon wear off again—I have already put them in a situation that, under ordinary circumstances, would have to be called adultery. Yet even now I trust her. What possible way is left to bring them closer, without forcing her to be unfaithful? I must try to think of one, although they— with Toshiko's help—will probably hit on something before I do.

I have said that Ikuko is secretive, but so am I. It's no wonder that Toshiko, taking after her parents, is secretive too. But Kimura is even worse. How extraordinary that the lives of four such sly, secretive persons should be intertwined. More extraordinary still, the four of us—all the while deceiving one another—are co-operating quite effectively. That is, each of us seems to have his own scheme in mind, but in fact we all have a single aim. We are doing our best to corrupt Ikuko.

March 30

❋

This afternoon Toshiko came over, and persuaded me to go along on a little trip to Arashiyama. Kimura-san—it's vacation time just now—was waiting for us at the Omiya streetcar terminal; we went on together from there. It seems that it was all Toshiko's idea. I felt very grateful to her.

We strolled along the bank of the river, took a boat as far as the Rankyo Hotel, then, after resting a bit near the bridge, went to look at the garden of the Tenryuji Temple. For the first time in ages I was breathing fresh, healthy air. I think I'd like to go on an outing of this kind more often. It's too bad my husband is such a bookworm.

Toward evening we started back. We left the streetcar at Hyakumamben and went our separate ways. The day had been so exhilarating that for once I didn't feel like drinking brandy.

March 31

❀

Last night my husband and I went to bed cold sober. Around midnight I let him see the toes of my left foot, exposing them beyond the edge of the blanket, out into the glare of the fluorescent lamp. He was quick to notice, and got into my bed. Then, bathed in that strong light and not in the least intoxicated, we made love. An astonishing performance. I could see that he was flushed with excitement.

Because of the vacation, he's usually home all day (and so is Madame Okada). Of course he goes out walking; he wanders about the neighborhood for an hour or two, and then comes home. He likes to walk, but I think he also likes to give me time to read his diary. Whenever he says: "I'll be back soon," I feel as if I've been told: "Be sure to read my diary!" That makes me all the more determined not to. But maybe, under the circumstances, I ought to give him a chance to read my own.

March 31

❀

Last night Ikuko amazed and delighted me. She didn't pretend to be drunk or even ask me to put out the light. After displaying herself in a most provocative manner, she deliberately set to work arousing me. I was surprised to find her so expert at the art of love. In time I suppose I'll understand the meaning of this.

The dizziness has been so bad that I began worrying, after all, and went to Dr. Kodama to have him check my blood pressure. I could see that it alarmed him. He said it was almost high enough to break his instrument. According to him, I need absolute rest—I ought to stop work at once.

April 1

✿

Today Toshiko brought over a Miss Kawai, who teaches dressmaking, and who also makes things to order. There's no tax, so she can do it for twenty or thirty percent less than the usual prices. Toshiko gets all her clothes from her. Except for my school uniforms, I've never worn Western clothing—my tastes are old-fashioned, and kimonos are becoming to my figure. But although I have no intention of changing styles at my age, I let Toshiko persuade me to order a dress from her. I know I can't keep it a secret, but I felt embarrassed and asked her to come this afternoon, while my husband was away. I had Toshiko and Miss Kawai pick out the fabric and the pattern. I said I'd like the skirt long—at least two inches below the knee—since my legs are a little bowed. Miss Kawai told me they couldn't really be called bowed—even Westerners' legs were often curved that much.

They showed me all sorts of samples, and pointed out a pattern in *Modes et travaux*, a gray and russet tweed ensemble. Both of them said I should try it, so I agreed. It seems it won't cost over ten thousand yen, but I'll have to buy shoes too, and a few accessories.

April 2

❁

Went out this afternoon. Back by evening.

April 3

❁

Went out at ten. Bought shoes at a shop on Kawaramachi. Back by evening.

April 4

❀

Went out this afternoon. Back by evening.

April 5

❀

Went out this afternoon. Back by evening.

April 5

❀

Ikuko's routine has changed. She goes out almost every afternoon—sometimes even in the morning—and comes home four or five hours later, in time for dinner. The two of us have dinner together. She usually won't drink—brandy doesn't seem to appeal to her any more. Perhaps the fact that Kimura is free just now has something to do with her new habits. I have no idea where she goes.

At two o'clock this afternoon Toshiko turned up unexpectedly, and asked: "Where's Mama?"

"She's always out around this time," I said. "Isn't she at your place?"

"I haven't seen anything of her," Toshiko replied, tilting her head doubtfully; "or of Mr. Kimura, either. Where do you suppose she goes?"

But I suspect that Toshiko herself is in on the secret.

April 6

❄

Went out this afternoon. Back by evening.

Lately I've been going out every day. My husband is usually here when I leave. He's shut up in his study, sitting crouched over his desk with an open book in front of him, as if he's absorbed in reading. I don't think he is, though. I imagine he's far too busy wondering what I do in the hours I spend away from home. Of course there's no doubt that while I'm gone he comes down to the sitting room, takes my diary out of the cabinet, and reads it. But unfortunately he finds it doesn't tell him anything—I've purposely been vague about my activities of the past few days.

Before leaving I go up to his study, open the sliding door a crack, and call in to say I'll be gone for a while. Then I steal down the stairs as if I were making an escape. Sometimes I only call from the stairs. He never turns to look at me; either he nods and murmurs "All right," or he doesn't answer.

I need scarcely say I don't go out just to let him read my diary. I've been meeting Kimura-san at a certain rendezvous. I go because I've wanted to lie in his arms—somewhere flooded by the healthy rays of the sun, at a time when my mind isn't dulled by liquor. It's true that I've been alone with him at Toshiko's place, away from my husband, but I've always been hopelessly drunk at the moment when our bodies touch. On January thirtieth I wrote about wondering "how much truth there was in my dream of Kimura-san" and, on March nineteenth, about being curious "to see for myself, without any interference from my husband, that naked body I'd always dreamed of." Those feelings, still unsatisfied, lurked in my heart. Whatever the cost, I wanted to gaze long and deep—fully conscious, and in broad daylight—at the man I knew to be the genuine, palpable Kimura-san, not just a phantom brought to me through my husband.

Joyfully, but with an eerie sense of having done this before, I discovered that Kimura-san, in the flesh, was the very man I've dreamed of sleeping with so many times since early this year. Once I wrote about "grasping his strong young arms," of being "pressed tight against his firm, resilient body"—above all, of being startled by his dazzlingly fair skin. Now I've actually seen him, and know what he's like. At last, beyond the shadow of a doubt, I have grasped his young arms, felt my breasts tight against his firm body, felt the warm, silky touch of his white skin.

But how strange that my illusions mirrored reality! I can't think it's only a coincidence that my dream-image of

Kimura-san corresponded so perfectly to the real man. I feel as if I'd known him from a former life, as if he had a mysterious power to haunt my dreams.

Now that his image has unmistakably come alive, I can separate him completely from my husband. Once and for all, I hereby strike out the words "you are part of him, the two of you really one." The only resemblance between them is that they both appear to be slightly built. In the nude Kimura-san looks very different. His chest is surprisingly deep and his whole body radiates vitality; he's not at all like my scrawny husband, with his bad complexion, his slack, sagging skin. There's a glossy sheen and freshness to Kimura-san's skin, a tinge of pink under the white, whereas my husband's dark, sallow skin seems dead; its waxy smoothness still nauseates me. My feelings about my husband used to be divided equally between love and hate, but the balance is tipping more and more toward hate. How many times a day I sigh to think what a miserable sort of man I married: if only Kimura-san were in his place!

Yet if I say that, having come this far, I still haven't crossed that last line—will my husband believe me? Whether he does or not, it's the truth. Of course I'm interpreting the "last line" in an exceedingly narrow sense; maybe I should say I've done everything *but* violate it. I was brought up by conventional-minded parents, and I can't escape their rigid way of thinking. Somehow I have the notion that no matter what happens, as long as I don't engage in what my husband likes to call "orthodox" sexual intercourse, I haven't really been unfaithful. And so I've remained faithful to him, in that sense, but I don't stop at anything that isn't covered by that strict definition. I'd prefer not to be specific, though.

April 8

❀

This afternoon I almost ran into Ikuko. I was going west on Shijo, several blocks past the Fujii Department Store, when I happened to see her leave a shop thirty or forty feet ahead. However, she turned and went the other way. I looked at my watch: it was half past four. To judge from the time, she should have been going east, toward home; I suppose she saw me coming and was trying to avoid me. She must have been startled, since I seldom venture out of the Higashiyama district. I hardly ever go downtown.

Quickening my pace a little, I caught up to within a few yards of her. But I didn't call, nor did she look back. We both kept on walking, the same distance apart. Meanwhile, I had glanced in at the window of the shop she had just left, a window full of ladies' accessories—lace and nylon gloves, all kinds of earrings, pendants, and the like. It occurred to me that she never wore Western clothes and wouldn't have any use for such things—but then I noticed, to my surprise, that pearl earrings were dangling from her ears.

When had she acquired a taste for wearing earrings with kimono? Had she just bought them and put them on in the shop, or was she in the habit of wearing them whenever she was out of my sight? Now and then, during the past month, I have seen her in one of those fashionable short *haori* called tea-jackets. And she had it on today. Before, she always refused to take up the latest styles, but I had to admit that this one was not unbecoming to her. What surprised me even more was that the earrings suited her so well. I recalled something Akutagawa Ryunosuke once wrote about the alluring pallor of the back of a Chinese woman's ears. My own wife's ears, seen from the back, were like that. They enhanced the pearls, and were enhanced by them—the effect was quite lovely. But I couldn't believe that this was her own idea. As usual, I had mixed feelings of jealousy and gratitude. It was chagrining to think that someone else had discovered this exotic aspect of her beauty, which I had failed to see. I suppose husbands are not so observant, because they look at their wives in a fixed way.

She crossed Karasumaru Avenue, and kept straight on. Besides her handbag, she was carrying a long, narrow parcel, probably from the shop she had just left. I couldn't tell what was in it. When I saw her going on down the next block I crossed the street and walked rapidly ahead, to let her know that I wasn't following her any more. Then I got on a east-bound streetcar at Horikawa.

She came home about an hour after me. The earrings were gone—in her bag, presumably. She was still carrying the parcel, but she didn't open it in my presence.

April 10

❀

I wonder if my husband's diary reveals anything about the state of his health. How much does it worry him? I have no way of finding out what he's thinking, of course, but for at least a month I've noticed that there's something wrong. Lately his complexion has been worse than ever—really ashen. He often falters going up and down the stairs. He has always had a strong memory, but he's becoming terribly forgetful; sometimes, talking on the phone, he can't think of a person's name, and he seems bewildered. When he's walking around the house he sometimes stops short and closes his eyes, or holds fast to a pillar.

Although he writes all his letters on formal letter paper, by brush, his writing is becoming dreadfully clumsy. (You'd expect a man's calligraphy to improve with age.) Frequently he's even wrong. I only see what is on the envelopes, but there's always a mistake or two. And the mistakes are glaring ones: he may give the wrong date, by several months, or put down something absurd for our own street number. Once he wrote "June" for "April," then crossed that out and neatly corrected it to "August." Worst of all, a letter to his uncle had two errors in the name itself. With dates and addresses, I quietly correct them before mailing; but this time I didn't know how to fix it, so I warned him, casually, that the name was wrong. He was obviously perturbed, but tried to seem calm. "So it is," he said, and put the letter on his desk without immediately correcting it. It's all very well about the envelopes, since I look them over carefully, but there's no telling what mistakes I'd find inside.

Maybe it's already common knowledge that he's behaving oddly. The other day I went to see Dr. Kodama—he's the only one I could consult about this—and asked him to persuade my husband to have a check-up. "That's something I've been wanting to talk to you about," he told me. It seems my husband himself was so worried that he went to see Dr. Noma, a professor on the medical-school faculty. Then, badly frightened by what he heard, he came to Dr. Kodama.

Dr. Kodama explained to me that, not being a specialist,

he couldn't make a definite diagnosis. "Still," he went on, "I was shocked to see how high his blood pressure was."

"How high was it?" I asked.

He hesitated a moment. "Perhaps I shouldn't tell you this," he said. "When I tried to measure it, my instrument nearly broke. It went over the top of the scale, and kept on climbing. I had to stop. I can't say how high it is."

I asked if my husband knew.

"He's been warned by Dr. Noma before," he answered, "but hasn't listened. I told him frankly that it was a dangerous condition." (I'm writing this because I don't think it matters if he reads it, since he's already heard it from Dr. Kodama.)

I suppose I'm to blame for having brought it on. If it hadn't been for my demands on him, he wouldn't have sunk to such depravity. When I talked to Dr. Kodama I had to blush. Fortunately he doesn't know the truth about our sexual relations. He seems to think I'm so passive that my husband's excesses are entirely his own fault. Probably my husband would say it all came about because he wanted to give me pleasure. I won't deny that; but for my part, I've done everything possible to fulfill my duty to him, I've put up with things that were really hard to bear. Toshiko would call me "a model wife." In a way, I think I am.

But there's no use trying to fix the blame, now that it's too late. We enticed each other; we urged each other on; we fought desperately, without quarter; and now at last, driven by an irresistible force, we've come to this.

I don't know whether I ought to mention it, or what may happen if he reads this, but the truth is, he isn't the only one whose health is bad. I'm not much better off myself. I began to be aware of it in January. Years ago, of course, when Toshiko was about ten, I started coughing up traces of blood, and the doctor warned me that I was showing symptoms of tuberculosis. But since that had turned out to be a mild case, I didn't worry about these new symptoms. (Yes, and the first time, too, I ignored the doctor's advice. It's not that I wasn't afraid of dying, but my instinct wouldn't let me dwell on it. I shut my eyes to the terror of death, and yielded blindly to sexual impulse. Although he was shocked at such recklessness, my husband soon gave in to me. I suppose I'd have died then, if I'd been unlucky. Somehow, as rash as I was, I got over it.)

And so this year, late in January, I had a premonition of illness; every now and then I felt a warm, itching sensation in my chest. One day in February, just as before, I coughed up a scarlet-flecked bit of phlegm containing a thread of blood. There wasn't much, but it happened two or three times. At the moment it seems to have subsided; I don't know when it may begin again. I'm sure I have a fever—my body is heavy, and my face and hands feel hot—but I don't intend to take my temperature. (Once I did, and it was 99.7°. I haven't taken it since.) I've also decided not to consult a doctor, though I've been having night sweats too.

Maybe this won't be any more serious than last time,

but it's not the kind of thing you can make light of. Luckily, as my doctor once told me, I have a strong stomach. He said people with chest trouble usually get thin: it was amazing I didn't lose my appetite. What worries me most is that my chest often aches quite severely, and by afternoon I feel exhausted. (To resist that feeling I press all the closer to Kimura-san. I can't overcome it without him.) Before, my chest didn't ache so badly, and I didn't feel such fatigue. Perhaps I'm gradually getting worse—I can't believe that this is only a trivial matter. Besides, I've done everything to ruin my health. They say drinking aggravates this illness; if that's so, it'll be a miracle if I recover. Now that I think of it, maybe I've let myself get drunk so often because I've had a feeling of despair, a feeling that I haven't long to live, anyway.

April 13

❀

I had thought that my wife might begin keeping different hours, which is exactly what she has done. Now that Kimura's vacation is over they can no longer meet in the afternoon. For a few days she stayed at home instead of going out immediately after lunch. However, yesterday at five o'clock Toshiko appeared, as if by previous arrangement, and Ikuko began getting ready to leave. I was in my study, but I soon realized what was happening.

A few minutes later she came upstairs and called to me through the door: "I'm leaving now, but I'll be home soon."

As usual, I merely said: "All right."

"Toshiko's here," she added, pausing on her way down. "You can have dinner with her."

"What about you?" I asked, somewhat annoyed.

"I'll eat when I get back," she said. "You can wait for me if you like."

But I told her not to hurry on my account. "I'll go ahead. You might as well have dinner out."

Suddenly I was curious to see what she was wearing. I got up quickly, went into the hall, and looked down the stairs. She had already reached the bottom, but I could see that she had on those pearl earrings. (Perhaps she would have put them on later if she had expected me to come out.) She was slipping on a pair of white lace gloves, too—I thought of the parcel she was carrying the other day. It seemed to embarrass her to be seen like this. Toshiko was just remarking how well the gloves suited her.

About half past six Baya came to say that dinner was ready. When I went down I found Toshiko waiting.

"You needn't have stayed," I told her. "I can eat by myself, you know."

"Mama said I ought to spend a little more time with

you," she said. I gathered that there was something she wanted to talk about.

It is true that I seldom have dinner alone with her, for of course Ikuko is usually here. Lately she's been going out a great deal, before dinner or after, but she makes a point of being home at dinnertime. Perhaps that is why I was feeling a certain loneliness, a sad, empty mood such as I have rarely experienced. And Toshiko's company only deepened my sense of loneliness; she was really being much too kind. Knowing her, I don't think it was accidental.

"Papa," she began, as we sat down at the table, "do you know where Mama goes?"

"I haven't the slightest idea," I said; "and I don't care to find out, either."

But she said flatly: "Osaka." Then she waited to see my reaction.

I almost blurted out "Osaka?"—but I stopped myself. "Is that so?" I said, as calmly as I could.

Toshiko went on to explain that the place she went to was five or six minutes' walk from the Kyobashi station, less than an hour from here by interurban express. "Shall I give you some more details?" she asked, and seemed quite ready to.

I tried to change the subject. "Never mind about that," I said. "How do you happen to know so much?"

"I helped find the place," she said coolly. "Mr. Kimura thought they'd be seen in Kyoto and wondered if I knew of somewhere not too far away. So I asked a sophisticated friend of mine, the sort of girl who knows all about such things." With that, she poured out a glass of brandy and offered it to me. I haven't been drinking recently, but she had brought the bottle of Courvoisier to the table. I took a sip, to hide my embarrassment.

"What do you think now, if I'm not being too inquisitive?" Toshiko said.

"Think about what?" I asked.

"Suppose Mama insists she still hasn't betrayed you," she said. "Would you believe that?" I asked whether her mother had told her anything like that.

"No, but I heard it from Mr. Kimura," she answered. "He says she's still being faithful to you—though I don't take that kind of nonsense seriously."

Toshiko poured another glassful. I accepted it without hesitation, and drank it down. I felt like getting drunk. "Do as you please," I said. "It's up to you whether you want to take it seriously or not."

"But how about *you?*" she asked.

"I trust Ikuko," I said. "No one has to defend her to me. Even if Kimura said he'd slept with her, I wouldn't believe it. She's not the kind to deceive me."

"Oh?" Toshiko gave a faint, muffled laugh. "Still, even supposing he hasn't 'slept with her,' in the way you mean, there are nastier ways of satisfying—"

"Will you stop it?" I said sharply. "Don't be so impudent: you talk like a sophisticated bitch yourself! Go on home! I don't need you around here."

"I'm going!" she said, flinging down her rice bowl. And she left.

My agitation at being caught off guard by her took a long time to subside. When she said "Osaka" I felt as if I had been kicked in the stomach—and the feeling lasted. Yet that doesn't mean I have never guessed what was going on. Perhaps the real shock was being confronted with something that I had done my best to ignore.

Of course it was the first time I had heard that they were meeting in Osaka. But where? I wondered. A small hotel, perhaps a disreputable one? I couldn't keep from imagining what kind of place it was, what their room was like, how they looked together.... "Asked a sophisticated friend of mine"?—somehow I was reminded of a cheap, cramped, one-room apartment. I pictured them in a high, Western-style bed; strangely enough, I felt I *wanted* them that way, rather than on the soft, matted floor of a purely Japanese room. "Some extremely unnatural method"—"other, nastier ways"—I could see them in all sorts of positions, a tangle of arms and legs. . . .

Doubts began to well up in me. Why had Toshiko made her disclosure? Had Ikuko suggested it? She may have written the same thing in her diary, and then become afraid that I wouldn't read it—or wouldn't admit I had. Perhaps she used Toshiko to force me to recognize that this time she had yielded herself completely. That was what worried me most. When Toshiko said: "I don't take that kind of nonsense seriously," hadn't Ikuko put the words into her mouth? Now that it's come to this, I realize how mistaken I was to reveal that "her physical endowment for it is equaled by very few women." I wonder how long she was able to resist the temptation to experiment with another man.

One reason why I haven't doubted her earlier is that she has never refused to sleep with me. Even when she has obviously just come from seeing him, she has never shown the slightest reluctance to let me make love to her. Far from it, she lures me on. I took this to mean that she wasn't sleeping with him. But I had overlooked her innate sensuality. Unlike most women, Ikuko welcomes repeated love-making—and can keep it up day after day. For anyone else, surely, it would be unbearable to repeat the act with a hated partner after leaving one you love. Yet even if she wanted to refuse me, her body would respond willingly to my embrace.

It was nine o'clock last night when she came home. I went into the bedroom at eleven, and found her already in bed. She was incredibly ardent, so ardent that I was forced into the passive role. In warmth, in eagerness, in responsiveness, she left nothing to be desired. Her seductive attitudes, her bold technique, the way she led us, step by step, to the most ravishing pleasure—all this proved how she abandoned herself to love.

April 15

❁

I can see that my brain is steadily deteriorating. Since January, when I became intent on satisfying Ikuko, I have found myself losing interest in everything else. My ability to think has so declined that I can't concentrate for five minutes. My mind teems with sexual fantasies. For years I have been a voracious reader, whatever the circumstances, but now I spend the whole day without reading a word. And yet, out of long habit, I continue to sit at my desk. My eyes are fixed on a book, but I scarcely read at all. To be sure, I am suffering from a visual disturbance that makes reading extremely difficult. The print looks double, and I have to go over the same line again and again.

Now at last I have been bewitched into an animal that lives by night, an animal good only for mating. By day, when I am shut up in my study, I feel intolerably tired and bored; at the same time, I am a prey to terrible anxiety. Going out for a stroll is somewhat diverting, but my dizziness gives me trouble in walking. I feel as if I am about to fall over backward. Even if I go out, I don't venture far from home. Leaning on my cane, I hobble about Hyakumamben, Kurodani, the Eikan Temple; I stay away from busy streets, and spend most of the time resting on benches. My legs are so weak that I soon become exhausted.

When I came back today Ikuko was talking to Miss Kawai, the dressmaker, in the sitting room. I was going to stop for a cup of tea, but she exclaimed: "Don't come in just now!" I peeped in anyway, and saw her trying on a foreign-style dress. She objected, and I went up to my study. Later I heard her calling to say that she would be gone for a little while. She seemed to be leaving with Miss Kawai.

From the second-floor window I looked at the two of them walking along together. It was the first time I had seen Ikuko in Western clothes. No doubt this is what she was getting ready for when she began wearing gloves and earrings with kimono. But, to tell the truth, her new dress is not very becoming. It doesn't seem to suit her. I should have thought that, compared with the squat, shapeless Miss Kawai, Ikuko would have looked attractive in such clothes. But Miss Kawai is accustomed to them, and wears them with a flair. My wife's earrings and lace gloves didn't suit her as well as they had before. Then they had seemed exotic, but today, with foreign dress, they struck me as unnatural, ill-assorted. There was a lack of harmony between her clothes, her accessories, and her figure.

These days it is becoming popular to wear Japanese things in a Western manner, but Ikuko does the opposite. You can see that she is built for kimono. Her shoulders are too sloping for Western clothes. Worse yet, her legs are bowed—slender and trim enough, but excessively curved out from knee to ankle. In silk stockings her ankles seem rather puffy. Moreover, the way she carries herself—her walk, the movements of her shoulders and trunk, the way she holds her hands, the tilt of her head—everything about her is pliant and feminine in the traditional Japanese style, a style that is suited to kimono.

All the same, I felt a strange voluptuousness in her slender, supple figure, her awkwardly curved legs. This was something that had been concealed from me when she wore kimono. As I watched her walk away I gazed admiringly at the distorted beauty of her legs below the tweed skirt. And I thought of tonight.

April 16

❀

This morning I went shopping, to the Nishiki Street market. For weeks now I've been out of the habit—I've left everything to Baya. But it seems unfair to my husband, somehow, as if I'm slighting my duty as a housewife. And so today I went. (It's true that I've scarcely had time for trips to Nishiki Street; I've been kept busy by a far more important matter.)

At the vegetable shop I always go to I bought garden peas, broad beans, and bamboo shoots. Seeing the bamboo shoots reminded me that the cherry-blossom season was over—gone before I'd even thought of it. Wasn't it last year that Toshiko and I went to look at the flowers together, walking along the canal from the Silver Pavilion to the Honen Temple? The blossoms along there must have fallen by now. But what a restless, uneasy spring this has been! The last two or three months have gone by in a twinkling, like a dream.

I was home by eleven, and went upstairs to change the flowers in the study, to put in some mimosa that Madame Okada sent over from her garden today. Apparently my husband had slept late; he came in while I was arranging the mimosa. He's always been an early riser, until quite recently.

"Did you just get up?" I said.

He asked if it was Saturday, and then: "I suppose you'll be out all day tomorrow." His voice sounded drowsy, as if he were still half asleep. (But I could tell that he was worried.) I murmured a vague reply.

About two o'clock I heard someone at the door, and found a man I didn't know standing there. He said he was a massage therapist from the Ishizuka Clinic. It seemed most unlikely that anyone at our house would have called such a person, but Baya came up and said she'd sent for him on my husband's orders. That was very odd. He's always disliked the notion of being touched by a stranger; this is the first time he's ever let a masseur near him. Baya said he'd been complaining that his shoulders were so stiff he could hardly turn his head, and she told him she knew a wonderful massage doctor. Wouldn't he just try him? It was like magic—after once or twice, he'd forget he'd ever had such troubles. He seemed to be in a great deal of pain, and asked her to send for him.

The man was about fifty, rather sinister-looking, thin, wearing dark glasses. I thought he might be blind, but he wasn't. Baya was upset when I referred to him as a masseur. "He'll get angry if you call him that," she said. "He's a doctor!"

As soon as he was in our bedroom the "doctor" had my husband lie down, and climbed on the bed himself to perform his treatment. He was wearing a clean white clinic coat, but he gave the impression of being dirty. I didn't like to see him there on the bed—I think it's quite natural to have an aversion to masseurs. And this one kept saying: "Pretty stiff, aren't you? I'll have those kinks out in no time!" He had a ridiculously self-important air.

After massaging my husband till four o'clock, he said: "You'll feel fine after another session or two. I'll be back tomorrow." Then he left.

"How do you feel?" I asked my husband.

"A little better," he said, "but it was quite an ordeal. My whole body aches from the pounding and squeezing."

I reminded him that the man would be back tomorrow.

"Well, let him try it once or twice more," he said. He did seem awfully stiff.

"I suppose you'll be out all day tomorrow," he remarked again. It was hard for me to tell him: "I'm going out now, too," but it couldn't be helped.

At half past four I changed into my new Western clothes, put on my earrings, and deliberately looked in at the bedroom, as much as to say: "I'm leaving."

"Are you going for a walk?" I asked him, to hide my embarrassment.

"Yes, I'll be leaving too," he said, lying there flat on his back, still worn out from the treatment.

April 17

❈

A day so critical for my husband is critical for me, too. Maybe what I write here will preserve the memory of it for the rest of my life. I'd like to put down all that's happened, minutely, concealing nothing. Still, it's best not to be too hasty. At this point I'd be wise to avoid going into detail about where and how I've spent my time.

Anyway, my Sunday plans were made long in advance, and I carried them out exactly as I'd intended. As usual I went to meet Kimura at our hotel in Osaka, and enjoyed a few hours of happiness with him. Today we were ecstatically happy, perhaps more than any of our other Sundays together. We made love in every conceivable way. I did whatever he wanted, yielding myself completely to him. I twisted my body into fantastic postures that would have seemed unthinkable with my husband. When on earth had I acquired such skill, such freedom? I couldn't help being astonished, though I knew I owed it all to Kimura.

Always, when we meet there, we abandon ourselves to love; we regret even the slightest pause, and never waste a moment in idle talk. But today Kimura suddenly fixed a sharp look on me, and asked: "What are you thinking, Ikuko?" (He's been calling me Ikuko for some time now.)

"Nothing," I said. But just then—an experience I'd never had at a time like that—my husband's face flashed into my mind. I couldn't imagine why.

As I was trying to erase that image, Kimura said: "It's your husband, isn't it? I seem to be worrying about him too." He went on to say how awkward he felt about visiting our house, though he really ought to call on us soon. In fact, he'd written home and asked them to send us some more mullet roe—hadn't it reached us yet?

That was all we said, and once again we plunged into our world of love. But now I wonder if I'd had a kind of premonition.

When I came home at five, my husband was out. The massage doctor had called again, Baya said, and had treated him at least half an hour longer than yesterday. She reported what the man had told him: the stiffness in his shoulders was a sign of high blood pressure, but doctors' medicines wouldn't do any good, not even from one of those fancy medical-school doctors. "You'd better leave it to me," he had said. "I'll guarantee to cure you. I'm not just a physical therapist, I use acupuncture and moxa, too. If massage doesn't work, I'll use the needles: it'll help your dizziness within a day. Even though your blood pressure *is* high, you shouldn't worry about having it measured all the time. As long as you do, it'll keep going higher and higher. Lots of people get along perfectly well at two hundred, or at two hundred and forty or fifty, without taking any special care of themselves. It's best not to worry. A little alcohol and tobacco won't do any harm. You'll get over it," he had reassured him. "Your high blood pressure is definitely not going to kill you."

According to Baya, my husband was quite taken with the man. He told him to come every day, for the time being, and said he'd stop going to the doctor.

At six-thirty he came back from his walk, and at seven we had dinner together. Baya cooked the things I bought at Nishiki Street yesterday; we had broad beans, garden peas with Koya bean curd, soup made out of the bamboo shoots. In addition, there was about a half-pound of tenderloin of beef. He's supposed to be on a vegetarian diet, but to cope with me he eats beef every day. Sukiyaki, grilled meats, roasts, all sorts of dishes—what he likes most is half-raw steak, dripping with blood. He seems to feel uneasy if he doesn't have it. I usually broil the steaks myself when I'm home, since they're hard to time.

I could see that the mullet roe had arrived; there was some on the table. Soon my husband suggested having a drink to go with it, and brought over the Courvoisier. But we didn't drink very much. The other day when he quarreled with Toshiko he nearly emptied the bottle; we finished off what was left with a glass apiece. Then he went back upstairs. At ten-thirty I told him the bath was ready. After he finished, I bathed—the second time today. I'd had a bath in Osaka, but took another for appearance' sake. That's happened before.

When I came into our room I found my husband already in bed. As soon as he saw me he turned on the floor lamp. Nowadays he likes to keep the bedroom dim, except when we're making love. Hardening of the arteries seems to be affecting his sight: he's bothered by flickering double and triple vision. Sometimes the strain is so bad he has to shut his eyes. That's why he turns the fluorescent lamp on full only at that special time. Now it has a stronger bulb, so it's quite powerful.

When he looked at me in that sudden glare of light, he blinked with astonishment. After bathing, I had put on my earrings. I got into bed, purposely lying so that he could see my jeweled ears. As trivial a thing as that, the merest novelty, is enough to arouse him. He calls me sex-mad, but I'm sure there's no other man so obsessed by it. From morning till night it's his one concern. He never fails to respond to the slightest hint; whenever he sees a chance, he takes advantage of it.

In a moment he was climbing into my bed, embracing me, showering kisses on my ears. I lay there with tight-shut eyes, letting him do as he pleased. And that sensation—being titillated by a "husband" I can no longer say I love—was not wholly unpleasant. Even while I was thinking how clumsy his kisses were, compared with Kimura's, the queer, ticklish sensation from his tongue didn't seem merely disagreeable. It *was* disagreeable; but it had a kind of sweetness, too, and I was able to enjoy its flavor. It's true I detest that man from the bottom of my heart; yet when I think how infatuated he is with me, I have an urge to drive him into paroxysms of desire. I'm a person who can keep love and lust completely separate. On the one hand, I treat him coldly, find him nauseating, even; on the other, I'm so eager to seduce him that before I know it I've seduced myself. At first I'm icily calm, absorbed in wondering how I can excite him further. Maliciously I watch him gasp as if he's losing his mind, and I'm intoxicated by the skill of my own technique. But then at last I find myself gasping the same way, as excited as he is.

Tonight I repeated with him, one after another, all the things I'd done with Kimura this afternoon. How very different it was—I began to feel sorry for my clumsy husband. Yet somehow, as this was going through my mind, I became just as aroused as I'd been in the afternoon. I locked my arms around him, embracing him as fiercely as I'd embraced Kimura. (I suppose he would say this proves how oversexed I am.) Again and again I clasped him, until I was on the verge of a climax. At that moment his body began to quiver; then he went limp, and collapsed heavily on me.

I knew instantly that this was serious. When I spoke to him, he only uttered a hollow, meaningless sound. I felt a warm liquid on my cheek—his mouth was open, and saliva was dribbling from it.

April 18

❁

I remembered what Dr. Kodama told me to do in case of an emergency like this. Gently, laboriously, I began to pull myself out from under the inert body. (He was settling forward, as if borne down by a crushing weight. Doing my best not to jolt him, I drew my head free. First, though, I took off his glasses. That blank face of his—

eyes half opened, muscles slack—had never been more repulsive.) I got out of bed and slowly, with great care, turned him on his back. Then I propped his head up with pillows. He was stark naked (so was I, except for my earrings); but since I knew he needed absolute quiet, all I did was to lay his night kimono over him.

The whole left side of his body seemed to be paralyzed. I looked to see what time it was: three minutes past one. It occurred to me to turn off the fluorescent lamp and use only the little night lamp, with a cloth to shade it. I telephoned Toshiko and Dr. Kodama, and asked them to come right away; I told Toshiko to wake the iceman and bring along fifteen pounds of ice. Although I meant to be very calm, the receiver trembled in my hand.

Toshiko got here about forty minutes later. I was in the kitchen looking for an ice bag; she came in, put the ice on the drainboard, and glanced sharply at me to see my expression. Then she turned away, casually, and began cracking the ice. I explained Papa's condition to her. She showed no emotion whatever, only nodding occasionally as if to say there was no use getting alarmed. After that we went to the bedroom and applied the ice bag to the side that wasn't paralyzed. We didn't exchange a single unnecessary word. We didn't even look at each other. . . . We tried not to look.

At two o'clock Dr. Kodama arrived. I had Toshiko stay at the bedside, and went to meet him. On our way to the room I hastily explained the circumstances of my husband's stroke—including something I hadn't mentioned to Toshiko. Once again I blushed.

Dr. Kodama's examination was very thorough. He asked for a flashlight, and used it to test the patient's eye reflexes. Then he wanted a chopstick. Toshiko brought a pair from the kitchen. "Now make the room a little brighter," he said, and had us turn on the fluorescent lamp. He rubbed the tip of a chopstick up the soles of the feet slowly, from heel to toe, repeating this several times. That was for Babinski's reflex, he told me later. When one of the feet reacts by bending back, it indicates that there has been a cerebral hemorrhage on the other side. In this case, he had to conclude that part of the brain had been cut off, somewhere on the right side.

Next he took off the light blanket I'd covered my husband with and rolled his night kimono up as far as his abdomen. For the first time Dr. Kodama and Toshiko realized that my husband had been naked. They both seemed to shrink from the sight of him—stretched out under that ugly glare. I felt more embarrassed than ever. It was hard to believe that only an hour ago that man had been lying with me. As often as he's looked at me in the nude, even photographed me, I had never looked at him this way before. Of course I could have if I'd wanted to, but I've tried to avoid it. I'd cling to him and shut my eyes. He has examined every inch of me, to the very pores of my skin, but I haven't known his body nearly as well as I know Kimura's. I haven't wanted to. I suspected it would only make me detest him all the more. It gave me a queer feeling to think I've been sleeping with such a miserable creature. And he called *me* bow-legged!

Dr. Kodama spread my husband's legs about half a yard apart. Then, with the chopstick, he rubbed both sides of the scrotum, just as he'd rubbed the soles of the feet. (Later he explained that he was testing the reflexes of the suspensory muscles.) He rubbed one side and then the other, several times each. The right testicle made a slow up-and-down motion, like the squirming of a live abalone, but the left one didn't seem to move. (Toshiko and I tried to look away. Finally Toshiko left the room.) Next he took his temperature and measured his blood pressure. The temperature was normal. Blood pressure: 190+. Apparently it had dropped a bit as a result of the hemorrhage.

For over an hour and a half Dr. Kodama stayed at the bedside to see how his patient was getting along. During that time he drew one hundred grams of blood from a vein in his arm and gave him an injection of Neophyrin, vitamins B-1 and K, and a fifty percent glucose concentrate.

"I'll call again in the afternoon," he said, "but it would be a good idea to have Dr. Noma look at him." That was something I'd intended to do anyway.

I asked if I should inform the relatives.

"I think you can afford to wait a little," he told me.

Dr. Kodama left at about four a.m. At the door, I asked him to send us a nurse as soon as possible.

At seven Baya came, and Toshiko went home to Seki-dencho. She said she'd be back in the afternoon.

As soon as Toshiko was gone I called Kimura. I told him what had happened to my husband, and added that for the present he'd probably better not come over. He was quite disturbed, and said he wanted to stop in to see him for a moment, at least. But I explained that it might upset him—in spite of his paralysis and loss of speech, he still seemed to be partly conscious. "Then let me come to the front door," Kimura said. "I won't go to his room."

Around nine o'clock my husband began to snore. It's an old habit of his, but today it was different, really dreadful. He seemed to have lapsed into a coma. I telephoned Kimura again to say there'd be no harm in looking in on him, if he continued like this.

Dr. Kodama phoned at eleven. "I've been in touch with Dr. Noma," he told me. "We'll be over to see the patient at two o'clock."

At twelve-thirty Kimura arrived, between classes. He went to the sickroom and sat at the bedside for about half an hour. I stayed too; Kimura sat in the chair, and I on the other bed (my husband was in mine). We exchanged a few words now and then. Meanwhile the snoring got louder and louder, until it seemed quite thunderous. Suddenly I wondered if it was genuine. I could see that Kimura noticed my misgivings, and even shared them, but of course neither of us said anything about it. At one o'clock he left. The nurse arrived—a pretty girl in her early twenties named Koike. Toshiko came too. At last I was free, so I went to the kitchen to eat. It was my first meal since yesterday.

At two Dr. Noma arrived, along with Dr. Kodama. Since morning my husband had developed a 100.8° fever. Dr. Noma seemed to be in general agreement with Dr. Kodama. He tested Babinski's reflex again, but not the other one (apparently it's called the scrotal reflex). He didn't think it wise to deplete the blood very much. And he gave Dr. Kodama some further advice, in technical language.

After the doctors had gone, the massage therapist turned up for another session. Toshiko sent him away, with a sarcastic remark about how his treatments had helped her father. That was because Dr. Kodama said, earlier, that the long, drastic massage might have brought on my husband's stroke. (I suppose he was trying to console me.) Baya apologized profusely. Introducing that man was a terrible thing to have done, she said.

A little after three Toshiko suggested I lie down for a while, and I decided it was a good chance to get some sleep. The bedroom was occupied, of course, and there was a good deal of coming and going through the sitting room. Toshiko's room was free, but she doesn't like anyone else to use it; she keeps her closet doors, bookcases, and desk drawers all locked tight. I've hardly ever set foot in it. So I came upstairs to the study, spread the bedding out on the floor, and lay down to sleep. I suppose the nurse and I will be taking turns here. But I had to admit that I was in no mood for sleep. I wanted to catch up with my diary—which I'd smuggled along with me, making sure not to let Toshiko notice. After spending an hour and a half at it, I finished the entry for the seventeenth. Then I hid the diary behind the bookshelf and went downstairs, as if I had just awakened. It wasn't quite five o'clock.

My husband had emerged from his coma. Now and then he opened his eyes a little and glanced around. I was told he'd been doing it for about twenty minutes. The coma had lasted since nine a.m., over seven hours. Miss Koike said she'd heard it was dangerous if it lasted twenty-four hours, and so he was getting along well. But the left side of his body still seemed to be paralyzed.

About five-thirty he began mumbling, as if he wanted to talk. I couldn't understand what he was trying to say, but he didn't sound quite as inarticulate as before. He moved his right hand slightly, pointing to the lower part of his abdomen. I guessed that he wanted to urinate, and gave him the bedpan. But he didn't pass anything. He seemed to be terribly irritated. He nodded when I asked if he wanted to make water, so I tried again—and again nothing came out. It must have been painful, since his urine had been collecting for such a long time. I decided that his bladder was paralyzed. After calling Dr. Kodama to get instructions, I sent out for a catheter, which Miss Koike used to draw off the urine. I could see that there was a great deal.

At seven we gave him a little milk and fruit juice through a straw.

At ten-thirty Baya went home. She said she couldn't stay overnight, because of her family. Toshiko asked if I needed her for anything. I knew that she was implying: "There's no reason why I shouldn't stay, except that it might be inconvenient for you." I told her she could do as she pleased; there was no special danger; the patient seemed to be holding his own. I could let her know if he took a turn for the worse. "Yes, I suppose so," she said, and at eleven she left for Sekidencho.

He seemed to be dozing, not sleeping very soundly.

April 19

❀

At midnight Miss Koike and I were sitting quietly together in the sickroom. We had turned the lamp away from my husband, and were passing the time reading newspapers and magazines. I urged her to go and rest for a little, but she didn't want to. About five o'clock, when it was already getting light, she finally went upstairs.

The sun began filtering in through the shutters, and it

seemed to disturb my husband's sleep. Suddenly I noticed that his eyes were open, staring in my direction. He seemed to be looking for me—I wonder if he really couldn't see me as I sat there beside him. He was trying to say something. All I recognized—or thought I recognized—was a single word. Maybe it was just my imagination, but he seemed to be saying "Ki—mu—ra." The rest was only a kind of gurgling sound, but that much seemed unmistakable. Maybe he'd have said the rest of it more clearly, too, if it hadn't been quite so embarrassing. After repeating it two or three times he stopped, and shut his eyes.

At seven Baya arrived, and then Toshiko. An hour later Miss Koike came downstairs.

At eight-thirty we gave him his breakfast: a bowl of thin rice gruel, an egg yolk, apple juice. I spooned it up for him. He seemed to want me, rather than Miss Koike, to take care of him.

A little after ten o'clock he wanted to urinate. I tried to get him to use the bedpan, but nothing came out. When Miss Koike tried to draw off the urine, he objected, and made a gesture as if to say: "Take that thing away!" All we could do was give him the bedpan again. After ten minutes there were still no results. He seemed terribly annoyed. Miss Koike brought out the catheter again, and talked to him as if she were trying to reason with a child. "You may not like this, but you'll feel a lot better afterward. Come on, you'll let me use it, won't you? You'll feel better right away."

He was trying to tell us something, trying to indicate it with his hands. All three of us—Miss Koike, Toshiko, and I—kept asking him what he wanted. We gathered that he was talking to me, and saying: "If the catheter has to be used, you use it. Have Toshiko and the nurse go away." At last Toshiko and I persuaded him that the nurse was the only one who could do it properly.

At noon we gave him his lunch. It was about what he'd had this morning, but his appetite seemed fairly good.

At twelve-thirty Kimura arrived. Today I only talked to him at the door. I told him that my husband was out of his coma, that he seemed to be gradually improving, that he'd mumbled something that sounded to me like "Kimura."

One p.m. A visit from Dr. Kodama. He said the patient was making satisfactory progress. We still had to be very careful, but if his recovery continued at this rate, everything would be fine. Diastolic blood pressure 165, systolic, 110. Temperature down to 99°. Again today he tested Babinski's reflex and the scrotal reflex. During the latter I wondered uneasily whether my husband would put up with it. But he did, staring off into space with glazed, expressionless eyes. Dr. Kodama also gave him an intravenous injection of dextrose, Neopyrin, and vitamins.

I've tried as far as possible not to let anyone know about his stroke, but the news has leaked out at school. This afternoon there were a number of telephone calls and visitors; people have begun sending fruit, flowers, and other such things, too. Madame Okada came over, and was all the more sympathetic when she learned that it was the same illness as her husband's. She left us some lilacs from her garden. Toshiko filled a vase with them, brought it into the sickroom, and placed it on a bedside table. "Papa, these are from Madame Okada's garden," she told him. We'd also received some mandarin oranges, which he likes. I squeezed them in the mixer and gave him the juice.

At three I left everything to Toshiko and Miss Koike, and came upstairs. After writing in my diary, I tried to get some sleep. Naturally I was very tired by then, and I slept soundly for about three hours.

Tonight Toshiko went home at eight, soon after dinner. Baya left at nine-thirty.

April 20

✿

One a.m. Miss Koike went upstairs to sleep, and I stayed alone with my husband. He had been dozing since early evening. About ten minutes after she left, though, I began to think he might really be awake. He was lying in the shadow, but I could hear him stirring and mumbling. Stealthily I peered over at him, and saw that, just as I'd imagined, he was lying there with his eyes open. He was looking in my direction, but beyond me. Those lilacs Toshiko had brought in—his eyes seemed fixed on them. The lamp was shaded so that it lighted up only a small part of the room; within that little pool of lamplight, barely enough for reading a newspaper, the lilacs were dimly glowing. He seemed to be staring blankly at their pale silhouette, as if he were lost in thought. It bothered me, somehow. Yesterday, when Toshiko told him they were from Madame Okada's garden, it occurred to me— though I can't say what prompted her to do it—that she needn't have mentioned it just then. I suppose he heard what she said. Even if he didn't, those flowers must have reminded him of the lilac bush in the garden at Sekiden-cho. And then he must have thought of Toshiko's cottage, and of all that had happened there at night.

It may have been only my imagination, but as I looked into his eyes I thought that fantasies of that sort were drifting in their vacant depths. Hurriedly I turned the lamp away from the flowers.

Seven a.m. I took the lilac vase out of the bedroom, replacing it with some roses in a glass bowl.

One p.m. A visit from Dr. Kodama. Temperature down to 98.2°. Blood pressure rising again: diastolic, 185, systolic, 140. To correct it, an injection of Neohypotonine.

Again today Dr. Kodama performed that scrotal-reflex test. I went to the door with him, and stepped outside to consult him about a few things. I told him that the paralysis of the bladder continued, so that Miss Koike had had to use the catheter again this morning; that my husband was annoyed every time she did it; that the slightest thing seemed to get on his nerves, but what especially irritated him was that his hands and legs and mouth didn't work the way he wanted them to.

Dr. Kodama says we should give him Luminal to calm him down and make sure he sleeps.

Today Toshiko didn't turn up until five p.m. About ten o'clock I began to hear my husband snoring—not that abnormal snoring of the day before yesterday, but the way he usually sounds when he's asleep. Apparently the injection of Luminal had already taken effect. Toshiko watched his face a moment, and remarked that he seemed to be having a good rest. She left soon after. Baya left too. I sent Miss Koike up to bed.

Toward eleven o'clock the phone rang. It was Kimura. "I'm sorry to bother you at this hour," he said. (Had Toshiko told him I'd be alone now?) He asked how my husband was getting along. I told him, and mentioned that he was sound asleep, under sedation.

"Could I just look in for a moment?" he asked. Look in at whom? I wondered.

"Yes, if you'll wait in the garden till I come out the back way," I answered, very softly, my mouth close to the telephone. "You mustn't ring the doorbell. If I don't come out, you'll know it isn't convenient, so please go on home."

Fifteen minutes later I heard a faint sound of footsteps in the garden. My husband's noisy breathing went on as steadily as ever. I brought Kimura in through the back door, and we talked for half an hour in the maid's room.

When I returned to my husband, he was still snoring peacefully.

April 21

❀

One p.m. A visit from Dr. Kodama. Diastolic blood pressure 180, systolic, 136. It's gone down a little, but he won't be out of danger until the diastolic is in the 170's with a difference of at least fifty between the two readings. But his temperature is finally back to normal. This morning he managed to pass urine, using the bedpan. His appetite is good; he eats anything I give him, though for the present he's on a soft diet.

At two o'clock I left Miss Koike in charge and went up to bed. After writing in my diary, I slept till five. When I came down, Toshiko had arrived. At five-thirty, half an hour before dinner, we gave him another injection of Luminal. Dr. Kodama advised us to give it to him regularly at this time, since it takes effect only after four or five hours. But he warned Miss Koike not to say that it was a sedative: she should let him think it was something to lower his blood pressure.

At six o'clock, when he saw the dinner tray, my husband started mumbling. Whatever he was saying, he repeated it two or three times. I spooned up some of the rice gruel for him, but he said it again, as if to hold back my hand. I thought perhaps he didn't like having me serve him, so Toshiko, and then Miss Koike, tried instead. But that wasn't it. Meanwhile, I'd gradually begun to understand him. Fantastic as it seemed, he was saying "Be-e-e-f st-e-eak." And as he said it he glanced quickly at me, with a look of appeal, then shut his eyes again. I could guess what was in his mind, but Miss Koike—and Toshiko?—probably couldn't. I shook my head at him, discreetly, to hint that he would have to wait, that he mustn't even think of such a thing now. I wonder if he understood. In any case, he let it go at that, and opened his mouth meekly to sip the gruel that I held out to him.

At eight o'clock Toshiko left; at nine, Baya. At ten he fell sound asleep and began snoring. I sent Miss Koike upstairs.

At eleven I heard footsteps in the garden. I brought him in the back way, to the maid's room. He left at twelve. The snoring continued.

April 22

❀

Not much change in his condition. His blood pressure was a little higher again. He sleeps well enough under sedation, but during the day his mind is clouded, and he's often irritable. Although Dr. Kodama says he needs at least twelve hours of sound sleep, he probably doesn't get more than six or seven. The rest of the time he seems to be merely dozing. On the whole, it's been my experience that he's not really asleep unless he's snoring—but now there are times when even his snoring sounds suspicious. Tomorrow, with the doctor's permission, we're going to begin giving him Luminal twice a day: once in the morning and once in the afternoon.

Toshiko and Baya left at their usual times. At ten o'clock the snoring began. At eleven I heard footsteps in the garden.

April 23

✤

It's been almost a week since he had his stroke. At nine a.m., when Miss Koike was taking the breakfast tray back to the kitchen, he saw that we were alone, and began trying to talk. "Di-a-ry, di-a-ry," he was saying. Compared with yesterday's "be-e-e-f st-e-e-ak," it sounded quite distinct. Again he repeated the word "diary." Evidently it was weighing on his mind.

"Do you want to write in your diary?" I asked. "But that's still too much for you!"

He shook his head.

"No?" I said. "It's not your diary, then?"

"*Your* diary . . ." he answered.

"Mine?" I exclaimed.

He nodded, and said: "You . . . what are you doing . . . about your diary?"

I pretended to be annoyed. "You know very well I've never kept a diary."

He smiled weakly, and nodded as if to say: "Yes, of course! I understand." It was the first time he had smiled for me, even faintly, but his smile was a rather perplexing one.

Miss Koike had her own breakfast in the sitting room; she came back at about ten o'clock. Then, without a word, she began getting ready to inject the Luminal into his arm.

"What's this?" he asked suspiciously. He'd never had an injection at this time in the morning.

"Your blood pressure is still a little high," she told him. "I'm giving you something to bring it down."

One p.m. Visit from Dr. Kodama. Around two-thirty, noticing that my husband had begun to snore, I went upstairs. When I came down at five the snoring had already stopped. According to Miss Koike, he slept less than an hour; after that he seemed to be dozing. Apparently he still can't rest very well in the daytime, even with a sedative. After dinner we gave him the second injection.

At eleven sharp I heard footsteps in the garden.

April 24

❋

This was the first Sunday after his stroke. We had two or three callers, but I didn't ask them in. Dr. Kodama didn't come to see him. No change in his condition.

Toshiko arrived about two o'clock, a good deal earlier than usual. She's been coming late in the afternoon, and staying only a few hours. Today, as she stood there beside her father, who was fast asleep, she said: "I thought you might have a lot of visitors." She was watching my face.

When I didn't answer, she went on: "Mama, don't you have any shopping to do? Why don't you go out for a little fresh air, now that it's Sunday?"

Was that really her own idea? I wondered. Maybe he asked her to suggest it. Of course he could easily have said something to me. Did he prefer to have Toshiko do it for him, or was she simply acting on her own suspicions? . . . Suddenly I could see him at our Osaka hotel, eagerly awaiting me, at that very moment. Suppose he actually *was* there—but then I checked myself. After all, it seemed most unlikely. Yet the notion kept coming back to me.

Clearly though, I didn't have time to go to Osaka. I couldn't possibly be away that long, at least not until next Sunday.

However, there was something else on my mind, so I told Toshiko I'd go to pick up a few things at the Nishiki market. "I'll be back in an hour," I said. It was three o'clock when I left the house.

I found a taxi and hurried down to Nishiki Street. First, to justify the trip. I bought wheat-gluten cakes, toasted bean curd, and some vegetables. After that I walked up Teramachi as far as Sanjo, and stopped in at the stationer's for ten large sheets of rice paper and a sheet of cardboard. I had them all cut to the size of my diary and carefully wrapped; then I put them in my shopping bag, under the vegetables. I went over to Kawaramachi Street for a taxi—but I mustn't forget to mention that I telephoned him from the market.

"No, I wasn't planning to go out at all today," he told me. He said it hesitantly, as if he thought I might be suggesting we meet. But we only talked for a few minutes.

I got home a little after four (I'd been gone just over an hour), hid the package of rice paper behind the umbrella rack, and took the shopping bag out to Baya in the kitchen. My husband still seemed to be asleep, though he wasn't snoring.

What had bothered me was his question about my diary. Why had he come out with that? Had he forgotten, in his confused mental state, that he wasn't supposed to know about it? Or was he saying: "I don't see any more need to pretend"? And when I tried to wriggle out of it by telling him I've never kept one, did that odd smile of his mean "Stop playing innocent"? Anyway, he obviously wanted to know if I'd kept up my diary. Next he will want to see it. Since he can no longer read it behind my back, he's begun to hint that he'd like my permission. I have to be ready for the time when he asks me openly.

As far as the entries up to the sixteenth of this month are concerned, I'm willing to show them to him whenever he likes. But he must never know that it doesn't stop there. "You've been reading my diary in secret," I'll tell him, "so there's no use hiding it any more. Look at it all you want, though it's hardly worth showing to you. As you'll see, it ends on the sixteenth. Since then, I've been far too busy to have time for keeping up a diary—not that I've done anything worth writing about."

But I'll have to prove it by showing him there are only empty pages after the sixteenth. With my new rice paper, I can divide the book at that point, add the proper num-ber of blank sheets, and rebind it in two volumes.

I'd missed my afternoon nap, so I went upstairs to rest for about an hour. When I came down at half-past six I brought along the diary and put it in the drawer of the sitting-room cabinet. Toshiko left after dinner, at eight o'clock. At ten I had Miss Koike go upstairs. At eleven I heard footsteps in the garden.

April 25

❀

At midnight I saw him out and fastened the kitchen door. Then I stayed in the bedroom about an hour, listening intently. As soon as I'd satisfied myself that my husband was asleep, I went to the sitting room and got to work rebinding my diary. When I finished I put the part with the old entries back in the cabinet drawer, and took the other upstairs and hid it behind the bookshelves. It was after two o'clock when I returned to the bedroom. He was still fast asleep.

One p.m. Visit from Dr. Kodama. No particular change. Lately his blood pressure has been fluctuating in the 180's. Dr. Kodama frowned, and said he wished it would go down a little further. As usual, my husband couldn't seem to sleep very well during the day.

At eleven I heard footsteps in the garden.

April 28

❀

At eleven, footsteps in the garden . . .

April 29

❀

At eleven, footsteps in the garden . . .

April 30

❁

One p.m. Visit from Dr. Kodama. He says Dr. Noma ought to have another look at the patient early next week.

May 1

❁

This was the second Sunday after his stroke. Again Toshiko arrived early, as I'd expected. She listened to make sure her father was asleep, then, in a low voice, urged me to go out shopping and get a little air.

"Should I?" I said, hesitating.

"Papa's all right," she assured me. "He's just fallen asleep. Go ahead, Mama, and stop in at Sekidencho on your way home. We've got the bath heated."

I guessed that there was something behind it. "Well, then, just for an hour or two," I said. It was about three o'clock when I left the house.

I went straight to Sekidencho. Kimura was there alone. He said Toshiko had phoned to ask him to come over for two or three hours, while she went to visit her father. She told him she'd promised to look after the house for Madame Okada, who was spending the day in Wakayama. The bath was stone cold.

For the first time in weeks we were able to have a few leisurely hours together. Yet somehow we felt restless; we couldn't seem to relax. . . . At five I left him there and hurried out to do my shopping at a nearby market. I was afraid my husband might have awakened.

"You're back early," Toshiko said. When I asked how Papa had been, she told me he'd slept amazingly well—more than three hours already. Sure enough, he was snoring loudly.

"Your daughter took care of the patient while I went for a bath," Miss Koike said, her pink, shiny face glowing as if she had just stepped out of the tub. So she had gone to the bathhouse! I couldn't help thinking Toshiko had seen to it. Of course it was Miss Koike's turn to go; we've only heated our own bath two or three times since my husband has been sick, and Baya, Miss Koike, and I have been going to the public bathhouse every other day or so, in the afternoon. Toshiko must have known that when she sent me out. It was careless of me not to have thought of it myself. I suppose I would have—and would have remembered that Miss Koike takes almost an hour at her bath—except that when Toshiko mentioned Sekidencho it made my heart leap, made me forget all about being cautious.

Now I've done it! I thought, as I left them to go upstairs for my nap.

I took the diary from its hiding place behind the bookshelves and examined it very carefully. I should have sealed it with Scotch tape, perhaps, but I hadn't dreamed of being *that* cautious. And so there was no way for me to find out—but I told myself I was only imagining things. I had let my suspicions carry me too far. How could anyone know I'd taken my diary apart and hidden this section of it upstairs? Looking at the matter that way gave me a sense of relief.

But at eight, when Toshiko left for Sekidencho, I started worrying again. I went to the kitchen and asked Baya if anyone had gone up to the study this afternoon. She surprised me by saying that Toshiko had. Apparently Miss Koike left about fifteen minutes after I did; then Toshiko went upstairs. She came down in a few minutes and went back to the bedroom. "She seemed to be talking to the master about something," Baya said.

"I thought he was asleep," I said.

"He woke up suddenly," she told me, and added that Toshiko went upstairs again later, but stayed only a moment. Then Miss Koike came back from the bath-house.

"But he was snoring when I got home," I objected.

"Not while you were gone," she said. "He fell asleep just before you came in."

I began to realize that my fears were not quite so groundless as I had supposed. Perhaps I should try to set down what Toshiko must have done today. At three o'clock, after managing to get rid of me, she sent Miss Koike off to the bathhouse. Then—whether or not my husband put her up to it—she hunted out my diary in the sitting-room cabinet and brought it to him. He noticed that it stops on April sixteenth, and told her there should be another book hidden somewhere—that's the one he wanted to see! Next she rummaged through the book-shelves in his study, found it, and brought it down to show him. Maybe she read it aloud to him. After that she took it upstairs and put it back in its hiding place. Miss Koike returned. Again he pretended to be fast asleep. At five I came home.

But, supposing I've guessed right, how shall I protect my diary now? I can't bring myself to give it up just because of a single blunder. Still, I've got to make sure it won't hap-pen again. From now on I'll stop writing upstairs during my nap time. Late at night, after my husband and Miss Koike are both asleep, I'll make a new entry, and then hide the book away in some really safe place.

June 9

❀

For a long time I've neglected my diary. I haven't touched it since May first—the day before my husband was carried off by another stroke. That is partly because his sudden death burdened me with all sorts of family duties; partly, too, it's because I lost the desire—perhaps I should say incentive—to go ahead with it. My reason for "losing incentive" remains unchanged, and so this may be my final entry. At least, I haven't yet decided to go on.

I do feel that a diary I've succeeded in keeping up for four whole months deserves to be brought to a conclusion, rather than simply dropped. But I'm not just being tidy. I think it will be worth my while, at this point, to look back once again at the conflict in our sexual life, and try to recall its various phases. If I compare his diary with my own I ought to be able to understand what really happened. Then there were a number of things I hesitated to put in writing while he was alive. I'd like to add them as a kind of postscript, to bring this account to a close.

As I've said, my husband died suddenly. I don't know

the precise time, but it was on May second—probably around three a.m. His nurse, Miss Koike, was sleeping upstairs, and Toshiko had gone back to Sekidencho. I was the only one left taking care of him. At two, since he was snoring peacefully, I slipped out to the sitting room, where I began making an entry in my diary. Until then— from the time he fell ill, that is—I'd done my writing during the afternoon. I'd go upstairs for my nap, and steal the chance to jot down what had happened the day before. But on Sunday, May first, I got the impression that this part of my diary, which I'd carefully hidden, was being read by Toshiko and my husband. I decided to change my habits, do all my writing late at night, and find a new hiding place. However, since I couldn't think of a good one, I left the diary in its usual place and went downstairs. That night, as soon as Toshiko and Baya were gone, I took it out again and tucked it away in the folds of my kimono. Soon afterward Miss Koike went to bed. I was worried because I still hadn't hit on a safe place for it. Of course I had the whole night to think of one; if necessary, I could even stuff it between the loose ceiling boards in the sitting-room closet.

At two a.m. on May second, then, I went to the sitting room, took out the diary I'd been carrying, and began writing. Some time later I realized with a start that my husband's breathing, so noisy until a few moments ago, had become inaudible. There was only a thin wall between us, but I'd been so absorbed that I hadn't noticed the silence. I became aware of it just as I finished writing these words: "Late at night, after my husband and Miss Koike are both asleep, I'll make a new entry, and then hide the book away in some really safe place."

I put down my brush and listened, my ears cocked toward the bedroom. But I couldn't hear anything, so I got up, leaving my diary on the table, and went to look at him. He was lying on his back, his face turned straight up. (That was the way he usually slept, with his gray, naked face—he never wore glasses after his stroke—in full view. I could scarcely avoid looking at it.) He seemed to be sleeping quietly. It was hard to tell, though, since a cloth had been draped over the lamp shade, and his head lay in the shadow.

I sat down for a moment and watched him, there in the gloom. But he seemed strangely quiet, so quiet that I uncovered the lamp and let the bare light strike his face. Then I saw that his eyes were half open, fixed in a rigid, slantwise stare. He's dead, I thought; and when I went over to touch his hand, it was cold. The clock said seven minutes past three. And so I can only be sure that he died sometime between two and three a.m. on May second. He must have died in his sleep, without pain. For a few moments, like a coward peering into the depths of an abyss, I held my breath and looked into that gray, naked face. Memories of our honeymoon night came flooding into my mind. Then I hastily covered the lamp again.

The next day both Dr. Noma and Dr. Kodama told me

they hadn't expected him to have another stroke so soon. Till about ten years ago, they said, most patients suffered their second attack of cerebral anemia after two or three— at the longest, seven or eight—more years, and the second one was usually fatal. Now, however, thanks to the progress of medicine, that was no longer true. Some people had one or two strokes and then recovered; some even survived three or four. With my husband, there was clearly danger of a relapse, because, unlike most educated men, he tended to ignore his doctor's advice. Still, they hadn't thought it would come so soon. He wasn't sixty yet; once he had regained his health, no matter how slowly, he ought to have been active for several more years—over ten years, if all went well. It was really quite unexpected . . . or so they said.

Of course I can't tell if they were being honest with me, but maybe they were. Doctors are never very accurate about predicting how long a man will live. As for myself, I felt it had happened more or less as I'd expected. It didn't come as a shock to me. I'm often wrong in my intuitions, more often than not, perhaps; but this time I guessed right. So did Toshiko, I imagine.

Now I want to reread our diaries and compare them, tracing the steps by which we came to this final parting. To be sure, he told me he began keeping a diary years ago, before we were married; maybe I ought to start there in order to study our relations thoroughly. But I'm not the kind of person for such a research project. I know there are dozens of diaries piled up in the closet in his study, so high you can't reach them without a ladder; but I don't have the patience to wade through those dusty old books. As he said himself, he used to be careful not to mention anything about our sexual life. It was in January that he began writing about it freely—almost exclusively—and that I began to contend with him by keeping a diary of my own. By comparing entries from that time on (and filling in what we left out), I ought to be able to see how we loved, how we indulged our passions, how we deceived and ensnared each other, until one of us was destroyed. I don't think there'll be any need for me to go further back.

In his New Year's Day entry he says that I am "furtive, fond of secrets, constantly holding back and pretending ignorance." That is perfectly true. On the whole, he was far more honest than I was—I have to admit that his diary has very few falsehoods in it. It has a few, though. For instance, he says: "It seems unlikely that she would dip into her husband's private writings. . . . I have decided not to worry about that any more." I saw at once that his real motive was just as he later admitted: "Secretly, I hoped that she was reading it."

The fact that he purposely dropped the key (on the morning of January fourth) proves that he wanted me to read his diary. Really, he needn't have bothered to tempt me. On January fourth I said: "I shall never read it. I haven't the faintest desire to penetrate his psychology, beyond the limits I've set for myself. I don't like to let others know what is in my own mind, and I don't care to pry into theirs." But that wasn't true—except when I said: "I don't like to let others know what is in my own mind." Soon after our marriage I got into the habit of glancing over his secret notebooks. Of course I'd "known about his diary for a long time." It's nonsense to say "I'd never dream of touching it."

In the past, though, he concentrated on what were, to me, dry-as-dust academic matters. And so I merely leafed through the pages now and then, for the mild satisfaction of reading something of my husband's behind his back. But ever since he "decided not to worry about that," I've naturally been drawn to his diary. As early as January second, while he was out on a walk, I discovered how it had changed. Still, it wasn't just because I like to "pretend ignorance" that I kept on being secretive about it. I could tell that that was what he wanted me to do.

I think he was being quite sincere when he called me his "beloved wife." I haven't the slightest doubt of his love. In the beginning I myself felt a passionate love for him. I can't deny that "I accepted a man who was utterly wrong for me," nor that "sometimes the very sight of him made me queasy." But that doesn't mean I didn't love him. Having had an "old-fashioned Kyoto upbringing," I "married him because my parents wanted me to, and I thought marriage was supposed to be like this." I had no choice but to love him. He was right to say I set great store by my "antiquated morality." Whenever I began to be sickened by him, I felt ashamed of myself. I thought I was behaving inexcusably toward my dead parents, as well as toward him; the more I loathed him, the more I tried to love him. And I succeeded. Driven by sexual hunger, I could do nothing less.

At the time, my only regret was that he didn't fully satisfy me. Instead of accusing him of weakness, though, I felt ashamed of my own lustful appetite. I was sorry about his declining vigor, and, far from blaming him, tried to be all the more devoted. But since January I've had to look at him in a new light. It's still not clear to me why he decided he would "begin writing freely." He said it was "out of frustration at never having a chance to talk to her about our sexual problems . . . because of her extreme reticence—her 'refinement,' her 'femininity,' her so-called modesty." He wanted to sweep away all that—but wasn't there another reason, too? I think there was, though I can't find anything clearcut about it in his diary. Maybe even he didn't understand his real motive.

Anyway, I learned that my "physical endowment for it is equaled by very few women." But then he said: "Perhaps I shouldn't mention this. At the very least, it may put me at a disadvantage." Why did he decide to run the risk? He said that the mere thought of it made him jealous, that he worried about what might happen "if another man knew of it." Yet he deliberately mentioned it in his diary.

I took that to mean he hoped I would give him cause to doubt me. And, later on, he wrote: "I secretly enjoyed being jealous. Such feelings have always given me an erotic stimulus; in a sense, they're both necessary and pleasurable to me" (January thirteenth). But I had already gathered that from his New Year's Day entry.

June 10

❀

On January eighth I wrote: "I violently dislike my husband, and just as violently love him. No matter how much he disgusts me I shall never give myself to another man."

For twenty years I'd felt obliged to suppress my dissatisfaction with my husband. That is why, in spite of a strict Kyoto upbringing, I allowed myself to write unpleasant things about him. Above all, though, I'd begun to understand that making him jealous was the way to make him happy—and that that was the duty of a "model wife." Still, I'd only said: "I violently dislike my husband"—and then added feebly: "I shall never give myself to another man." Maybe I already loved Kimura without realizing it. All I did—fearfully, and in a roundabout way at that—was to drop a disturbing hint. And I did it reluctantly, from a sense of duty.

But my feelings changed when I read his entry of the thirteenth: "Stimulated by jealousy, I succeeded in satisfying Ikuko. . . . I want her to make me insanely jealous. . . . Not that there shouldn't be an element of danger—the more the better."

My thoughts turned suddenly to Kimura. On the seventh my husband had written: "Although Ikuko may believe that she is merely acting as a chaperone, I think she finds Kimura extremely attractive." But that had only repelled me, made me think that, no matter what he said, I couldn't possibly be so immoral. When it came to being told "the more the better," I had a change of heart. I'm not sure whether he said it because he realized—before I did—that I liked Kimura, or whether it was what he said that began to stir my interest. Even after I knew I was drifting into love with Kimura, I went on deceiving myself, as long as I could, that I was doing it reluctantly, for the sake of my husband. Yes, I was already drifting into love, but I told myself I was only trying to show a little interest in another man.

On the first night I fainted (January twenty-eighth, that is) I could no longer explain my feelings for Kimura that way; all I could do was try to conceal my suffering. I slept straight through to the morning of the thirtieth. He wrote: "Of course she may have been only shamming." I certainly wasn't shamming, though I can hardly say I remained unconscious all that time. I suppose he was right in calling me half awake; but as to whether I was "really delirious" when I murmured Kimura's name, or whether "that was only a subterfuge," I'd say it was somewhere between the two. It's true I was "dreaming of making love with Kimura"; but just then I became vaguely—only vaguely—aware that I'd called his name. How shameful of me! I thought. Yet as much as it embarrassed me to have my husband hear such a thing, I *did* feel, too, that what had happened was for the best.

But the case was different on the following night (the thirtieth), even though he said: "She murmured Kimura's name again—was she having that same dream, that same delusion, just as she had had before?" That night I did it intentionally. I can't say I'd formed a definite purpose—maybe I was dreaming a little, after all—but that haziness helped to still my conscience. "Should I, perhaps, interpret it as a kind of ridicule?" he wondered. Maybe he was right. I was trying to tell him how I longed to be in Kimura's arms instead of his, and how I wished he would bring the two of us together. That is what I wanted him to understand.

On February fourteenth Kimura told my husband about the Polaroid camera. "But how did he guess that I would be pleased to learn about such a camera? That puzzles me." It puzzled me, too. I hadn't guessed that my husband wanted to take nude photographs of me. Even if I had, I couldn't have said so to Kimura. At that time I was being carried to bed by him, drunk, nearly every night; but I never had a private talk with him, much less tell him anything about our sexual life. The truth is I had no other relations with him—I didn't have the chance. Personally, I was inclined to suspect Toshiko. She's the only one who could have given him the hint.

On February ninth she asked permission to live alone, in Sekidencho, saying she wanted a quiet place to study. It wasn't hard to imagine that "a quiet place" meant somewhere away from her parents' bedroom. She must have been peering in night after night at that garishly lighted spectacle—what with the roaring of the stove, we couldn't have heard her footsteps. I suppose she saw my husband stripping me naked and doing all sorts of lewd things. And I suppose she told Kimura about it. Later my suspicions were more or less confirmed, but I'd already guessed as much from my husband's diary of the fourteenth. Toshiko probably knew what was going on—and reported it to Kimura—even before I did.

But why did Kimura tell my husband about that special camera, as if to suggest photographing me in the nude? I haven't asked him yet, but perhaps he was trying to curry favor. Besides, he must have hoped to see the pictures someday. Probably that was his main reason. I suppose he expected my husband to turn from the Polaroid to the Zeiss Ikon, and to want him to do the developing.

On February nineteenth I wrote: "I cannot imagine what is in Toshiko's mind." That wasn't quite accurate. As I've said, I already felt sure she'd told Kimura what went on in our bedroom, and I realized, too, that she was in love with him. That's why she was "secretly hostile to me." It's true she worried about my health, and hated her father for "forcing me to satisfy his sexual demands." But when she saw him bringing Kimura and me together, and saw us indulging his strange whim, she began to hate me too. I suspected that very soon. Toshiko is wily, and knows that "though she's twenty years younger, she's actually not as attractive as I am in face or figure." Knowing, too, that Kimura was falling in love with me, she decided to act as go-between for us; then, at leisure, she could devise a scheme of her own. That much was clear to me. Yet even now I'm not sure how closely she and Kimura worked together. For instance, I don't think she moved to Seki-dencho merely to get away from home: the fact that Kimura was living nearby must have had something to do with it. Was it his idea or hers? He said she made the arrangements ("I only followed her lead")—but I wonder if that was true. I'm afraid I still don't trust him.

At heart, I was as jealous of Toshiko as she was of me. But I tried not to let anyone notice it, nor to betray it in my diary. That was partly out of my natural secretiveness; even more, though, it was because I felt superior to her, and my pride was involved. Most of all, I was afraid my husband might think that I had reason to be jealous, that I suspected Kimura of being interested in her. My husband wrote: "If I were he, and had to say which of the two I found more attractive, I have no doubt that, despite her age, I would choose the mother." But he added: "I can't tell about him. . . . He may be trying to improve his chances by ingratiating himself with Ikuko."

I didn't want to revive any notions of that kind. I wanted him to think of Kimura as completely infatuated with me, ready for any sacrifice on my account. Otherwise, his own jealousy would have been weakened.

June 11

❀

On February twenty-seventh my husband said: "I was right, after all! Ikuko has been keeping a diary. . . . I got an inkling of it several days ago."

I'm sure he knew it long before, and was reading it behind my back. Of course I'd written: "I won't make the mistake of letting him suspect what I'm up to." But I was lying. I wanted him to read it. It's true I wanted to "talk to myself," too, but that wasn't really why I began keeping a diary. Being so secretive—using rice paper, sealing the book, and all that—was simply my natural way of going about it. Although he ridiculed me for it, he was just as bad. We knew we were reading each other's diaries, and still we set up all sorts of barriers, to make it as difficult and uncertain as possible. We preferred to be left in doubt. I didn't mind the trouble, since I was catering to both our tastes.

On April tenth I mentioned his illness for the first time. "I wonder if my husband's diary reveals anything about the state of his health. . . . For at least a month I've noticed that there's something wrong." Actually, he began writing about it on March tenth; but I think I noticed it even earlier, though I pretended I hadn't. I was afraid of worrying him, especially because he might feel he had to give up sexual intercourse. It's not that I wasn't concerned about his health, but the need to gratify my desire seemed far more urgent. Using Kimura to inflame his jealousy, I did all I could to make him forget his fear of death.

In April, though, my feelings slowly began to change. All through March I'd written that I was still stubbornly defending the "last line," and I did my best to convince him of it. In fact, it was on March twenty-fifth that I surrendered that last "paper-thin" defense. The next day I invented a harmless conversation with Kimura to put in my diary. I think it was early in April, around the fourth or the fifth, that I made a grave decision. Enticed into immorality, I'd been sinking lower and lower, but until then I'd deceived myself that it was only because I couldn't refuse what my husband wanted. I'd told myself I was behaving like a devoted wife, even from an old-fashioned moral point of view. But then I threw off the mask of self-deception, and frankly admitted I was in love with Kimura.

On April tenth I wrote: "He isn't the only one whose health is bad. I'm not much better off myself." Of course I wasn't at all sick—I had something else in mind. It's true that "when Toshiko was about ten, I started coughing up traces of blood, and the doctor warned me that I was showing symptoms of tuberculosis." But luckily "it turned out to be a mild case," and has never bothered me since. As for my statements that "one day in February, just as before, I coughed up a scarlet-flecked bit of phlegm containing a thread of blood," that "by afternoon I feel exhausted" and "my chest often aches quite severely," that this time I was afraid I might be "gradually getting worse"—those were all downright lies. I was trying to lure him into the shadow of death. I wanted him to think I was gambling my own life, and that he ought to be willing to risk his.

From then on my diary was written solely for that purpose. I didn't just write, though; sometimes I acted out my symptoms. I did everything I could to excite him, to keep him agitated, to drive his blood pressure higher and higher. (Even after his first stroke I kept on playing little tricks to make him jealous.) Long before, Kimura had hinted that my husband seemed on the verge of collapse. To me—and no doubt to Toshiko—his opinion meant more than any doctor's.

But why did I go so far as to scheme against my husband's life? Why did such an appalling thought come to me? Was it because anyone, no matter how gentle, would have been warped by the steady pressure of that degenerate, vicious mind of his? Maybe, deep down in me, I'd always been capable of it. It's something I'll have to think about. Yet I do feel, after all, that I can claim to have given him the kind of happiness he wanted.

I still have a good many suspicions about Toshiko and Kimura. She said she found the Osaka hotel for us—through "a sophisticated friend" of hers—"because Mr. Kimura wondered if I knew of somewhere." Was that really all there was to it? She herself may have used that hotel with someone—may be using it even now.

According to Kimura's plan, he'll marry Toshiko when the mourning period is over. She'll make the sacrifice for the sake of appearances; and the three of us will live here together. That is what he tells me. . . .

Diary of a Mad Old Man

❊

June 16

❀

This evening I went to the Kabuki. All I wanted to see was *Sukeroku*, I had no intention of staying for the rest of the program. Kanya as the hero didn't interest me, but Tossho was playing Agemaki and I knew he would make a beautiful courtesan. I went with my wife and Satsuko; Jokichi came from his office to join us. Only my wife and I knew the play, Satsuko never saw it before. My wife thinks she may even have seen it with Danjuro in the lead, she isn't sure. But I have vivid memory of seeing him in it. I believe that was around 1897, when I was thirteen or fourteen. It was Danjuro's last Sukeroku; he died in 1903.

We were living in the Honjo district of Tokyo in those days: I still remember passing a famous print shop there—what was the name of it?—with a triptych of Sukeroku in the window.

I suppose this was Kanya's first attempt at the role, and sure enough his performance didn't appeal to me. Lately all the actors cover their legs with tights. Sometimes the tights are wrinkled, which spoils the effect completely. They ought to powder their legs and leave them bare.

Tossho's Agemaki pleased me very much. I decided it was worth coming for that alone. Others may have acted the part better, but it is a long time since I have seen such a beautiful Agemaki. Although I have no homosexual inclinations, recently I've come to feel a strange attraction toward the young Kabuki actors who play women's roles. But not off stage. They don't interest me unless they're made up and in feminine costume. Still, if I stop to think of it, I must admit to a certain inclination.

When I was young I had an experience of that kind, though only once. There used to be a handsome young actor of female roles called Wakayama Chidori. He made his debut at the Masago Theater in Nakasu, and after he got a little older he played opposite Arashi Yoshizaburo. I say "older," but he was around thirty and still very beautiful: you felt as if you were looking at a woman in the prime of life, you wouldn't have believed it was a man. As the daughter in Koyo's *A Summer Gown*, I found her—or rather him—utterly captivating. Once I remarked jokingly to a teahouse mistress that I'd like to ask him out some evening, dressed just as he was for the stage, and maybe even see what he was like in bed. "I can arrange it for you," she told me—and she did! Everything went perfectly. Sleeping with him was exactly like sleeping with a geisha in the usual way. In short, he was a woman to the very last, he never let his partner think of him as a man. He came to bed in a gaudy silk undergarment, and still wearing his elaborate wig lay there in the darkened room with his head on a high wooden pillow. It was a really strange experience, he had an extraordinarily skillful technique. Yet the fact is that he was no hermaphrodite, but a splendidly equipped male. Only, his technique made you forget it.

But as skillful as he was, I have never had a taste for that sort of thing, and so my curiosity was satisfied after a single experience. I never repeated it. Yet why, now that I am seventy-seven and no longer even capable of such relations, have I begun to feel attracted, not to pretty girls in trousers, but to handsome young men in feminine attire? Has my old memory of Wakayama Chidori simply been revived? I hardly think so. No, it seems to have some connection with the sex life of an impotent old man—even if you're impotent you have a kind of sex life. . . .

Today my hand is tired. I'll stop here.

June 17

❀

Let me add a little more about what happened yesterday. Although it was raining last night—the rainy season has begun—I found the heat oppressive. Of course the theater was air-conditioned, but that kind of air conditioning is very bad for me. It made the neuralgia in my left hand ache more than ever, and the numbing in the skin got worse too. I always have trouble from my wrist to my fingertips, but last night it hurt up to the elbow joint, and sometimes even beyond, all the way to my shoulder.

"There, didn't I tell you so?" my wife said. "But you wouldn't listen to me. Do you still think it was worth coming? To a second-rate performance like this?"

"Oh, it's not so bad. Just to look at that Agemaki helps me forget the pain."

Her reproaches made me all the more stubborn. However, my arm was getting a bad chill. I was wearing a silk mesh undergarment, an unlined kimono of a thin, porous wool, and over that a summer cloak of raw silk; in addition, I had my left hand in a gray woolen glove and was holding a pocket warmer wrapped in a handkerchief.

"I understand what Father means," Satsuko said. "Tossho's wonderful!"

"Darling—" Jokichi began, but changed his tone. "Satsuko, do you really appreciate his acting too?"

"I don't know about his acting, but he's beautiful to look at. Father, how about coming to the matinee tomorrow? They're doing the Teahouse scene of *The Love Suicides at Amijima*—he'll be marvelous in it! Wouldn't you like to go tomorrow? The longer you wait, the hotter it'll be."

To tell the truth, my arm was bothering me so much I had thought of giving up the matinee program, but my wife's nagging made me want to come again out of sheer perversity. Satsuko was amazingly quick to grasp how I felt. The reason she is in disfavor with my wife is that in cases like this she ignores her and tries to ingratiate herself with me. I suppose she likes Tossho well enough, but probably she is more interested in Danko, who was to play the hero.

The Teahouse scene on today's afternoon program began at two o'clock and finished around twenty past three. It was hotter than yesterday, with a broiling sun. I was worried about the heat too, but especially about the effect of that extreme air conditioning on my arm. Today the chilling would be all the worse. Our chauffeur wanted us to start out early. "We didn't have any trouble last night," he said, "but at this time of day we're bound to run into a demonstration somewhere or other, around the Diet Building or the American Embassy." We had to leave at one o'clock. There were only the three of us, Jokichi didn't come.

Fortunately we arrived without too much delay. The curtain-raiser was still going on. We went into the restaurant to wait until it was over. Satsuko and my wife had ice cream, so I ordered some too, but my wife stopped me. The Teahouse scene included Tossho as Koharu, Danko as Jihei, and Ennosuke as Magoemon. I remember seeing it years ago at the Shintomi Theater with Ennosuke's father playing Magoemon, and the former Baiko as Koharu. Danko's Jihei was very intense, I could tell he was putting all he had into it; but he was too intense, too strained, he ended by being tight and nervous. Of course that was only to be expected of a young man in such a major role. You can only hope that his efforts will eventually lead to something. But I should think he would have chosen a role from the Edo repertory, instead of trying to play an Osaka character. Tossho was beautiful today too, though I have the feeling he was better as Agemaki. We didn't stay for the third piece on the program.

"As long as we've come this far, let's stop in at a department store," I said, expecting my wife to object. She did.

"Don't you think you've had enough air conditioning? It's so hot you ought to go straight home!"

"You see how this is?" I showed her the tip of my snakewood cane. "The ferrule came off. I don't know why, but they never last very long. Two or three years at the most. Maybe I can find a cane I like at Isetan."

Actually, I had something else in mind, but I didn't mention it. "Nomura, do you think we can avoid the demonstrations on the way back?"

"I think so, sir." According to our chauffeur, one faction of the Students' Federation was out today: it seems they had planned to gather at Hibiya Park at two o'clock and march toward the Diet Building and the Metropolitan Police Headquarters. We'd be all right if we stayed away from that part of town, he said.

Men's furnishings were on the third floor; they didn't have a cane I liked. I suggested stopping at the second floor to see the special women's fashion exhibit. The summer sale was on, and the whole store was crowded. They were showing all sorts of summer clothes in the "Italian style" by famous *haute couture* designers. Satsuko kept exclaiming how marvelous they were, and didn't want to leave. I bought her a Cardin silk scarf for three thousand yen.

"I'm dying to have one of these, but they're just too expensive!" She was sighing with admiration over an imported handbag of beige suède, its frame studded with imitation-looking sapphires. The price was twenty-odd thousand yen.

"Have Jokichi get it for you. He can afford a thing like that."

"It's no use. He's too stingy."

At five o'clock I suggested going down to the Ginza for supper.

"Where on the Ginza?" my wife asked.

"Let's go to Hamasaku. I've been hungry for eel lately."

I had Satsuko phone in for seats at the counter. I told her to call Jokichi too and ask him to meet us there at six, if he could. Nomura said the demonstrators would come to the Ginza around ten o'clock before breaking up. If we went right away we could be home by eight and avoid any trouble. All we had to do was go downtown by circling around the other side of the palace, and we'd have nothing to worry about. . . .

June 18

❀

(Continued from yesterday.)

We reached Hamasaku by six. Jokichi was already there. My wife and I sat side by side, then Satsuko and Jokichi, in that order. While we drank green tea, the young people had beer; our appetizer was chilled bean curd, but theirs was different, to go with their drinks. I asked for fish salad too. For the *sashimi* course my wife and Jokichi had thin-sliced sea bream, and Satsuko and I ordered *hamo* eel with plum sauce. I was the only one who had broiled eel, the other three preferred broiled sweet-fish; we all had mushroom custards and sautéed egg plant.

"I think I'd like something else," I said.

"Are you serious?" my wife asked incredulously. "Haven't you eaten enough?"

"It's not that I'm hungry, but whenever I come here I get a craving for Kyoto food."

"I see they have *guji*," Jokichi said.

"Father, would you like to finish this?" Satsuko's *hamo* was almost untouched. She had eaten only a slice or two of it, meaning to give the rest to me. To be honest, perhaps I went there last night with the expectation—or was it the object?—of getting her leftovers.

"That's fine, but I gobbled mine up so fast they've already taken away my plum sauce."

"I have some of that left too." Satsuko handed the sauce dish over to me along with the eel. "Or shall I order another one for you?"

"Never mind. This will do."

In spite of showing so little interest in the *hamo* Satsuko had smeared her plum sauce around untidily—not a very ladylike way of eating. Maybe she did it on purpose.

"Here's the part of the sweetfish you like," my wife said. She has a special talent for extracting its bones neatly, and she puts them aside with the head and tail and eats up every scrap of flesh, leaving her plate as clean as if a cat had licked it. She is also in the habit of saving the viscera for me.

"You can have mine too," Satsuko offered. "But I'm clumsy at eating fish, so it isn't as neat as mother's."

That was an understatement. The remains of her sweet-fish were even messier than the plum sauce. It seemed to me that this might have a meaning too.

During our conversation Jokichi remarked that he would be going to Hokkaido on business in a few days. He expected to be there about a week, and he told Satsuko she could come along if she liked. After thinking it over for a moment, Satsuko said she'd always wanted to see Hokkaido in the summer but would pass it up this time—she had promised Haruhisa to go to a boxing match on the twentieth. Jokichi said "Oh?" and let it go at that. We got home around seven-thirty.

This morning, after Keisuke left for school and Jokichi for his office, I walked out to the pavilion in the garden. It's about a hundred yards to the pavilion, but my legs have been weakening lately, every day it seems a little harder to walk. The dampness of the rainy season has something to do with it, though I didn't have this much trouble last year. My legs aren't as painful or sensitive to cold as my arms, but they feel oddly heavy and tend to get in each other's way. At times the heaviness is centered in the kneecap, at times in the instep or in the soles of my feet; it changes from day to day. The doctors have different opinions about it too. One of them tells me that I am still showing traces of the mild stroke I had some years ago, that it produced a slight cerebral change which is affecting my legs. And when I had an X-ray examination I was told that my cervical and lumbar vertebrae were warped out of line, and advised to begin lying on an inclined bed with my neck suspended, as well as to wear a temporary collar-like plaster cast around my neck. I can't stand being cramped and squeezed like that, so I've been trying to put up with the trouble in my legs. Even though walking is hard for me, I have to walk at least a little every day. I've been warned that if I don't I will soon lose the use of my legs altogether. To avoid falling I steady myself with a bamboo cane, but usually Satsuko or the nurse or someone comes along with me. This morning it was Satsuko.

"Satsuko, here." While I was resting in the pavilion I took a tightly folded packet of money out of the sleeve of my kimono and slipped it into her hand.

"What's this?"

"Twenty-five thousand yen. You can buy the handbag you saw yesterday."

"That's sweet of you!" She quickly tucked the money away into her blouse.

"But maybe my wife will suspect I bought it for you, if she catches you with it."

"Mother didn't see this one when we were in the store. She was walking ahead of us at the time."

Now that I think of it, Satsuko was perfectly right. . . .

June 19

❀

Although today is Sunday, Jokichi left on his business trip from Haneda Airport this morning. Satsuko went out of the house soon after him, in the Hillman. It's become her private car—the way she drives, the rest of us are afraid to ride with her. She wasn't going to the airport. She was going to the movies downtown to see Alain Delon, probably with Haruhisa again. Keisuke moped around the house alone. He seemed to be waiting impatiently for Kugako and her children, who were coming over from Tsujido.

Dr. Sugita visited me a little after one p.m. I had been in so much pain that Miss Sasaki decided she ought to telephone him. According to Dr. Kajiura's diagnosis at the Tokyo University Hospital, the damage to my brain is almost entirely repaired by now—the pains I suffer indicate the onset of a rheumatoid or neuralgic condition. On Dr. Sugita's advice I went to the Toranomon Hospital the other day for an orthopedic examination, with X rays. They startled me by saying that it might be cancer, since the pain in my arm was so severe and the area around the cervical vertebrae was cloudy; and they even took tomographic X rays of my neck. Luckily, I didn't have cancer, but I was told that the sixth and seventh cervical vertebrae were deformed. So were the lumbar vertebrae, but not as much. Since this was what caused the pain and numbing in my arm, the way to cure it was to make a smooth, slippery board, put sliding wheels under it, and incline it to about thirty degrees; at the beginning I would lie on it for about fifteen minutes morning and evening with my neck in a "Glisson's sling" (a kind of neck sling made to order by a specialist in medical appliances) to stretch my neck by the weight of my body. If I kept up this exercise for two or three months, gradually increasing its length and frequency, I ought to feel better. In all this heat I have no desire whatever to do such a thing, but Dr. Sugita urged me to try it, for want of a better treatment. I don't know whether I will or not, but I have decided to call in a carpenter and a medical appliance man and order the equipment.

Kugako came around two o'clock. She had her two younger children with her, the other one was at a baseball game or somewhere. Akiko and Natsuji went immediately to Keisuke's room. It seems they're planning to go to the zoo. Kugako stuck her head in to say hello, and is now busy chattering away with my wife in the sitting room, just as she always does.

Today I have nothing else to write about, so I'll try to set down a few of the thoughts that have been preying on my mind.

Perhaps everyone is like this in his old age, but lately I never spend a day without thinking of my own death. In my case, though, it's hardly anything new. I've done it for a very long time, since my twenties, but now more than ever. Two or three times a day I think to myself: Maybe I'll die today. Not that I am necessarily frightened by such thoughts. When I was young they did terrify me, but now they even give me a certain pleasure. I let my imagination picture the scene of my last moments, and what will follow my death. Instead of having the service in the funeral hall at the Aoyama Cemetery, I want my coffin to lie in the ten-mat room facing our garden. That will be convenient for the people who come to offer incense: they can go from the main gate to the inner gate and follow the stepping-stones. I don't care for that Shinto-style music with reed pipe and flageolet, but I'll have someone like Tomiyama Seikin sing "The Moon at Dawn." I can almost hear his voice now:

> *Half-hidden by the pines along the shore*
> *The moon sinks toward the sea—*
> *Have you awakened from this world of dreams*
> *To dwell in the pure radiance of Paradise?*

I'm supposed to be dead, but I feel as if I can hear it anyway. I can hear my wife crying too. Even Itsuko and Kugako are sobbing, though I've never been able to get along with them. Satsuko is sure to be calm—or maybe she'll surprise everyone by crying. At least she may pretend she is. I wonder how my face will look when I'm dead. I'd like it to be as plump as it is now, even to the point of being a bit repulsive. . . .

Just as I got this far, my wife came in with Kugako and announced that Kugako had a favor to ask of me.

This was the "favor." Kugako says their eldest son Tsutomu has found a sweetheart and wants to get married. He's really too young for it, he's only in his second year at college, but they've decided to let him go ahead. Still, they feel uneasy about having the young couple go off on their own to an apartment, so they'd like to have them live at home until Tsutomu has graduated and found a job. But their present house at Tsujido isn't large enough for that. Even now it's uncomfortably small for Kugako and her husband and their three children. And if Tsutomu brings in a wife, sooner or later there'll be a baby. Under the circumstances, they want to move to a little roomier and more modern house—and right there in Tsujido, five or six blocks away, the very house they've been looking for has come on the market, and they're trying to raise the money to buy it. They need two or three more million yen. They can scrape up another million somehow, but anything over that will be awkward at present. Of course she isn't asking her father to give it to her. They mean to borrow it from a bank, but she wonders if I couldn't help out by lending them the twenty thousand yen they'll need for the advance interest. They'll pay it back before the end of next year.

"You've got some stocks, haven't you?" I said to her. "Can't you sell them?"

"If we sell our stocks we'll be left penniless!"

"Of course you will!" my wife chimed in. "You mustn't touch that money!"

"Yes, we want to keep it for an emergency."

"What are you talking about? Your husband's still in his forties. How can you be so timid at that age?"

"Kugako's never asked you for anything since the day she was married," my wife said. "This is the first time. Don't you think you ought to let her have it?"

"She says twenty thousand yen, but what'll they do if they can't pay the next quarterly installment?"

"Let's not worry about that till the time comes."

"In that case there'll be no end to it."

"Kugako's husband certainly isn't going to cause you any trouble. He just says he'd like a little help now, so they won't lose the house."

"Don't you think you could find the interest money for them?" I asked my wife.

"The very idea of asking me for it! When you bought Satsuko the Hillman!"

That annoyed me, and I made up my mind to refuse. Then I felt better.

"Well, let me think it over," I said.

"Can't you give them an answer today?" my wife insisted.

"I've got a lot of expenses just now."

Muttering something between themselves, the two left the room.

What a time to break in and interrupt me! Well, suppose I pursue my thoughts a little further.

Until I was in my fifties there was nothing I dreaded so much as premonitions of death, but now that is no longer true. Perhaps I am already tired of life—I feel as if it makes no difference when I die. The other day at the Toranomon Hospital when they told me it might be cancer, my wife and Miss Sasaki seemed to turn pale, but I was quite calm. It was surprising that I could be calm even at such a moment. I almost felt relieved, to think that my long, long life was finally coming to an end. And so I haven't the slightest desire to cling to life, yet as long as I live I cannot help feeling attracted to the opposite sex. I am sure I'll be like this until the moment of my death. I don't have the vigor of a man like Kuhara Fusanosuke who managed to father a child at ninety, I'm already completely impotent. Even so, I can enjoy sexual stimulation in all kinds of distorted, indirect ways. At present I am living for that pleasure, and for the pleasure of eating. Satsuko alone seems to have a vague notion of what is in my mind. She's the only one in the house who has even the faintest idea. She seems to be making little experiments, subtly and indirectly, to see how I react.

I know very well that I am an ugly, wrinkled old man. When I look in the mirror at bedtime after taking out my false teeth, the face I see is really weird. I don't have a tooth of my own in either jaw. I hardly even have gums. If I clamp my mouth shut, my lips flatten together and my nose hangs down to my chin. It astonishes me to think that this is my own face. Not even monkeys have such hideous faces. How could anyone with a face like this ever hope to appeal to a woman? Still, there is a certain advantage in the fact that it puts people off guard, convinces them that you are an old man who knows he can't claim that sort of favor. But although I am neither entitled nor able to exploit my advantage, I can be near a beautiful woman without arousing suspicion. And to make up for my own inability, I can get her involved with a handsome man, plunge the whole household into turmoil, and take pleasure in *that*.

June 20

❀

Jokichi doesn't seem to be so much in love with Satsuko any more. Maybe his love has been cooling ever since Keisuke was born. Anyhow, he's often away on business trips, and when he's in Tokyo he spends most of his evenings at banquets and entertainments, and doesn't come home till late at night. He may have found someone new, though I'm not sure about that. Nowadays he seems to be more interested in work than women. There was a time when he and Satsuko were passionately in love; I suppose he's inherited his fickleness from me.

My wife was opposed to the marriage, but I believe in letting people do as they please, so I didn't interfere. Satsuko said she used to be a chorus girl in the Nichigeki Music Hall. That was only for about half a year—what did she do afterward? I have the impression that she worked in a night club somewhere, perhaps in the Asakusa district.

"Do you do any toe dancing?" I once asked her.

"No, not any more," she said. "I took lessons for a year or two, though, thinking I wanted to be a ballerina. I wonder if I could still dance at all."

"Why did you give it up, if you studied that long?"

"But it spoiled my feet, they looked simply awful!"

"So you gave it up?"

"I can't bear having my feet like that."

"Like what?"

"Oh—just horrible! The toes all callused and swollen, the toenails coming off."

"But your feet are pretty now."

"They used to be a lot prettier! The calluses made them so ugly that when I stopped dancing I tried everthing—pumice stone, emery boards, and what not, day after day. And they *still* aren't the way they used to be!"

"Really? Let me see."

I was quick to make the most of this chance to touch her bare feet. She stretched both legs out on the sofa and peeled off her nylons to show me. I put her feet on my lap and clasped each of her toes in my hand, one by one.

"They feel soft to me!" I said. "You don't seem to have any calluses."

"You're not looking hard enough! Try pressing over there."

"Here?"

"You see? I still haven't got rid of them completely. A ballerina's a pitiful creature, if you think about her feet!"

"You mean even Lepeshinskaya has trouble with her feet?"

"Of course she does. When I was practicing, the blood would often drip out of my ballet shoes. And it isn't just your feet, you lose all the softness here in your calf—you get hard, bunchy muscles like a laborer. It makes you flat-chested too, your breasts disappear, and your shoulder muscles are as tough and hard as a man's. Even chorus girls begin to get that way, though luckily I didn't."

Obviously it was her figure that made her so intriguing to Jokichi, but she seems to have brains too, although she never finished school. She hates to be outdone: after coming to our house she studied till she could rattle away in broken French and English. She likes driving automobiles and is crazy about boxing, but on the other hand she has an unexpected taste for flower arrangement in the classical style. Twice a week the son-in-law of the Issotei family of Kyoto comes to Tokyo to teach, bringing all sorts of rare flowers along, and she has a lesson from him. Today striped pampas grass, lizard's tail, and a kind of sax-ifrage were arranged in a shallow celadon bowl in my room. The hanging scroll is a piece of calligraphy by Nagao Uzan:

Willow catkins fly, my friend has not yet returned.
The plum blossoms and the warbler were lonely, my empty dreams
   remain.
I have spent ten thousand coppers for the wine of the Capital.
I stand by the balustrade in the spring rain, looking at peonies.

June 26

Last night I seem to have eaten too much chilled bean curd: after midnight I began to have a stomach ache, and got up two or three times with diarrhea. I took three tablets of Entero-Vioform but I'm still not over it. I am spending most of today in bed.

June 29

❀

This afternoon I asked Satsuko to take me out for a drive around the Meiji Shrine. I thought I had escaped, but my nurse saw us leaving and said she'd come along. The whole thing was spoiled. We were home in less than an hour.

July 2

❀

For the last few days I've felt that my blood pressure is rising again. This morning it was up to 180. Pulse 100. At the nurse's urging, I took two tablets of Serpasil and three of Adalin. The pain and chilling in my hand is acute too. Although it seldom keeps me awake, last night it woke me up and I had Miss Sasaki give me an injection of Nobu-lon. I find that Nobulon works for me, as far as that goes, but it has unpleasant aftereffects.

"The collar and sliding bed are here. Would you like to try them?"

I'm not very eager, yet the way I feel makes me willing to give them a trial.

July 3

❀

Today I tried on my neck cast. It's a kind of thick plaster collar that holds your chin up. It doesn't hurt, but you can't move your head an inch—right, left, up, or down. All you can do is stare straight in front.

"It's like some hellish torture instrument, isn't it?" I said.

Since this is Sunday, Jokichi and Keisuke were here to see the show too, along with Satsuko and my wife.

"Poor Father!" Satsuko said. "You look miserable."

"How long at a time do you wear that thing?" Jokichi asked.

"I wonder how many days it'll take," my wife added.

"Shouldn't you give it up, Father? It's just too cruel at your age!"

I could hear their gabbling voices all around me, but I couldn't turn my head to see their faces.

Finally I decided to stop wearing the collar and try the sliding bed and neck traction—that so-called Glisson's sling. Fifteen minutes every morning and evening, at first. My chin hangs in a cloth sling, which is a good deal more comfortable than the collar, but I still can't move my head, I lie staring up at the ceiling.

"That's fifteen minutes," Miss Sasaki announced, looking at her wristwatch.

"End of round one!" Keisuke cried, and went scampering off down the hall.

July 10

It's a week since I began using traction. Meanwhile I've lengthened the sessions from fifteen minutes to twenty, and I've had the slope of the platform made so steep that there's a fairly strong pull on my neck. But it doesn't do any good. My hand hurts as much as ever. According to the nurse, it looks as if I'll have to keep it up for a few months before I see any improvement. I doubt if I'll be able to stand it that long.

Tonight the whole family came in to talk it over with me. Satsuko said traction was too much for an old man, at least in this hot weather, so I ought to put it off and try to find a different treatment. One of her foreign friends told her the American Pharmacy has a medicine for neuralgia called Dolosin. He said it wasn't a real cure for neuralgia, but three or four tablets taken several times a day would certainly kill the pain, Dolosin was absolutely effective. And so she had bought some for me—wouldn't I try it?

My wife suggested having acupuncture from Dr. Suzuki of Denenchofu; maybe the needles would cure me, so why not call him? She was on the telephone a long time. Dr. Suzuki told her he was extremely busy, and hoped I could come to his house; otherwise, he'd visit us three times a week. He couldn't tell until he examined me, but, judging from what she said, he thought he'd be able to correct the condition. It would probably take two or three months. Dr. Suzuki has helped me before: once when I had been suffering from heart palpitations, which no one else could seem to cure, and again when I was bothered by dizziness. So I decided to ask him to start his treatments next week.

I have had a naturally strong constitution. From boyhood till my early sixties I was never really sick, except once when I spent a week in the hospital for minor rectal surgery. At sixty-two or -three I began to have warning symptoms of high blood pressure, and at sixty-six or -seven I was in bed for a month after a light cerebral hemorrhage; yet it was only after celebrating my seventy-fifth birthday that I became acquainted with severe physical pain. At first it began in my left hand and traveled to my elbow, then from elbow to shoulder, then from my feet to my legs. I have had trouble with both legs, every day I find it a little harder to walk. No doubt most people wonder what I have left to live for, the way I am—sometimes I wonder myself. But strangely enough, and I suppose I must be considered fortunate, I have nothing to complain about as far as sleep and appetite and bowel movements are concerned. I'm not allowed to have alcohol or stimulants or salty foods, but my appetite is exceptionally good. I'm told there's no objection even to beefsteak or eel, as long as I don't overdo it, and I enjoy whatever I eat. When it comes to sleeping, I almost sleep too much: counting my nap, I get about nine or ten hours a day. And I have two bowel movements every day. Although I pass a good deal of urine and have to get up two or three times in the night, I never lie sleepless afterward. Barely awake, I go to the lavatory, and as soon as I am back in bed I fall fast asleep. Once in a while the pain in my hand wakens me, but before long, as I lie there drowsily aware that it hurts, I drop off to sleep again. When it is really painful I have an injection of Nobulon and go back to sleep at once. This capacity of mine is what has kept me alive. Without it, I imagine I would have died long ago.

"You talk about your hand hurting, and not being able to walk," some people even say, "and yet you're enjoying life well enough, aren't you? You can't be in so much pain."

But I am. Of course there are times when the pain is acute and times when it isn't; it doesn't remain constant, there are even times when I have no pain at all. It seems to vary according to the weather, the humidity, and so on.

It's odd, but even when I am in pain I have a sexual urge. Perhaps especially when I am in pain. Or should I say that I am more attracted, more fascinated by women who cause me pain?

Probably you could call it a masochistic tendency. I don't think I've always had it—it's something I've developed in my old age.

Suppose there are two women equally beautiful, equally pleasing to my aesthetic tastes. A is kind and honest and sympathetic; B is unkind, a clever liar. If you ask which would be more attractive to me, I'm quite sure that these days I would prefer B. However, it won't do unless B is at least the equal of A in beauty. And when it comes to beauty I have my own tastes, a woman has to have just the right kind of face and figure. Above all, it's essential for her to have white, slender legs and delicate feet. Assuming that these and all the other points of beauty are equal, I would be more susceptible to the woman with bad character. Occasionally there are women whose faces reveal a streak of cruelty—they are the ones I like best.

When I see a woman with a face like that, I feel her innermost nature may be cruel, indeed I hope it is. That's the feeling Sawamura Gennosuke used to give me playing female Kabuki roles. I could detect it in the face of Simone Signoret in *Les Diaboliques*, and in the face of Honoo Kayoko, the young actress one hears so much about these days. Perhaps they are merely acting, but if I found a woman who was really bad, and if I could live with her—or at least live in her presence, on intimate terms with her—how happy I would be!

July 12

Even with a woman of bad character, though, her badness mustn't be obvious. The worse she is, the cleverer she has to be. That is indispensable. Of course there are limits: kleptomania or homicidal tendencies would be hard to put up with, yet I can't rule them out entirely. I might be all the more attracted to a woman knowing that she was a sneak thief—in fact I doubt if I could resist getting involved with her.

When I was at the University I knew a law student

named Yamada Uruu. Later he worked for the Osaka Municipal Office; he's been dead for years. This man's father was an old-time lawyer, or "advocate," who in early Meiji defended the notorious murderess Takahashi Oden. It seems he often talked to his son about Oden's beauty. Apparently he would corner him and go on and on about her, as if deeply moved. "You might call her alluring, or bewitching," he would say. "I've never known such a fascinating woman, she's a real vampire. When I saw her I thought I wouldn't mind dying at the hands of a woman like that!"

Since I have no particular reason to keep on living, sometimes I think I would be happier if a woman like Oden turned up to kill me. Rather than endure the pain of these half-dead arms and legs of mine, maybe I could get it over and at the same time see how it feels to be brutally murdered.

Does my love for Satsuko come from my impression that there is something of Oden in her? She is a bit spiteful. A bit sarcastic. And she is a bit of a liar. She doesn't get along very well with her mother-in-law or sisters-in-law. She's cold toward her child. When she was a young bride she didn't seem so malicious, but the difference in the last three or four years has been striking. Perhaps to some degree it is because I have deliberately egged her on. She wasn't always like that. Even now I suppose she is good at heart, but she has come to pride herself on being bad. No doubt that is because she realizes how much her behavior pleases me. Somehow I am much more affectionate toward her than toward my own daughters, I prefer to have her on bad terms with them. The more spiteful she is to them the more she fascinates me. It's only recently that I've got into this state of mind, but my attitude is becoming increasingly extreme. Is it possible that physical suffering, that inability to enjoy the normal pleasures of sex, could distort a man's outlook this much?

I am reminded of a quarrel that occurred here the other day. Although Keisuke is six by now and in his first year at school, there haven't been any children after him. My wife is suspicious of Satsuko, and says she must be doing something artificial to avoid pregnancy. Secretly, I believe that it may very well be true, but I have always denied it to my wife. Apparently she's so disturbed that she has appealed to Jokichi more than once. But he only laughs, and won't discuss it with her.

"You're all wrong," he says.

"I'm sure of it. I can tell!"

He laughs, and says she should ask Satsuko in that case.

"What is there to laugh at? This is serious! You mustn't be so soft on Satsuko—she's making a fool of you!"

Finally the other day Jokichi called in Satsuko to defend herself before my wife. Now and then I could hear Satsuko's high-pitched voice. The quarrel went on for about an hour, and at last my wife came and asked me if I wouldn't please step into the other room with them a moment. However, I didn't, so I don't know exactly what happened; but I heard later that Satsuko was so nettled by my wife's sarcastic remarks that she struck back sharply.

"I'm not that crazy about children!" she would answer. Or: "What's the use of having so many children, with all this nuclear fallout?"

But my wife refused to give in. "You talk disrespectfully to Jokichi when we're not around!" she said, flying off at a tangent. "And he calls you Satsu and carries on like a doting husband even in front of others. I'll bet you're responsible for that too!" There seemed to be no end to the argument. By that time both Satsuko and my wife were in such a passion that Jokichi couldn't handle them.

"If you hate us so much we'd better go and live somewhere else! Isn't that right, Jokichi?"

For once my wife was speechless. She knew as well as Satsuko that I wouldn't hear of it.

"Father can get along, with you and Miss Sasaki to take care of him. Don't you think so, Jokichi? Shouldn't we leave?" Now that my wife was thoroughly beaten, Satsuko was rubbing it in. That finished the argument. I was sorry I hadn't gone in to see it.

Today my wife came to my room again. She seemed quite downcast, the quarrel was still rankling in her mind. "I expect the rains will be ending soon," she said.

"We haven't had much this year, have we?"

"It's already time to buy offerings for Bon. That reminds me, what are you going to do about your grave?"

"There's no need to be in a hurry! As I told you the other day, I don't want to be buried in Tokyo. I was born and reared in this city, but it's becoming impossible. If you have your grave here you never know when they'll move it somewhere else, for one reason or another. And anything as far out as the Tama Cemetery might as well not be in Tokyo at all. I don't want to be buried in such a place."

"I understand that, but you told me you decided on Kyoto, and you'd settle it by the middle of August."

"That still leaves a month. I could even have Jokichi go for me."

"Would you be satisfied without seeing the place yourself?"

"The way I've been feeling, I don't think I can go in all this heat. Maybe I'll put it off till fall."

Two or three years ago my wife and I had a Nichiren priest give us our posthumous Buddhist names. But I dislike that sect and want to change to the Pure Land or the Tendai. My chief objection is that Nichiren household shrines always have a kind of clay-doll image of the Founder, wearing a floss-silk hood, and you have to worship it. If I can, I want to be buried at a temple like the Honenin or the Shinnyodo in Kyoto.

Satsuko walked in then, around five o'clock. As she was saying hello, she suddenly found herself face to face with my wife, and they greeted each other with ridiculously polite bows. My wife soon disappeared.

"You've been out all day," I said to Satsuko. "Where did you go?"

"I was shopping here and there, and had lunch with Haruhisa at a hotel grill, and then went to a dress shop for a fitting. After that I met Haruhisa again, and saw *Black Orpheus. . . .*"

"You've got quite a sunburn on your right arm."

"That's because I drove out to Zushi yesterday."

"With Haruhisa?"

"Yes. But he's good for nothing, I had to do all the driving."

"When you're sunburned in a single place like that it makes the rest of you look whiter than ever."

"The steering wheel's on the right, so that's the way it gets when you drive all day."

"You seem a little flushed, as if you're excited about something."

"Do I? I wouldn't say I'm excited, but Breno Mello was rather wonderful!"

"What are you talking about?"

"The Negro star of *Black Orpheus!* It's a movie from that Greek myth, with a Negro playing the lead, and it takes place in Rio de Janeiro at carnival time."

"So you thought it was good?"

"They say Breno Mello's an amateur who used to be a soccer champion. In the movie he plays a streetcar driver— now and then he winks at a girl as he goes along. What a wink!"

"It doesn't sound like the kind of thing I'd care for."

"Do me a favor and come see it."

"You mean you'll go again, with me?"

"Will you come then?"

"All right."

"I'd go any number of times. It's because he reminds me of Leo Espinosa—I was a great fan of his."

"*Another* queer name!"

"Espinosa's a Filipino boxer who once fought a world flyweight title match. He's a Negro too, though not as handsome. Somehow Breno Mello affects you the same way, especially when he winks! Espinosa is still fighting, but he isn't so good any more. He used to be marvelous! That's who I was reminded of."

"I've only been to one boxing match in my life."

Meanwhile my wife and Miss Sasaki had come in to tell me it was time for my sliding bed, and Satsuko purposely began to rave about him all the more.

"Espinosa's a Negro from the Island of Cebu, with a honey of a left jab. He shoots his left straight out, and snaps it back the instant it lands. Swish, swish—you can't imagine how fast he snaps back that arm! It's beautiful, swishing in and out! And he keeps giving sharp little whistles when he's on the attack. Most boxers weave right or left if the other man throws a jab, but Espinosa bends back from the waist. He's amazingly supple!"

"And you're fond of Haruhisa because he's so dark, is that it?"

"Haruhisa's got a hairy chest, though, and Negroes don't have much hair on their bodies. When they sweat all over their skin gets slippery and shiny—really fascinating! Father, I'm definitely going to drag you off to a match some day!"

"I don't imagine there are many handsome boxers."

"A lot of them have flattened noses."

"Which is better, boxing or wrestling?"

"Wrestling is more of a show—they get all bloodied up, but they don't really mean business."

"They draw blood even in boxing, don't they?"

"Of course they do! Sometimes a smashed mouthpiece comes flying out, and there's blood all over. But it isn't done on purpose, the way it is in wrestling; you don't often see blood except when a man knocks his head into the other one's face—what they call heading. Or else when an eyelid gets cut."

"Do you actually go to look at such things?" Miss Sasaki broke in. My wife was standing there aghast. She looked ready to flee.

"I'm not the only one, lots of women go to them."

"It would make *me* faint!"

"You get excited when you see blood. That's part of the fun!"

I had begun to feel an excruciating pain in my left hand. And yet I also felt an acute sense of pleasure. As I looked into Satsuko's malicious face the pain—and the pleasure—became more and more intense.

July 17

❀

Last night, soon after we ended the Bon Festival ceremonies by putting out our gate fires, Satsuko left the house. She said she was taking the late express to Kyoto, to see the Gion Festival. Haruhisa went yesterday to begin filming it, though it was awfully hot for that kind of job. The TV company was staying at the Kyoto Hotel, and Satsuko at her sister-in-law's house in Nanzenji. "I'll be back on Wednesday," she said. Since she's not likely to get along with Itsuko, I dare say she'll only sleep there.

"When are you coming to Karuizawa?" my wife wanted to know. "It'll be noisy once the children arrive, you ought to come as soon as you can. They say Tokyo will be at its hottest around the twentieth."

"I wonder what I should do this year—it's too boring to stay as long as I did last summer. And I've got an engagement with Satsuko on the twenty-fifth, to see an Orient featherweight title match at the Korakuen Gym."

"You won't admit your age, will you? You'll be lucky if you don't get hurt, going to a place like that."

July 23

❀

I keep a diary merely because I enjoy writing, I don't intend to show it to anyone. My sight has been failing so badly that I can't read as much as I want, and since I have no other way to amuse myself I like to write on and on, if only to kill time. I write in large characters, with a brush, so that my script will be easy to read. To avoid embarrassment I lock my diary up in a small cashbox. I have accumulated five such boxfuls by now. I suppose I really ought to burn all this some day, but there may be an advantage to saving it. When I look at one of my old diaries I am astonished to find how forgetful I have become. The events of a year ago seem entirely new to me, my interest never flags.

Last summer, while we were away at Karuizawa, I had the bedroom and bath and lavatory remodeled. As forgetful as I am, I remember that very well. But in looking through last year's diary I see that I omitted the details. Now something has come up that makes it necessary to fill in a few of them.

Until last summer my wife and I slept side by side in a Japanese-style room, but last year we replaced the mats with a wood floor and put in two beds. One is mine, and the other has become Nurse Sasaki's. Even before that my wife used to sleep alone in the sitting room now and then, and since remodeling we have regularly slept apart. I get up early and go to bed early, but my wife sleeps late and likes to stay up late at night too. Although I prefer a Western-style toilet, she says that she has trouble unless it's the low Japanese style. And there were various other reasons to remodel, such as the convenience of the doctor and nurse. So our lavatory, the next room down the corridor to the right, was fitted with a chair-type water closet and reserved for my own use, and we cut a door in the wall between it and my bedroom. We also made substantial changes in the bath, which is on the other side of the bedroom: the new one was fully tiled, including the tub, and we even installed a shower. This was at Satsuko's request. We put in a door between the bath and the bedroom too, but if necessary you can lock the bathroom from inside.

I should add that the room beyond the lavatory is my study (we opened a door between these rooms as well), and the one beyond that is the nurse's room. The nurse sleeps in the bed next to mine at night, but during the day she is usually in her own room. Day and night my wife stays in the sitting room just around the corridor, and spends most of her time watching TV or listening to the radio. She seldom comes out unless she has something in particular to do. Jokichi and his wife and Keisuke have the second floor, which includes a guest room furnished in Western style. Apparently the young people have decorated their living room quite luxuriously, but since I am so unsteady on my feet I hardly ever venture up our winding staircase.

There was some dispute when we remodeled the bathroom. My wife insisted on a wooden tub, arguing that the water wouldn't stay hot as long in a tile one and that the tiles would be uncomfortably cold in winter. But I accepted Satsuko's suggestion (without mentioning her whim to my wife) and had the whole thing done in tile. Still, that was a failure—maybe I should say a success—because it turned out that wet tiles are dangerously slippery for an old person. Once my wife skidded on the new floor and took a fine thumping fall. And once when I grasped the edge of the tub to help myself out of it, my hand slipped and I couldn't get my legs under me. Since I can only use one hand, that was a really awkward situation for me to be in. I had drainboards laid over the floor, but I couldn't do anything about the tub.

Anyway, there was a new development last night.

Miss Sasaki goes to stay overnight with her family once or twice a month; she leaves in the evening and comes back before noon the next day. On nights when she is away my wife takes her place in the bed next to me. I am accustomed to retiring at ten, immediately after my bath.

Ever since her fall my wife won't assist me in bathing, so Satsuko or the maid does it, but they're not as skillful or helpful as Miss Sasaki. Satsuko is diligent enough in getting things ready, but then only stands back and watches, without helping properly. About all she will do is give the sponge a swipe down my back. When I get out of the water she dries me with a towel from behind, sprinkles baby powder over me, and turns on the electric fan. Whether out of modesty or repulsion, she never comes around in front. Finally she helps me into my bathrobe and bundles me off to the bedroom, after which she hurries away down the corridor. She all but tells me that the rest is my wife's duty, she isn't responsible for it. I can't help wishing she would occasionally spend the night in my bedroom too, but, perhaps because my wife keeps an eye on her, Satsuko is deliberately brusque.

My wife dislikes sleeping in someone else's bed. She changes all the sheets and blankets, and lies down uneasily. Because of her age she has to make two or three trips a night to relieve herself, but she says that a foreign-style toilet won't do, so she goes all the way to the Japanese one. She grumbles that it keeps her from getting a good night's sleep. Secretly I have been expecting that Satsuko would soon be asked to take her place on a night when Miss Sasaki was away.

Last night, by accident, that is what happened. Miss Sasaki had asked for the night off and left at 6 p.m. After dinner my wife began to feel ill, and went to her room to lie down. Naturally Satsuko had to stay with me as well as help me bathe. At first she was wearing knee-length toreador pants and a polo shirt with a bright blue Eiffel Tower design. She looked wonderfully fresh and smart. Maybe it was only my imagination, but she seemed to be scrubbing me with unusual care. I could feel the touch of her hands here and there, on the neck, the shoulders, the arms.

After taking me to my bedroom, she said: "I'll be right back—just wait a minute, will you? I want a shower too." Then she went into the bathroom again. I had to wait about half an hour. As I sat on the edge of the bed waiting, I felt strangely nervous. At last she reappeared in the bathroom door, but this time she had on a salmon-pink seersucker dressing gown and Chinese-looking satin slippers embroidered with peonies.

"Sorry to be so long." As she walked into the room the door from the corridor opened and Oshizu brought in a folded rattan chair. "Father, haven't you gone to bed yet?" Satsuko asked.

"I was just going to, my dear. But why do you want a thing like that?" When my wife isn't around I tend to speak to Satsuko in a more intimate way than usual. Often I do it consciously, though it seems natural enough when we are alone. Satsuko herself, if there are only the two of us, talks to me in a curiously impudent manner. She is quite aware of how to please me.

"You go to bed too early for me, so I'm going to sit here and read."

She unfolded the rattan chair into a kind of chaise longue, sprawled out in it, and opened a book she had brought with her. It looked like a French language text. She had shaded the lamp with a cloth to keep the light out of my eyes. No doubt she dislikes Miss Sasaki's bed too, and meant all along to sleep in the chair.

She was lying there stretched out, so I lay down too. I have an air conditioner in my bedroom, but I keep it turned as low as I can, to avoid chilling my arm. For the past few days the weather has been so sultry and humid that the doctor and nurse say it's best to use it, if only to dry the air. Pretending to be asleep, I was actually watching the little pointed tips of Satsuko's Chinese slippers, which were peeping out below her gown. Such delicately tapering feet are rare for a Japanese.

"Father, you're still awake, aren't you? Miss Sasaki says she hears you snoring as soon as you go to bed."

"For some reason I can't sleep tonight."

"Because of me?"

When I didn't answer, she giggled and said: "It's bad for you to get excited!" And then, after a pause: "Maybe I'd better give you some Adalin."

It was the first time Satsuko had been so coquettish, which *did* excite me.

"That's hardly necessary."

"Never mind, I'm getting it for you!"

While she was gone to find the medicine I had a bright idea.

"Here you are! I wonder if two will be enough." She shook two pills from the Adalin bottle into a saucer, and then went to bring a glass of water from the bathroom.

"Now, open wide! Aren't you pleased it's me giving it to you?"

"Yes, but don't hand it to me on a saucer—pick it up in your fingers and put it in my mouth."

"I'll go wash my hands then." And out she went into the bathroom again.

"The water will spill," I said, as soon as she came back. "While you're at it, why not give it to me mouth-to-mouth?"

"Don't be ridiculous! You won't get anywhere being fresh!" Before I knew it she popped the pills nimbly into my mouth and poured water in after them. I had meant to pretend to fall asleep, but in spite of myself I really did.

July 24

❀

I went to the lavatory twice last night, at about two and four o'clock. Sure enough, Satsuko was asleep in the rattan chair. The lamp had been turned off, and the French book was on the floor. Because of the Adalin I can barely remember those two trips in the night. This morning I woke up at six as usual.

"Are you awake, Father?" Satsuko is a late riser, and I was surprised to see her sit up briskly the moment I stirred.

"Were *you* awake already?" I asked.

"I was the one who couldn't sleep last night!"

When I raised the window shade she hastily fled to the bathroom, as if she didn't want to let me see her face so soon after getting up.

Around 2 p.m., while I was still lying in bed listlessly after an hour's nap, I suddenly saw the bathroom door open halfway and Satsuko's head emerge. Only her head— I couldn't see the rest of her. She had on a vinyl shower cap, and her whole head was dripping wet. I could hear the hiss of the water.

"Sorry to run away so early this morning. I'm just taking a shower—I thought you'd be having your nap, and peeked in to see."

"This must be Sunday. Isn't Jokichi here?"

Instead of answering, she said: "Even when I'm in the shower I never lock this door! It can be opened any time!"

Did she say that because I invariably take my own bath in the evening, or because she trusts me? Or was she saying "Come on in and look, if you want!"? Or: "A silly old man doesn't bother me in the least"? I have no idea why she made a point of saying such a thing.

"Jokichi's home today. He's busy getting ready for a barbecue supper in the garden."

"Is somebody coming?"

"Haruhisa and Mr. Amari, and some of Kugako's family too, I think."

It isn't likely that Kugako will visit us for a while, after what happened. If any of them come, it'll probably be just the children.

July 25

❀

Last night I made a big mistake. It was about half past six when the barbecue began in the garden, but it seemed so gay and lively that I felt like joining the young people. My wife did her best to stop me, warning me I'd get a bad chill if I went to sit on the grass at that time of day. But Satsuko urged me to come.

"Just for a little while, Father!" she said.

I had no appetite for the bits of lamb and chicken the others were devouring, and no intention of eating such things. What I really wanted was to see how Haruhisa and Satsuko behaved together, but about half an hour after going out I began to get a chill in my legs and hips. That was partly because my wife's warning had made me nervous. At last even Miss Sasaki, apparently hearing about it from my wife, came to the garden and cautioned me. Then I turned stubborn, as usual, and refused to move. But I knew the chill was getting worse. My wife understands me well enough not to be too persistent. However, Miss Sasaki seemed so alarmed that finally, after holding out another half hour, I got up and went back to my room.

That wasn't the end of it. Around two o'clock this morning I was awakened by an extreme itchiness in my urethra. When I hurried to the toilet to urinate, I saw that the urine was milky. I went back to bed, and fifteen minutes later needed to urinate again. The itchy feeling still hadn't gone away. The same thing happened twice more, until Miss Sasaki gave me four tablets of Sinomin and warmed the area with a hot-water bottle, after which it began to get better.

For the past several years I have suffered from enlargement of the prostate (they called this gland by a different name in my youth, when I had a venereal disease): occasionally the urine accumulates too long, and a few times it has had to be drawn off with a catheter. They say that stoppage of the urine is frequent among old men, but at best mine doesn't flow freely; I find it very embarrassing to stand at a urinal in a theater rest room, for example, with men lined up waiting behind me. Someone told me that surgery to correct an enlarged prostate was possible until the middle seventies, I ought to go ahead and have the operation. "You can't imagine how much better you'll feel," he said. "It'll come spurting out the way it did when you were young—you'll feel as if you've regained your youth!" But others warned me against it, since the operation was a difficult, unpleasant one; and by now, having put it off so long, I am apparently too old. Still, my condition was improving until I blundered and had this relapse. The doctor tells me I ought to be careful for a while. Sinomin has harmful side effects after prolonged use, so I am to take four tablets at a time, three times a day, but not to continue it more than three days. Every morning without fail I must have my urine examined, and if there are any bacteria in it I am to drink *ubaurushi*.

As a result I am giving up the Korakuen title match tonight. The urethral obstruction was a good deal better this morning, so I could have gone, but Miss Sasaki wouldn't hear of it. "The very idea of being out at night!" she exclaimed.

"Poor Father!" Satsuko said, passing by. "Too bad you'll miss it. I'll tell you all about it when I get back!"

Against my will, I had to stay quietly at home and submit myself to Dr. Suzuki's needles. A rather long, painful session, from two-thirty till four-thirty, but during it I had a twenty-minute rest.

School is over for the summer, so Keisuke will soon be going to Karuizawa, along with the children from Tsujido. Kugako and my wife will take them. Satsuko says she'll come next month, and hopes they'll look after Keisuke in the meantime. Next month Jokichi can spend about ten days there too. Probably even Kugako's husband will be able to come then. My nephew Haruhisa says he's much too busy with TV work; an art designer has free time in the day, but he's always tied up at night. . . .

July 26

❀

Lately this has been my daily routine. I get up at 6 a.m. and go to the lavatory. As I urinate, I catch the first few drops in a sterilized test tube. Next I bathe my eyes in a solution of boric acid. Then I carefully gargle and rinse out my mouth with a baking-soda solution, clean my gums with a chlorophyll dentifrice, and put in my false teeth. I go for about a half-hour walk in the garden, after which I lie on the sliding bed for traction, now also half an hour. Breakfast is the one meal I have in my bedroom. A glass of milk, a slice of toast with cheese, vegetable juice, fruit, tea—and a tablet of Alinamin. Next I go to my study to look at the newspaper, to write in my diary, and, if I have any time left, perhaps to read a book. But I often spend the whole morning on my diary, and sometimes part of the afternoon or evening. At 10 a.m. Miss Sasaki comes into the study to take my blood pressure. About once every three days I get an injection of 50 mg. of vitamins. Lunch at noon in the dining room, usually a bowl of noodles and a fruit. From 1 to 2 p.m., a nap in the bedroom. Three times a week, on Monday, Wednesday, and Friday, from two-thirty to four-thirty, acupuncture by Dr. Suzuki. Beginning at five o'clock, another half hour of traction. A stroll in the garden at six. Miss Sasaki accompanies me on my morning and evening walks, but occasionally Satsuko takes her place. At six-thirty, dinner. I am supposed to eat only a small bowl of rice but a variety of meat, fish, and vegetables, so we have all sorts of dishes, including some to please the young people. We all seem to eat different things, and often at different times. After dinner I listen to the radio in my study. For fear of harming my eyes, I don't read at night, and I hardly ever look at television.

I keep remembering what Satsuko confided to me the day before yesterday, on Sunday afternoon. Around two o'clock, when I had awakened from my nap and was lying in bed listlessly, she stuck her head out of the bathroom and told me: "Even when I'm in the shower I don't lock this door! It can be opened any time!"

Whether calculated or not, these words from her own lips aroused my interest. That night we had the barbecue, yesterday I spent the day recuperating, and still her words haunted me. At two o'clock this afternoon I woke from my nap and went to the study, then came back to my bedroom at three. I know that recently Satsuko has been taking a shower at this time, whenever she is home. Just as an experiment, I stealthily gave the bathroom door a little push. Sure enough, the catch had been left open. I could hear the sound of the shower.

"Do you want something?"

I had only touched the door, barely enough to move it, but she seemed to notice instantly. I was taken aback. However, after a moment I mustered up my courage.

"You said you never lock the door, so I tried it to see." As I spoke, I peered into the bathroom. Satsuko was standing under the shower, but her whole body was concealed by striped green and white shower curtains.

"Now do you believe me?"

"I believe you."

"What are you doing out there? Come on in!"

"Is it all right?"

"You want to, don't you?"

"I have no special reason, I'm afraid."

"Now, now! Keep calm! If you get excited you'll slip and fall."

The drainboards were taken up, and the tiled floor was wet from the shower. Careful of my footing, I entered the room and shut the door behind me. Now and then, between the shower curtains, she let me see a flicker of a shoulder, a knee, the tip of a foot.

"Maybe I'd better give you a reason!"

The shower stopped. Turning her back toward me, she exposed the upper part of her body between the curtains.

"Take that towel and wipe my back, will you? Be careful, my head's dripping!" As she pulled off her vinyl cap a few drops of water splashed on me.

"Don't be so timid, put some energy into it! Oh, I forgot, your left hand's no good. Well, rub as hard as you can with your right."

Suddenly I grasped her shoulders through the towel. And then, just as I gave her a tongue-kiss on the soft curve of her neck at the right shoulder, I got a stinging slap on my cheek.

"Fresh, aren't you, for an old man?"

"I thought you'd allow that much."

"I'll allow nothing of the kind. Next time I'll tell Jokichi."

"I'm sorry."

"Please go away!" But then Satsuko became very solicitous. "Now don't be upset! Take it easy—you mustn't slip!"

As I groped for the door I felt the gentle touch of her fingertips against my back. I went and sat on the bed to catch my breath. Soon afterward she came in wearing her seersucker gown, her peony-embroidered slippers peeping out below.

"I'm awfully sorry for what I did."

"Never mind, it didn't amount to anything."

"Did it hurt?"

"No, but I was a little startled."

"I'm quick to slap a man's face, it's just the way I react."

"That's what I thought. You must have slapped lots of men."

"But it's wrong of me to hit *you*!"

July 28

❀

Yesterday was out of the question, because of my acupuncture treatment, but at three o'clock this afternoon I put my ear to the bathroom door again. The catch was open. I could hear the shower running.

"Come on in—I've been waiting for you!" Satsuko said. "I'm sorry about the other day."

"That's more like it."

"When you're old you can get away with a lot."

"After taking that slap, I think I deserve some kind of compensation."

"It isn't funny. Promise you'll never do a thing like that again!"

"Still, you ought to be willing to let me kiss you on the neck."

"I don't like to be kissed on the neck."

"Where *would* you like it?"

"I won't stand for it anywhere. It made me feel queasy the rest of the day, as if I'd been licked by a garden slug."

I swallowed hard, and said: "I wonder how you'd feel if Haruhisa did it."

"I'll hit you again! I mean it! Last time you only got a little tap."

"You needn't be so restrained."

"My hand can sting! If I really hit you, you'll see stars!"

"But that's what I'd like."

"You're impossible! A second-childhood terror!"

"I'm asking you again: If you won't have it on your neck, where *will* you have it?"

"You can do it once if it's below the knee—only once, mind you! And just your lips, don't touch me with your tongue!"

She was completely hidden behind the shower curtains, except for one of her legs below the knee.

"You look as if you're going to be examined by a gynecologist."

"Silly!"

"You're being very unreasonable, telling me to kiss you without using my tongue."

"I'm *not* telling you to kiss me—I'm just letting you touch me with your lips! That's enough for an old man like you."

"You might at least turn off the shower."

"Certainly not. It'll make my skin crawl unless I wash off immediately."

It tasted like a drink of water instead of a kiss.

"Speaking of Haruhisa, Father, I'm supposed to ask you a favor."

"What's that?"

"Haruhisa wants to come here for a shower occasionally, because of the heat. He told me to ask you if it would be all right."

"Can't he take a bath at his TV station?"

"He could, but there's one bathroom for the performers and one for everybody else, and it's so dirty he doesn't like to use it. He has to go down to a bathhouse near the Ginza, but if he can use our shower it'll save him a lot of trouble. He said I should ask you about it."

"You ought to decide for yourself, a thing like that. You don't have to ask me."

"Actually I did smuggle him in once, not long ago. But he says he thinks it's bad to slip in that way."

"It's all right with me. If you want to ask anybody's permission, ask my wife's."

"Won't you speak to her for me, Father? I'm afraid of her!"

That's what she says but Satusko is actually more concerned about me than about my wife. Because it's Haruhisa, she thinks she has to ask special permission. . . .

July 29

❊

As usual, the acupuncture session began at half past two this afternoon. I lay on my back in bed, and Dr. Suzuki sat on a chair beside me to perform his treatment. Although he takes care of everything himself, even to getting out his needles and sterilizing them in alcohol, he always has an apprentice standing behind. So far I haven't felt any improvement either in the chill in my hand or in the numbing in my fingertips.

Almost half an hour later Haruhisa burst in from the corridor.

"Excuse me, Uncle Tokusuke, I'll only be a minute. I'm sorry to bother you while you're being treated, but Satsu tells me you gave your permission the other day, and I wanted to let you know how grateful I am. I'm already taking advantage of your kindness, so I just thought I'd stop in and thank you."

"There's no need to ask permission, for a little thing like that. Come whenever you like."

"Thanks very much. I'll be coming often from now on, though not every day. . . . By the way, you're looking well lately!"

"What! I'm getting more decrepit all the time— Satsuko says I'm in my second childhood!"

"But Satsu admires you, she tells me you never seem to age."

"Nonsense! Here I am putting up with these needles just to keep myself alive a little longer."

"I can't believe it's as bad as that. You've got many more years ahead of you. . . . Well, I'll be running along now, as soon as I've said hello to my aunt."

"Busy as ever, I see. And in all this heat! Why don't you stay and relax a while?"

"Thanks very much, but I'm afraid I can't."

Shortly after Haruhisa left, Oshizu brought in a tray with refreshments for two. It was time for the rest period. Today she served them custard pudding and iced tea. Afterward the treatment was resumed, and continued till half past four.

As I lay waiting for Dr. Suzuki to finish, I was thinking of other matters.

I wonder if there isn't more to Haruhisa's wanting to come for a shower, I wonder if he hasn't some scheme in mind. Maybe Satsuko put him up to it. Even today, didn't he make a point of coming to see me while the doctor was here? Perhaps he thought: If I do, I can get out of the old man's clutches more easily. I once overheard him say he was busy at night but could get away any time during the day. And so he'll probably come for his bath in the afternoon, about when Satusko is taking hers. In short, he'll come while I'm in the study, or while I'm in the bedroom having acupuncture. Surely that door isn't left open when he's in the shower, it must be locked then. I wonder if Satsuko doesn't regret establishing such a bad precedent.

Another thing weighs on my mind. In three days, on the first of August, my wife, Keisuke, Kugako and her children, and our second maid Osetsu will leave for Karuizawa. Jokichi says he will go to Osaka the following day, come back to Tokyo on the sixth, and join the others in Karuizawa on Sunday the seventh, to stay a little over a week. That ought to be very convenient for Satsuko. As far as she is concerned, she says she'll go to Karuizawa occasionally for a few days, beginning next month. "Even if Miss Sasaki and Oshizu are with him, it worries me to leave Father behind in Tokyo—besides, the pool at Karuizawa is too cold for swimming! It's all right to go once in a while, but don't ask me to spend a long time there. I'd rather go to the beach." That convinced me I had to arrange to stay in Tokyo.

"I'll be leaving ahead of you," my wife said to me. "How soon will you come?"

"Let's see, what should I do? I've been thinking of keeping on with Dr. Suzuki, now that I've started."

"But didn't you say he hasn't done you a bit of good? Why not stop till it's cooler, anyway?"

"No, I think I'm beginning to feel better. It would be a pity to stop now, after less than a month."

"Then you don't intend to come at all this year?"

"Oh, no. I'll come sooner or later!"

With that, I succeeded in weathering her questions.

August 5

❀

At half past two Dr. Suzuki arrived, and started treating me immediately. The rest period began a little after three. Oshizu brought in refreshments: mocha ice cream and iced tea. As she was leaving I asked casually: "Didn't Haruhisa come today?"

"Yes, sir, but he must be gone by now." She seemed rather evasive.

Dr. Suzuki ate very slowly; between each spoonful of ice cream he took a sip of tea.

"Excuse me," I said, getting down from the bed and going over to the bathroom door. I tried the doorknob, but it was locked. To satisfy my curiosity I went into the lavatory, then out to the corridor and back across to the bathroom, and tried that door. It was open. The dressing area was empty. However, Haruhisa's socks and trousers and sport shirt were there. I even looked inside the curtains, but the shower stall was empty too. Still, a great deal of water had been splashed over the tiled floor and walls, they were dripping wet. So Oshizu was embarrassed and lied to me! I thought. But where was he? And where on earth was Satsuko? I was on my way to look for them at the bar in the dining room when I met Oshizu about to go upstairs with a tray holding two glasses and two bottles of Coca-Cola.

Oshizu turned pale, and stopped at the foot of the steps. Her hands were trembling as she held the tray. I felt embarrassed too. It was odd for me to be prowling around the house at this hour.

"So Haruhisa's still here?" I asked, trying to sound lighthearted and cheerful.

"Yes, sir. I thought he'd gone . . ."

"Oh?"

". . . but he was cooling off upstairs."

Two glasses and two bottles of Coca-Cola. Both of them were "cooling off" upstairs—whether or not he took his shower alone. Since his clothes were lying in the dressing area, he must have changed into a bath kimono. We have a guest room on the second floor, of course, but I wondered where they were. It was natural enough to lend him a kimono; still, with my wife away and three downstairs rooms empty, it hardly seemed necessary to take him up there. No doubt they thought I would be under treatment till four-thirty, and not likely to leave my bed.

After watching Oshizu go up the stairs, I returned directly to my room and lay down again. I had been gone less than ten minutes. The doctor was just finishing his ice cream.

Dr. Suzuki got out his needles once more. For the next hour or so I was at his mercy. At four-thirty he left, and I went back to my study. Meanwhile, Haruhisa had plenty of time to steal down the stairs and leave the house without my knowledge. But they had miscalculated too: not only did I unexpectedly come out to the corridor, I happened to run into Oshizu. Yet otherwise they might not have learned that I knew what was going on, perhaps it was not such bad luck after all. If I were to be even more suspicious, I could say that Satsuko, knowing I suspect her, guessed that I might go spying during my rest period. She may have deliberately allowed me the opportunity, having planned in advance to send Oshizu on an errand at just that time. Maybe she thought it would eventually be to her advantage to let the old man know, and so it would be charitable to get him used to the idea as soon as possible.

In my imagination I could hear Satusko saying: "Never mind! You needn't hurry away. Just relax and stay for a while."

From four-thirty till five, rest. Five till five-thirty, traction. Five-thirty till six, rest. And in the meantime, possibly before I finished my treatment, the upstairs guest had left. Whether Satsuko left with him or even felt too embarrassed to show her face, I hadn't seen her since lunch. (For the last three days I have been able to take my meals alone with her.) At six o'clock Miss Sasaki came to remind me of my walk in the garden. As I was stepping down from the veranda Satsuko appeared from somewhere and said she would go with me today.

"When did Haruhisa leave?" I brought up the subject the moment we reached the arbor.

"Soon after that."

"After what?"

"Soon after we had our Coca-Cola. I told him it would only look worse if he left so fast, once you knew he was here."

"Surprisingly timid, isn't he?"

"He kept saying you'd be sure to misunderstand, and begging me to explain it to you."

"That's enough. I don't need to hear any more about it."

"Go on and misunderstand if you want! But we simply went upstairs for a Coke, because you get a breeze up there! That sounds strange to an old-fashioned person, I suppose. Jokichi would understand."

"Don't worry, I don't care what happened."

"But *I* care!"

"Let me ask you this—aren't you misunderstanding *me*?"

"What do you mean?"

"Even supposing—just supposing, mind you—that there was something between you and Haruhisa, I wouldn't be inclined to notice it."

Satusko gave me a dubious look, but didn't answer.

"I wouldn't breathe a word of it to my wife or Jokichi. I'd keep your secret to myself."

"Father, are you telling me to go ahead?"

"Maybe I am."

"You're out of your mind."

"Maybe. Is this the first time you've realized how I feel, a bright girl like you?"

"But where do you get such ideas?"

"Now that I can't enjoy the thrill myself any more, I can at least have the pleasure of watching someone else risk a love affair. It's a pitiful thing when a man sinks that low."

"So you get a little desperate, because you've lost all hope for yourself?"

"And jealous too! You ought to feel sorry for me."

"You're clever all right. I don't mind feeling sorry for you, but I refuse to be sacrificed for your pleasure!"

"It's not much of a sacrifice—won't you be getting your own pleasure out of it? And won't yours far exceed mine? A man in my condition is really to be pitied!"

"Careful, or you get another slap!"

"Let's not try to deceive each other. Of course it doesn't have to be Haruhisa. Amari or anyone would do."

"Whenever we come to the arbor you start this kind of talk. Come on and finish your exercise—you need to clear your head too. Look! Miss Sasaki's watching from the veranda."

The path was barely wide enough for two abreast, and it was further narrowed by overgrown *hagi* bushes.

"Hang on to me, and don't get caught in the foliage."

"We ought to link arms."

"That's absurd, you're too short." Satsuko, who had been on my left, suddenly went around to the other side. "Lend me your cane. Here, hold on with your right hand." As she spoke, she thrust her shoulder toward me, and taking my cane, began brushing aside the sprays of *hagi*. . . .

August 6

❀

(Continued.)

"I wonder how Jokichi feels about you these days."

"I'd like to know myself! What do you think, Father?"

"I have no idea. I try not to think too much about Jokichi."

"So do I. Even if I ask, he looks annoyed and won't tell me the truth. But I'm sure he doesn't love me any more."

"What do you think he'd do if you had a lover?"

"He said I shouldn't worry about him—if I found somebody else, it couldn't be helped. . . . He seemed to be joking at the time, but I believe he's serious."

"He's just being proud. Any man will say that, when his wife tells him she may take a lover."

"Apparently he has a girlfriend of his own, somebody with a past like mine, from a cabaret. I told him I'd give him a divorce if he'd let me see Keisuke, but he says he doesn't want one—he'd feel sorry for Keisuke but even sorrier for *you*."

"He's making fun of me."

"So he knows all about you, Father! I haven't said a word to him, though."

"Well, he's my son after all."

"It's a funny way to show his devotion!"

"Actually, he's still attached to you. He's using me as a pretext."

The fact is, I know hardly anything about Jokichi, my own son and heir. There must be very few fathers so ignorant of their precious sons. I know that he graduated in economics from Tokyo University and went into Pacific Plastic Industries. However, I don't have a very clear idea of the kind of work he does. I understand that his company buys synthetic resins from Mitsui Chemicals or somewhere, and manufactures things like photographic film, polyethylene film, and molded plastic articles such as buckets and mayonnaise tubes. The factory is around Kawasaki, but the main office is in downtown Tokyo, in Nihombashi, and Jokichi has a position in the business department there. They say he may soon become the department manager, but I don't know what his salary is.

Although he will be my successor, at present I remain the head of the Utsugi family. It seems he bears part of our household expenses, but we still depend chiefly on my income from real estate and stock dividends.

Until a few years ago my wife took care of the monthly household accounts; since then Satsuko has been in charge. According to my wife, she is surprisingly good at figures and keeps a sharp eye on the tradesmen's bills. She often goes to the kitchen to inspect the refrigerator—the maids quake when they hear her name. Being fond of novelties, she had a garbage disposal installed last year, but now she regrets it. Once I heard her give a tongue lashing to Osetsu because she threw in a sweet potato that, in Satsuko's opinion, "could probably still be eaten."

"If it's spoiled, can't you give it to the dog?" she asked witheringly. "You all seem to amuse yourselves tossing in whatever you like. I should never have bought it."

My wife says that Satsuko nags the maids to cut down expenses as much as possible, and then puts the savings into her own pocket; she makes everyone else feel pinched, yet indulges in all sorts of personal luxuries. Sometimes she has Osetsu run up figures on the abacus, but usually she does it herself; she also deals with the accountant who is in charge of our tax matters. As busy as she is with her various family responsibilities, Satsuko will take on any kind of extra task around the house and make short work of it. Jokichi must be very pleased with her ability. By now she occupies a firm position in the

Utsugi household; in that sense, she has also become indispensable to Jokichi.

When my wife opposed the marriage, Jokichi told her: "You talk about how Satsuko was a dancer, but I'm sure she'll be good at running the house. I can tell she has the ability." But he must have been making a wild guess, he could hardly have had such foresight. After coming here as his wife, she began to show just how capable she was. Until then, Satsuko herself probably didn't realize it.

At first, though I consented to it, I didn't think their marriage would last very long. I've always felt that Jokichi takes after me in being as susceptible to women—and as fickle—as I was in my younger days. But now it doesn't seem quite so simple. Obviously he isn't as infatuated with her as he was when they were married. Still, to my eyes, she is even lovelier now. It's almost ten years since she came to our house, and every year she seems more beautiful. It was especially striking after she had Keisuke. Nowadays she no longer has an air of cabaret vulgarity. Of course when the two of us are alone she sometimes deliberately slips into that manner. Probably she used to do the same thing with Jokichi while they were so close, though it seems unlikely these days. Instead, I suppose my son values her for her ability at managing household affairs, and worries about how inconvenient it would be to lose her. When Satusko is playing innocent she seems to have all the qualifications of a model wife. Her speech and movements are spirited, she is highly intelligent; and yet she has warmth and charm, and knows how to get along with people. No doubt she impresses everyone that way, to Jokichi's secret pride. And so I can't believe he will want to leave her. Even if she seemed to be misbehaving he might pretend not to notice, as long as she did it skillfully.

August 7

✿

Last night Jokichi came home from Osaka; he leaves for Karuizawa this morning.

August 8

✿

From 1 to 2 p.m. I had my nap, and then stayed in bed waiting for Dr. Suzuki. Meanwhile I heard a knock on the bathroom door, and Satusko calling.

"Father, I'm going to lock this!"

"He's coming, is he?"

"Yes." She stuck her head out for a moment, but promptly banged the door shut and locked it. Though I had only a glimpse of her I noticed a cold, sulky look on her face. Evidently she had already taken a shower; water was dripping from her vinyl cap.

August 9

✿

This was not Dr. Suzuki's day to come, but I couldn't resist staying in the bedroom after my nap anyway. Again I heard a knock, and Satsuko's voice.

"I'm going to lock this!"

She was half an hour later than yesterday, and didn't look in at me. Shortly after three o'clock I tried the doorknob. It was still locked. At five, while I was under traction, I heard Haruhisa call out as he went by.

"Thanks again, Uncle! I'm taking advantage of it every day!"

Unfortunately I couldn't see the expression on his face as he said that.

At six, on my way out for a walk in the garden, I asked Miss Sasaki whether Satsuko was here.

"I think I heard the Hillman leave a little while ago, sir," she said, and went to ask Osetsu. "It seems Mrs. Utsugi did go out," she told me when she came back.

August 10

❀

From 1 to 2 p.m. I had my nap. Then there was a repetition of what happened the day before yesterday.

August 11

❀

No acupuncture. However, things were different from the other day.

Instead of "I'm going to lock this!" Satsuko stuck her

head out and said: "The door's open!" She looked bright and cheerful, for a change. I could hear the shower running.

"You're not expecting him?"

"No, come on in."

I did as I was told. She was already hidden behind the shower curtains.

"Today you can kiss me." The shower stopped. A leg appeared between the curtains.

"You look as if you're going to be examined again!"

"That's right, nothing above the knee. But didn't I stop the shower for you?"

"As a reward? Isn't that a little stingy?"

"If you don't like it, go away. I'm not forcing you." Then she added: "Today I'll let you use your tongue too."

I crouched over just as I had on the twenty-eighth of July, glued my lips to the same place on her calf, and slowly savored her flesh with my tongue. It tasted like a real kiss. My mouth kept slipping lower and lower, down toward her heel. To my surprise, she didn't say a word. She let me do as I pleased. My tongue came to her instep, then to the tip of her big toe. Kneeling, I crammed her first three toes into my mouth. I pressed my lips to the wet sole of her foot, a foot that seemed as alluringly expressive as a face.

"That's enough."

Suddenly the shower came on; water streamed over my head, face, that lovely foot. . . .

At five, Miss Sasaki informed me that it was time for traction. "My, but your eyes are red!" she exclaimed.

In recent years the whites of my eyes have tended to be bloodshot, at best they have a definite pinkish tinge. If you look carefully, you can see an extraordinary number of tiny red blood vessels below the cornea. I once had my eyes examined to find out if there might be any danger of hemorrhaging, and was told that such a hemorrhage would not be serious, the condition was natural at my age. However, it is true that when my eyes are bloodshot my pulse is also rapid and my blood pressure is high.

Miss Sasaki immediately took my pulse. "It's over 90!" she said. "Has anything happened?"

"No, nothing special."

"Let me check your blood pressure."

She insisted on having me lie down on the sofa in my study. After I had rested for ten minutes she fastened the rubber tube around my right arm. I couldn't see the reading on the gauge, but it was easy to make a rough guess from the look on her face.

"Aren't you feeling a little sick?"

"Not particularly. Is it high?"

"It's around 200."

When she says that, it's usually higher—maybe even ten or twenty degrees higher. Still, readings in that range don't alarm me as much as they do the doctor, since I have more than once experienced it as high as 245. And I am resigned to the fact that my end may come at any moment.

"This morning it was perfectly normal, 145 over 83—
I wonder why it shot up like that. I just can't understand
it. Did you strain yourself over a bowel movement?"

"No, no."

"Hasn't *anything* happened? It doesn't make sense."
Miss Sasaki shook her head doubtfully.

I said nothing, though I knew the cause only too well.
The feel of Satsuko's sole still lingered on my lips, I
couldn't forget it if I tried. I dare say it was when I crammed
her toes into my mouth that my blood pressure reached
its height. Certainly my face burned and the blood rushed
to my head, as if I might die of apoplexy that very instant.
Dying! Long as I had been prepared for death, the
thought of "dying" frightened me. I told myself that I *had*
to calm down, that I mustn't let myself be excited, and yet
I went on blindly suckling at her feet. I could not stop.
No, the more I tried to stop, the more insanely I suck-
led—and all the while thought I was dying. Waves of
terror, excitement, pleasure surged within me; pains as
violent as a heart attack gripped my chest. . . . That must
have been more than two hours earlier, but my blood
pressure had evidently remained high.

"Why don't you give up traction for today?" Miss Sasaki
suggested. "I think you ought to rest." She insisted on leading me back to the bedroom, and having me lie down. . . .

At 9 p.m. Miss Saski came in with the blood-pressure
apparatus again.

"I'd like to try once more."

Fortunately it was back to normal: systolic 150+, diastolic 87.

"That's better!" she said. "What a relief—it was up to 223 over 150!"

"I suppose it does that now and then."

"That's awfully high, even if it's just now and then! But of course it didn't last long."

Miss Sasaki wasn't the only one who had worried. Secretly I gave an even deeper sigh of relief. And yet the thought lurked in my mind that, as things were going, I ought to be able to keep on with this crazy behavior. It's scarcely the kind of erotic thriller Satusko likes in the movies or on TV, but I can't deprive myself of at least this much of an adventure. I don't care if it kills me.

August 12

❁

Haruhisa came a little after 2 p.m., and seems to have stayed two or three hours. As soon as she finished dinner Satsuko went out. She said she wanted to see Martin La Salle in *Pickpocket* downtown, and then go to the pool at the Prince Hotel. I can imagine how she would look in a low-cut bathing suit, her bare white shoulders and back gleaming in the rays of the floodlights.

August 13

❁

Again today, at around 3 p.m., I had my little erotic thriller. But today my eyes didn't become red. My blood pressure seems normal too. A slight disappointment. Something is lacking unless my eyes get bloodshot and my blood pressure goes over 200

August 14

❁

Tonight Jokichi came home alone from Karuizawa. He says that tomorrow (Monday) he will be going back to work.

August 16

❁

Satsuko went swimming at Hayama yesterday. She tells
me she hadn't been to the beach all summer, because of
looking after me, and she simply must have a tan. Since
Satsuko is as fair as the average Caucasian, her skin sun-
burns easily. Today her neck and chest were dyed crimson
in a V-shaped pattern; where she was covered by her
bathing suit was unbelievably white. No doubt it was to
show off the contrast that she invited me into the bathroom. . . .

August 17

❁

Apparently Haruhisa came again today.

August 18

❀

Another erotic thriller. But it was a little different from the earlier ones. Today she came in wearing high-heeled sandals, and kept them on while she took her shower.

"Why are you wearing those things?"

"At any nude show the girls come out in sandals like these. Doesn't it appeal to you, since you're so crazy about my feet? There's practically nothing to them."

That was well enough, but then something else happened.

"Shall I let you do some necking today, Father?"

"What's 'necking'?"

"Don't you know? That's what you were doing the other day."

"Kissing on the neck?"

"Of course! It's a kind of petting!"

"You'll have to explain that too."

"Old people are a real nuisance! It means to caress and pet someone all over. And then there's 'heavy petting'—I can see I have a lot to teach you."

"So you'll let me kiss your neck?"

"As long as you're properly grateful."

"I couldn't be more grateful. But why am I so lucky? I'm worried about the consequences."

"That's the way to look at it! Just don't forget that!"

"Well, what are they?"

"Oh, go ahead with the necking first."

The temptation was too strong. For over twenty minutes I indulged myself in what she called "necking."

"Now I've got you! You can't say no after that."

"What are you asking?"

"Brace yourself—don't panic!"

"What on earth *is* it?"

"There's something I've been wanting lately."

"Well, *what?*"

"A cat's-eye."

"A cat's-eye? You mean a jewel?"

"That's right. But a little one won't do—I want a ring with a big stone, the kind a man wears. And I've finally found one in the Imperial Hotel arcade. That's the one I've set my heart on."

"How much is it?"

"Three million yen."

"*How* much?"

"Three million yen."

"You're joking."

"I am *not* joking!"

"That's more money than I can spare."

"I know very well you've got it. You can easily let me have that much. So I told them I'd made up my mind, I'd be back for it in a few days."

"I didn't realize necking was so expensive."

"But it isn't just for today—you can do it any time you like from now on."

"Still, it's only necking. A real kiss would be worth something, though."

"How you talk! And you said you couldn't be more grateful!"

"But this is serious. What'll we do if my wife sees it?"

"Do you think I'd let that happen?"

"Anyway, I can't afford it. You're being too hard on this old man!"

"You look happy, all the same!"

I believe I *was* looking happy. . . .

August 19

They say a typhoon is coming. Perhaps that is why my hand hurts so badly, and why I am having more trouble using my legs. The Dolosin Satsuko bought me relieves the pain somewhat; I take it three times a day, three tablets at a time. Since it is taken orally, I prefer it to Nobulon. But what I find annoying is that, like aspirin, it makes me sweat profusely.

Early in the afternoon Dr. Suzuki telephoned to say he would like to cancel our appointment because of the possibility of a typhoon. I said it was all right with me, and went to my study. Satsuko came in immediately.

"I'm here for what you promised," she said. "After that I'm going to the bank, and then straight to the hotel."

"There's a typhoon on its way, you know. Why do you have to go at a time like this?"

"I'm not waiting till you change your mind—I want to see that stone on my finger as soon as I can."

"Now that I've promised it, I won't go back on my word."

"Tomorrow is Saturday, so if I sleep late I won't get to the bank on time. Never put a good thing off, they say."

I had wanted to use the money for another purpose.

During my childhood—I can't remember the exact year—we left the house in Honjo where our family had lived for generations to move to Nihombashi in downtown Tokyo. After the great earthquake of 1923 we moved out to our present house in the Mamiana section of Azabu. It was my father who built it, but he died in 1925, when I was in my early forties. Mother died only a few years later, in 1928. I said that father built our Azabu house; however, because there was already an old man-

sion on the site (the residence of the Meiji statesman
Haseba Sumitaka was supposed to have been somewhere
around here) he merely left part of it intact and remodeled the rest. Father had retired by then, and my parents
lived quietly in the old wing, loving the tranquility of its
setting. We had to remodel again after the house was damaged in the war, but the old part miraculously escaped burning. By now it is too dilapidated to be of any use; I want
to tear it down and replace it with a modern Western-
style wing, for myself and my wife, but so far she has
opposed the idea. We shouldn't wantonly destroy the
place where my father and mother spent their last years,
she says; we ought to preserve it as long as possible. Since
she would go on talking like that forever, I decided to
force her consent and call in the wreckers.

Even without an addition our house is large enough to
accommodate the whole family, but it is inconvenient for
carrying out certain schemes of mine. In building a new
wing for us, I planned to separate my bedroom and study
as far as possible from my wife's bedroom and provide her
with an adjoining lavatory. She was to have her own bathroom too, "for her convenience," a purely Japanese one
with a wooden tub. My bath would be tiled and include a
shower.

"What's the use of putting two baths in our part of the
house?" she asks. "I can share the old one with Oshizu
and Miss Sasaki."

"Oh, you might as well allow yourself a little luxury. At

our age there aren't many pleasures left besides a nice long soak in the tub."

My aim was to see that my wife stayed in her own room as much as possible, instead of wandering all around the house. While I was at it, I wanted to remodel the whole building to a single story; but Satsuko wasn't in favor of that, nor did I have enough ready cash. Reluctantly I decided to content myself with the new wing. The three million yen Satsuko had demanded was to go toward building it.

Satsuko returned soon. "Here I am!" she said, coming in like a triumphant general.

"Did you buy it already?"

Without a word she held the ring out to me on her palm. Sure enough it was a superb cat's-eye. I realized that my dreams of a new wing had dwindled to that speck of light on her soft palm.

"How many carats is it?" I put it on the palm of my own hand."

"Fifteen."

Instantly the old pain in my left hand flared up again. I hastily swallowed three tablets of Dolosin. As I watched the exultant look on Satsuko's face, the pain seemed almost unbearably rapturous. How much better than building a new wing!

August 20

❁

Increasingly heavy wind and rain from Typhoon No. 14. However, I left for Karuizawa this morning as I had planned. Satsuko and Miss Sasaki came along, the latter in a second-class car. Miss Sasaki kept worrying about the weather, asking if I wouldn't put the trip off till tomorrow, but neither Satsuko nor I would listen to her. Both of us were in a curiously reckless mood, as if to say: Let the typhoon blow! We were under the spell of the cat's eye. . . .

August 23 ·

❁

Today I expected to go back to Tokyo with Satsuko; but my wife said that, what with the children's school beginning soon, they had decided to leave on the twenty-fourth—wouldn't I stay till tomorrow, so we could all go back together? That dashed my hopes for traveling alone with Satsuko.

August 25

✿

I was supposed to begin traction again this morning, but have decided to give it up. It hasn't helped after all. I think I'll stop acupuncture too at the end of the month.

Satsuko left promptly this evening to go to the Kora-kuen Gym.

September 1

✿

Today the weather is fine, in spite of its being Typhoon Day by the old almanac. Jokichi is flying down to Fukuoka, to stay for the rest of the week.

September 3

❀

It is really beginning to feel like autumn. After last night's shower the sky is beautifully clear. Satsuko has arranged the seven autumn wildflowers in the entrance hall, and tall millet stalks and cockscombs in the alcove of my study. While she was at it, she changed the hanging scroll too. The new one has a Chinese verse composed and written by Nagai Kafu.

For seven autumns I have lived in Azabu Valley.
Frost lingers; the old tree shelters the Western Hall.
Laughing, I set myself tasks all week long.
I sweep leaves, air my books, and then air my winter clothes.

Kafu has always been one of my favorite novelists, though his calligraphy and Chinese poetry leave something to be desired. I bought this scroll from a dealer years ago; it may not even be genuine since there are said to be some extremely clever forgeries of his work. The Western-style frame house in which he lived until it was burned down during the war stood only a little way from here. Hence "For seven autumns I have lived in Azabu Valley."

September 4

Toward dawn this morning—I think it was around five a.m.—I heard a cricket chirping somewhere. It was only a faint chirp-chirp, and I was half asleep, but I could hear it go on and on. This is already the cricket season; still, it was strange to be able to hear one from my bedroom. Although we occasionally have crickets in our garden, they would hardly be audible to me in bed. I wondered if one had found its way into my room.

It reminded me of my childhood. We were living in Honjo, I was about five or six, and as I lay in bed in my nurse's arms a cricket would be chirping just outside. Perhaps it was hiding behind a stepping-stone in the garden, or beneath the veranda, as it shrilled away its clear ringing note. There was never more than one of them, never the large numbers that gather when you have bell crickets or pine crickets. But that one insect had a really shrill, penetrating chirp. As soon as she heard it my nurse would say: "Listen, Tokusuke! It's already autumn. There's a cricket!" Then she would imitate its cry with some nonsense syllables. "Isn't that the way it goes? When you hear that, it's autumn!"

Maybe it was only my imagination, but as she talked I felt a chilly draft up the sleeves of my white cotton night kimono. Although I disliked a stiffly starched kimono, the one I wore at night always had the characteristic sweet-sour odor of starch. That odor and the cricket's chirp and the chill of an autumn morning linger in my mind together as a blurred, distant memory. Even now, when I am seventy-seven, a few chirps at dawn revivify that old memory of the odor of starch, the way my nurse talked, the touch of a stiff night kimono against my skin. Half dreaming, I feel as if I am still at our house in Honjo, still lying in bed in my nurse's arms.

But this morning, as my mind gradually cleared, I realized that I was hearing it in this familiar room, where my bed stands side by side with Nurse Sasaki's. Still, that was odd. There could scarcely be a cricket in my room, nor was I likely to hear one from outside, with all the doors and windows closed. Yet it was certainly chirping. I strained my ears to listen. So that was it! I tried to listen more closely. Of course, that was what I had heard.

I had been listening to the sound of my own breathing. This morning the air was dry, my old throat was parched, and I seemed to be catching cold; as a result, each time I breathed in or out I produced a chirping sound. I wasn't sure whether it came from my throat or from the back of my nose, but apparently it occurred as my breath passed a certain point in that region. The chirping sounded as if it came from outside my body—I couldn't believe that I myself was the source of that tiny cricket-like note. Yet when I deliberately breathed in and out, there was no mistaking it. Fascinated, I did it over and over again. The harder I breathed, the louder the sound, as if I were blowing a whistle.

"Are you awake, sir?" Miss Sasaki asked, sitting up in bed.

"Listen, do you recognize this?" I made the chirping sound again.

"It's only your breathing."

"Oh? You've heard it before?"

"Of course I have. I hear it every morning!"

"Do you mean to say I've been making a noise like this every morning?"

"Didn't you know you were?"

"Maybe I *have* been hearing it in the mornings lately. I've been so groggy I thought it was a cricket."

"It's not a cricket, it comes from your throat, sir. There's nothing unusual about it. When a person gets older his throat dries out and he's likely to make a whistling noise when he breathes. Old people often do that."

"So you knew what it was all along?"

"Yes, I've been hearing it every morning these days—a tiny little voice going chirp-chirp!"

"I feel like doing it for my wife."

"She knows all about it."

"Probably Satsuko would laugh."

"I'm sure she's heard it too."

September 5

❀

Early this morning I dreamed about my mother. That is very unusual for me. Probably it came from thinking of the cricket and my old nurse yesterday at dawn. In the dream my mother appeared at her youngest and most beautiful, as far as I can remember her. I wasn't sure exactly where we were, but it must have been our house in Honjo. Mother was wearing a black silk crepe coat over a fine-patterned gray kimono, the kind of clothes she always wore when she was going visiting. I don't know where she meant to go, or even what room she was in at that time. Perhaps she was sitting in the parlor, since I saw her take an old-fashioned pipe and tobacco pouch out of her sash and begin to smoke. But soon she seemed to have left the house: she was walking along with nothing but straw sandals on her feet. Her hair was dressed in the ginkgo-leaf style, gathered with a string of coral beads and decorated with a round ornamental pin of coral and a tortoise shell comb inlaid with mother-of-pearl. Although I could see her coiffure in such detail, somehow her face was hidden. Like most women of her time, Mother was quite short, about five feet or so; I suppose that explains why I saw the top of her head instead of her face. Yet I knew beyond a doubt that it was Mother. Unfortunately she neither looked at me nor spoke to me. I didn't attempt to talk to her either. Perhaps I was afraid she would scold me. Since we had relatives nearby, it occurred to me that she might be on her way there. I saw her only for a moment, then the scene dissolved into a mist.

Even after I was awake I let my mind dwell on the dream image of my mother. Possibly one fine day in the mid-1890's, when I was a small child, Mother happened to meet me just as she had left our house and was walking down the street. That impression may have been revived in my dream. Curiously, though, she alone was young—I was as old as I am now, and tall enough to look down on her. Still I felt that I was a child, and that she was my mother. And I seemed to be back in Honjo, around 1894 or 1895. I suppose that sort of thing is typical of dreams.

Mother knew her grandson Jokichi, but because she died in 1928, when Jokichi was four, she never knew the girl who became his bride. Since even my wife had so violently opposed his marriage to Satsuko, I wonder what my mother might have done. Probably the marriage would never have taken place. No, from the very first an engagement with a former chorus girl would have been unthinkable. Supposing she had known that such a marriage was followed by the infatuation of her own son with her grandson's wife, by my squandering three million yen to give her a cat's-eye in return for the privilege of "petting"—Mother would have fainted with horror. If Father were alive he would have disowned both Jokichi and me. And I wonder how she might have reacted to Satsuko's appearance!

People called Mother a beauty, when she was young. I remember her very well in those days—until I was fourteen or fifteen she was as beautiful as ever. When I compare that memory of her with Satsuko, the contrast is really striking. Satsuko is also called a beauty. That was the main reason why Jokichi married her. But between these two beauties, between the 1890's and now, what a change has taken place in the physical appearance of the Japanese woman! For example, Mother's feet were beautiful too, but Satsuko's have an altogether different kind of beauty. They hardly seem to belong to a woman of the same race. Mother had dainty feet, small enough to nestle in the palm of my hand, and as she tripped along in her straw sandals she took extremely short, mincing steps with her toes turned in. (I am reminded that in my dream Mother's feet were bare except for her sandals, even though she was dressed to go visiting. Perhaps she was deliberately showing off her feet to me.) All Meiji women had that pigeon-like walk, not just beauties. As for Satsuko's feet, they are elegantly long and slender; she boasts that ordinary Japanese shoes are too wide for her. On the contrary, my mother's feet were fairly broad, rather like those of the Bodhisattva of Mercy in the Sangatsudo in Nara. Also, the women of her day were short in stature. Women under five feet were not uncommon. Having been born in the Meiji era, I am only about five feet two myself, but Satsuko is an inch and a half taller.

Make-up was very different in those days too, and very simple. Married women—nearly all women over eighteen—shaved off their eyebrows and dyed their teeth black. By late Meiji the custom had almost disappeared, but it lasted until my childhood. Even now I remember the peculiar metallic odor of tooth dye. I wonder what Satsuko would think if she saw my mother made up like that. *She* has her hair set in a permanent wave, wears earrings, paints her lips coral pink or pearl pink or coffee brown, pencils her eyebrows, uses eye shadow on her eyelids, glues on false eyelashes and then, as if that isn't enough, brushes on mascara to try to make them look still longer. During the day she elongates her eyes with a dark brown pencil, and at night uses eye shadow blended with Chinese ink. She gives the same kind of attention to her nails—it would take far too long to describe the whole process.

How the Japanese woman has been transformed in the last sixty-odd years! I can't help marveling at what a long

time I have lived, at what innumerable changes I have
seen. Suppose Mother knew that her son Tokusuke, born
in 1883, is alive today and is shamefully attracted to a
woman like Satsuko—to her granddaughter at that, the
wife of her own grandson—and finds pleasure in being
tantalized by her, even sacrificing his wife and children to
try to win her love! Could she possibly have imagined
that now, thirty-two years after her death, her son would
have become such a lunatic, and that such a woman would
have joined our family? No, I myself had never dreamed
it would turn out this way. . . .

September 12

❊

Around four o'clock this afternoon my wife and Kugako
came in. It has been a long time since I saw Kugako in this
room. Ever since I refused her on June 19 she has had
nothing to do with me. Even when my wife and Keisuke
left for Karuizawa she met them at the station, instead of
coming to our house, and when I went to join them later
she did her best to avoid me. Today she obviously had
something on her mind.

"Thank you for putting up with the children again this summer."

"What is it you want?" I asked her bluntly.

"Nothing, really. . . ."

"Oh? The children were looking fine."

"They had a wonderful time at Karuizawa."

"Maybe it's because I see so little of them, but they'd grown out of all recognition."

Then my wife broke in. "By the way, Kugako heard something interesting, and wanted to tell you too."

"Is that so?" She's here to be nasty, I thought.

"You remember Mr. Yutani, don't you?" my wife went on.

"The Yutani who went to Brazil?"

"It's his son—the young man who came to Jokichi's wedding in his father's place."

"How do you expect me to remember that? What about him?"

"I don't remember him either, but Kugako says he's a business friend of her husband's, and they've been seeing him and his wife occasionally."

"I asked what about him!"

"Well, it seems Mr. and Mrs. Yutani dropped in last Sunday, saying they happened to be in the neighborhood. But Mrs. Yutani is such a gossip, Kugako wonders if she didn't come just to tell her."

"Tell her *what?*"

"Oh, I think you'd better hear that from Kugako."

I was sitting in my armchair and they were standing, but then they settled down with a sigh on the sofa facing me. And so Kugako, who is only four years older than Satsuko but already seems middle-aged, took the story from there. She calls Mrs. Yutani a gossip, but when it comes to gossiping she can hold her own.

"On the twenty-fifth of last month, the night after we got back from Karuizawa, there was a featherweight title match at the Korakuen Gym, wasn't there?"

"How would I know a thing like that?"

"Well, there was! It's the night the Japanese bantam title-holder Sakamoto Haruo won the first Orient championship, by knocking out the top-rank Thai bantam—"

Kugako glibly rattled off a long, exotic name, a name I couldn't even say in one breath. It would leave me tongue-tied. A woman who can talk like that is in an altogether different class.

"Anyway, it seems Mr. and Mrs. Yutani went early, in time for the opening bout. At first the two ringside seats on their right were empty, she says; and then just before the title match an awfully chic young lady came in, flourishing automobile keys in one hand and a beige handbag in the other, and sat down next to her. Who do you think that was?"

I didn't answer.

"Mrs. Yutani says she hadn't seen Satsuko since the wedding, seven or eight years ago, so it would only be natural for Satsuko to forget what she looked like, or not even notice a person like herself in all that crowd. 'But I couldn't forget *her*,' Mrs. Yutani said. 'She's unforgettable—more beautiful than ever. But just as I was thinking I ought to speak to her, and ask if she wasn't Mrs. Utsugi, a man I didn't know came squeezing in and sat down next to Satsuko on the other side.' Mrs. Yutani says he seemed to be a friend of hers; they started chatting away together, so she had no chance to introduce herself."

I still didn't say a word.

"Well, that's all right, I suppose—at least I'll let Mother tell you that story."

"It certainly isn't all right!" my wife broke in again.

"Mother, will you please tell him about that yourself? I'd rather not. Anyway, Mrs. Yutani says the first thing she noticed was the cat's-eye shining on Satsuko's finger. Satsuko was next to her, and it was easy enough to see *that* stone! She says it must have weighed over fifteen carats—even if it's a cat's-eye, you don't often come across such a huge splendid jewel. I didn't know Satsuko had a ring like that, and mother says she's never seen it either. When do you suppose she bought it?"

Kugako paused and waited for me to answer. "That reminds me," she went on, "wasn't there a scandal when Kishi was Prime Minister about buying a cat's-eye in Indo-China or somewhere? The newspapers said it cost two million yen. Jewels aren't so expensive in Southeast Asia, so a stone like that ought to be worth twice as much in Japan. In that case Satsuko's must be really something!"

"Who do you think bought it for her?" my wife put in.

"Anyhow, because it was such a splendid stone, so terribly brilliant, Mrs. Yutani must have kept staring at it with wide-open eyes. Satsuko seemed to feel uneasy, she took a pair of lace gloves out of her handbag and slipped them on. But the cat's-eye shone through all the more brilliantly—you see, her gloves were delicate French handmade lace, and black lace at that! Maybe she wore them on purpose, to enhance the effect. My, but you were sharp-eyed, I told Mrs. Yutani; but she says Satsuko was sitting just on her right, with the ring on her left hand, so she couldn't avoid looking at it. That cat's-eye glowing through the black lace almost made her miss the boxing match!" . . .

September 13

❀

(Continued.)

"Tell me, how could Satsuko have had such a thing?" My wife suddenly began pressing me hard. Again I didn't answer. Then she asked: "Well, when did you buy it for her?"

"Does it matter when?"

"Indeed it does! In the first place, how did you happen to have that much money on hand? And you told Kugako you were hard up because you had a lot of expenses!"

I was silent.

"Is that what you meant by expenses?"

"That's exactly what I meant." For the moment my wife and Kugako were shocked speechless. "I'm telling you that even if I have money to give Satsuko I haven't any for Kugako."

After delivering a hammer blow like that, I happened to think of a good excuse. "You remember when I wanted to tear down the old wing and rebuild," I told my wife, "and how you were against it?"

"I certainly was! Who on earth would agree with you, when you show such lack of respect for your parents?"

"All right, then. My parents must be rejoicing in their graves to think what a devoted daughter-in-law they have. So I saved all the money I'd put away for that."

"Even if you did, why should you be so extravagant for Satsuko?"

"What's wrong with buying her a ring? She's not a stranger, she's our own son's wife! My parents would be proud of me for being so generous."

"But it would have cost even more to build a new wing. You must have some of the money left."

"Of course I have. I only spent part of it on the cat's-eye."

"Well, what are you going to do with the rest?"

"I'll do anything I please with it—you needn't go meddling in my affairs!"

"But what do you mean to use it for? That's all I'm asking."

"Oh, I haven't quite made up my mind. She's been saying how nice it would be if we had a swimming pool, so maybe the next thing I'll do is build one. That ought to delight her."

My wife didn't utter a word. She stared at me in astonishment.

"I wonder if you can build a pool so quickly," Kugako said. "It's already close to autumn."

"They say it takes a long time for the concrete to dry— even if we start work right away we'll need about four months. Satsuko looked into the whole thing."

"Then it won't be finished before winter."

"That's why there's no special hurry. We can take our time and finish around next March or April. It's just that I'd like to get it done a little early, to see how pleased she'll look."

That silenced Kugako too. "And Satsuko won't have one of those ordinary little family-sized pools," I added. "She wants one at least twenty by fifteen meters, so that she can practice water ballet. She says she wants to give me a solo performance! It's as if I'm building the pool just for that."

"Anyway, I'm sure it will be very nice," Kugako said

dryly. "Even little Keisuke will be delighted to have a pool at his house."

"She's not the kind to give any thought to Keisuke," my wife spoke up. "She won't even help him with his homework, he has to have a student tutor him. And his grandfather is just as bad—I feel sorry for the poor child!"

"Well, once you have a pool Keisuke will jump in too! I hope you'll let my own children use it often."

"Of course! The oftener the better." She was going to get even with me after all! Naturally I couldn't forbid the pool to Keisuke or her children, who love to swim. However, they have school until late June, and in July I'll pack them off to Karuizawa. The real problem will be Haruhisa.

"And how much will the pool cost?" That was what I had expected to hear, but in their confusion Kugako and my wife forgot to ask me that vital question. I felt somewhat relieved. Furthermore, they must have meant to keep pressing their attack, first wringing out a confession about the cat's-eye and then bringing up the relations between Satsuko and Haruhisa. But apparently they hesitated, for fear the quarrel might become too serious, and then missed their chance completely when I bowled them over with my high-handed retort. However, I don't see how I can keep the matter from coming up sooner or later. . . .

Today is an auspicious one, according to the old calendar. This evening Jokichi and Satsuko went to a friend's wedding, though they rarely go out together anymore. Jokichi wore a dinner jacket, Satsuko a formal kimono. For some reason Satsuko chose to dress in Japanese style, in spite of the lingering heat. That was rare too. She had on a kimono of white silk crepe with a design of tree branches in graded tones of pink against a pale blue shadow-like pattern. Through the sheer crepe you could see the shimmer of a blue lining.

"How do you like it, Father?" she asked as she came in.

"Turn around once, all the way."

Her sash was a seamless figured silk gauze, with an inwoven yellowish and gold design in the style of Kenzan on a silver-threaded azure ground. It was tied in a fairly small knot, and the end seemed to hang down a little lower than usual. The inner sash was of white silk gauze tinted a faint pink, the sash band a rope-like twist of gold and silver threads. She wore a dark green jade ring, and was carrying a small white beaded handbag.

"Japanese clothes aren't bad either, now and then. It's clever of you not to wear earrings or a necklace."

"You know quite a bit about it, don't you, Father?"

Oshizu came in with a sandal box, took out a pair of evening sandals, and set them down before her. Satsuko, who had been wearing slippers, deliberately stepped into them before my eyes. Her sandals were of silver brocade with triple-layered heels, pink on the underside of the thong. Since they were brand-new, it was hard to fit the thong between her toes properly. Oshizu perspired as she crouched there helping her. At last Satsuko was satisfied, and took a few steps in them for me. She likes the way they set off her trim ankles. Probably that is why she wore Japanese dress, and why she came in to let me see the effect.

September 16

❀

Day after day the heat continues—it's unusually hot for mid-September. Maybe the weather explains why my legs are so heavy and swollen. My feet seem to swell even worse than my legs: when I press the lower part of my instep the flesh sinks in alarmingly, and it stays that way a long time. The fourth and fifth toes of my left foot are completely paralyzed, and swollen up underneath like grapes. As for the feeling of dead weight, it is bad enough above the ankles, but the worst of it is in the soles of my feet. Both feet—not just the left one—feel as if they're stuck to an iron plate. When I walk, my legs get so much in each other's way that I find it difficult to maneuver. If I try to step down from the veranda into my garden clogs, I am never able to do it smoothly. Invariably I totter and

lose my balance, so that one foot lands on the stepping-
stone, or even on the bare ground. Although such symptoms are nothing new to me, they have become especially
noticeable of late. Miss Sasaki worries about them, and
frequently tests my knee reflexes for signs of beriberi. But
that doesn't seem to be the trouble.

"You ought to have Dr. Sugita give you a thorough
examination," she keeps telling me. "And you'll need an
electrocardiogram, it's been quite a while since you've
had one. Somehow I feel uneasy about these swellings."

Furthermore, I had an accident this morning. I was out
for my walk in the garden with Miss Sasaki leading me by
the hand, when suddenly our collie, who was supposed to
be in his kennel, came bounding out and sprang up at me.
The dog only meant to play, but I was as badly startled as
if I'd been attacked by a wild beast. Before I had a chance
to protect myself I was knocked flat on my back. It happened on the lawn, so it didn't hurt very much; still, I got
a jarring thump on the head. I tried to stand up but
couldn't at first—it took several minutes for me to retrieve
my stick and struggle to my feet. Meanwhile the dog was
jumping up playfully at Miss Sasaki. Satsuko heard her
shriek and came running out in her negligee.

"Leslie! Here!" As soon as she scowled at him, the collie quieted down and trotted obediently after her to the
kennel, wagging his tail.

"Are you hurt?" Miss Sasaki asked me, brushing off the
skirts of my light cotton kimono.

"No, but I'm so old and shaky I'm helpless against an animal that size."

"It's a good thing you landed on the grass."

Jokichi and I have always liked dogs, but we had only small ones—Airedales or dachshunds or Spitzes—until after his marriage. I think it was about six months after the wedding that Jokichi said he wanted a Borzoi, and before long he brought home a magnificent one. Then he hired a trainer to give the dog regular daily lessons. There was so much work involved in caring for him—feeding, bathing, brushing, and the like—that my wife and the maids grumbled constantly. To be sure, my old diary entries say it was all done for Jokichi, yet now I realize that Satsuko must have been behind it.

Two years later the Borzoi caught distemper and died; this time Satsuko frankly announced that she wanted another dog to replace him, and asked the pet shop to find her a greyhound. She called this one Gary Cooper and lavished affection on him, often taking him out on walks or having Nomura drive the two of them around town together. The maids said the young mistress seemed more attached to Gary Cooper than to little Keisuke. However, the greyhound turned out to be an old one the pet shop had passed off on her, and he soon died of filariasis. This collie is her third dog. According to its pedigree, the sire was born in London and named Leslie, so she decided to call the puppy Leslie too. I am sure I recorded all this in my diary at the time. Satsuko is as fond of Leslie as she was of Gary Cooper, but Kugako or someone seems to have urged my wife to get rid of him. For the last two or three years there has been more and more talk at our house about the disadvantages of having a big dog.

"Now you know why I said so!" my wife complained. "A few years ago you were strong enough to keep your footing if a dog that big jumped up at you, but not any more. Even a cat could tumble you over, let alone a dog. And our garden isn't all lawn—there's the sloping path, and the steps and the stepping-stones. What if you had a bad fall at one of those places? As a matter of fact, I heard of an old gentleman who was in the hospital for three months, and still wears a cast, just from tripping over a shepherd dog! That's why I've been hinting for you to have Satsuko give up that collie—if I asked she wouldn't listen."

"But it would be cruel to make her get rid of an animal she's so fond of. . . ."

"It still isn't worth risking your own safety."

"Suppose I had her give him up, what could we do with a huge dog like that?"

"Somebody would want him, I'm sure."

"Maybe so, if he was a puppy, but a dog that size is hard to take care of. Besides, I'm rather fond of Leslie myself."

"I expect you're afraid Satsuko would be cross with you. Don't you ever worry about getting hurt?"

"Why can't *you* ask her? If Satsuko is willing, I won't object."

Actually, my wife doesn't dare ask her either. Day by day the power of "the young mistress" has increased, so that by now it's hard to say how fierce a quarrel there might be over getting rid of a dog. When she thinks of that, my wife isn't going to blunder into opening hostilities.

To tell the truth, I don't particularly care for Leslie. I realize that I merely pretend to like him, because of Satsuko. Somehow it puts me in a bad humor to see her go out riding side by side with that dog. It's only natural for her to ride with Jokichi, and I can accept the situation even if she's with Haruhisa; but the very fact that you can't be jealous of a dog makes it all the more irritating. And yet Leslie's features are aristocratic, he has a certain air of nobility. Perhaps he's more handsome than that rather negroid-looking Haruhisa. Satsuko has him nestle close to her in the car; and even if she drives she keeps one arm around his neck, snuggling her cheek against his. That must seem offensive to anyone.

"She only does that when you are looking, sir," Nomura says. If that is so, maybe it's one of her ways of teasing me.

I am reminded that once, wishing to curry favor with her, I tried to cajole Leslie in her presence, and threw cookies to him over the fence of his kennel. But Satsuko was annoyed.

"What are you doing, Father?" she said sharply. "Please don't give him anything without asking me. Oh, look! He's so well trained he won't touch your cookies!" And she went inside the fence to Leslie, made a great show of fondling him before my eyes, stroking his cheek, almost kissing him, and grinned as if to say, "Jealous, aren't you?"

I wouldn't mind being injured if that would bring Satsuko pleasure, and a mortal injury would be all the better. Yet to think of being trampled to death, not by her but by her dog . . .

At 2 p.m. Dr. Sugita came. Miss Sasaki seems to have felt obliged to report my accident immediately.

"I hear you had a bad fall."

"It was nothing much."

"Anyway, suppose I take a look at you."

He had me lie down and began by examining my arms and legs minutely. The rheumatic-like pains in my shoulders and elbows and kneecaps have bothered me for some time, they weren't Leslie's fault. Fortunately I don't appear to have suffered any injury. Dr. Sugita examined my back, had me take deep breaths, and tapped my chest repeatedly as he listened to my heart. Finally he got out a portable cardiograph and made an electrocardiogram.

"I don't think you need to worry," he said before leaving. "I'll let you know the results later on today."

He telephoned his report this evening.

"The new cardiogram doesn't show anything serious," he said. "Of course there's bound to be a certain amount of change in a man of your age, but nothing abnormal. What you really need one of these days is a kidney test."

September 24

❀

Yesterday Miss Sasaki asked to spend the night with her family. It was the first time since last month, so I couldn't very well refuse. However, it meant that she would come back around noon on Sunday. That was convenient for her, allowing her a quiet Sunday morning at home, but I had to see what Satsuko thought. Ever since July my wife has told me she'd like to be excused from substituting for the nurse at night.

"Why not let her go?" Satsuko said. "She's probably been looking forward to it."

"It's all right with you, then?"

"Why do you ask?"

"Tomorrow's Sunday, you know."

"Of course it is. What of it?"

"Maybe you'll say it makes no difference, but hasn't Jokichi been doing a lot of traveling lately?"

"So what?"

"It's just that he's home this weekend for once."

"Well, what about that?"

"He'd probably like to sleep late with his wife!"

"So even the naughty old man feels like looking out for his son sometimes, is that it?"

"To make amends, I suppose."

"Anyway it's none of your business. Jokichi would tell you he'd rather you weren't so kind."

"I wonder."

"It's all right, you needn't worry on his account. You're an early riser, so I'll take Miss Sasaki's place tonight and go to him after you wake up."

"You'll rouse him out of a sound sleep."

"Don't be silly, he'll be lying there waiting."

"I give up!"

At half past nine I took my bath, and at ten I went to bed. As usual Oshizu carried in a rattan chaise longue for Satsuko.

"Are you going to sleep in that chair again?"

"I'll be perfectly comfortable, Father. Please be quiet and go to sleep."

"You'll catch cold on a thing like that!"

"Don't worry, I'll use lots of blankets. Oshizu will see to it."

"If I let you catch cold I'll feel guilty toward Jokichi—yes, and not only Jokichi."

"Such a nuisance! You seem to need Adalin again."

"Maybe I'll need more than two tablets."

"Nonsense! Last month two were quite enough. As

soon as you swallowed them you fell into a dead sleep, with your mouth wide open, drooling."

"I must have been a sight."

"I'll leave that to your imagination. But listen, Father, why don't you take out your false teeth when I sleep here? I know very well you usually do!"

"It's more comfortable to have them out at night, but it makes me look horribly ugly. I don't mind being seen by my wife or Miss Sasaki, though."

"Do you think I've never seen you like that?"

"Maybe you have."

"Last year you were in a coma for half a day, remember?"

"Did you see me then?"

"It doesn't matter whether you wear false teeth or not. But it's ridiculous to try hiding it!"

"I'm not eager to hide it, I just don't want to be unpleasant to others."

"But you think you can hide it if you don't take them out!"

"All right, I *will!* You'll see what I look like."

I got out of bed and went over to stand before her. Then I took out both my upper and lower plates, put them in the denture box on the night table, and clenched my gums hard, shriveling up my face as much as I could. My nose flattened down over my lips. Even a chimpanzee would have been better-looking. Time after time I smacked my gums open and shut, and licked my yellow tongue around in my mouth. Satsuko kept her eyes fixed steadily on that grotesque spectacle.

"Your face doesn't bother me in the least!" she said, taking a mirror out of the night-table drawer. "But have you ever had a good look at yourself? Let me show you. . . . See!" She held the mirror up to my face. "Well? What do you think?"

"It's incredibly ugly."

After looking at myself in the mirror, I looked at Satsuko. I could not believe that we were creatures of the same species. The uglier the face in the mirror, the more extraordinarily beautiful Satsuko seemed. If that ugly face were only uglier, I thought regretfully, Satsuko would look even more beautiful.

"Come on, let's go to sleep, Father. Back to bed, please."

"I'd like some Adalin," I said as I lay down.

"You don't think you can sleep tonight?"

"Being with you always excites me."

"Once you've seen that face you ought to realize there's nothing to get excited about."

"But it makes looking at you even more exciting. I suppose you can't understand that psychology."

"Frankly, I can't."

"What I'm saying is that the uglier I am the more ravishingly beautiful you look."

Hardly listening, Satsuko went out for the Adalin.

When she came back she had an American cigarette—a Kool—in her other hand.

"Open wide! You musn't get addicted, so I'm just giving you two tablets again."

"Can I have them mouth-to-mouth?"

"Remember that face!" At least she slipped them in with her own fingers.

"When did you take up smoking?"

"I've been smoking upstairs now and then, on the sly." A lighter glistened in her hand. "I don't particularly like to smoke, but it's a kind of accessory, you know. And tonight I want to get rid of the bad taste in my mouth."

September 28

On rainy days the trouble in my arm and in my legs is worse than ever, indeed I can feel the change coming from the day before. When I got up this morning I was suffering intensely from the numbness in my arm and from the swellings and heaviness in my legs. Because of the rain I couldn't go out in the garden, but it isn't easy for me even to walk along the veranda. I soon totter and lose my balance, and am in danger of falling off. The numbness in my arm extends from elbow to shoulder; at this rate I am afraid I may become paralyzed on one side of my body.

After about six o'clock this evening the chilling in my arm was even worse. It felt insensible, as if it were packed in ice. No, not just insensible, when chilling gets this bad you experience something akin to pain. And yet people tell me it isn't cold to the touch, my arms seems as warm as usual. I alone am aware of the unbearable chilling. This happened before, usually in the depth of winter; it's rare for me to get this way in September. To combat a chill like this I have my whole arm wrapped in a hot steaming towel, down to the tips of my fingers, wrap thick wool flannel over that, and apply a couple of pocket warmers. Even then, my arm chills through in about ten minutes, so hot water is kept at my bedside and the towel is soaked and wrapped again. This procedure has to be repeated five or six times, with a constant replenishment of the hot water. I had it done again tonight, and at last the chill was somewhat relieved.

September 29

❀

Last night, thanks to a fairly long application of hot towels, the pain in my arm diminished and I was able to have a good sleep. But when I woke up around dawn I noticed that my arm was hurting again. The rain had stopped and the sky was beautifully clear. If only I were in good health, how exhilarating a fine autumn day like this would have seemed! It exasperated me to think how much I would have enjoyed it even a few years ago. I took three tablets of Dolosin.

At 10 a.m. Miss Sasaki measured my blood pressure. It had dropped to systolic 105, diastolic 58. At her urging, I drank a cup of tea and ate two crackers with a little Kraft cheese. About twenty minutes later she measured it again. It was up to 158/92. It isn't good to have such a rapid change.

"Do you think you ought to keep on writing like that?" Miss Sasaki asked, seeing me at work on my diary. "I'm afraid it's bad for you."

I don't let her read these pages if I can help it, but I

need her services so often that she must have some notion of what is in them. Perhaps before long I'll be having her prepare the ink.

"Even if it hurts a little, writing is a diversion for me. If it hurts too much I'll stop, but for the present I'm better off keeping busy. You can leave now."

At 1 p.m. I lay down for a nap, and dozed about an hour. When I woke up I was drenched in perspiration.

"You'll catch cold," Miss Saski said, coming in to change my sweat-soaked cotton underwear. I felt unpleasantly sticky on my forehead and around my neck.

"Dolosin is all right, but I can't stand this heavy sweating. I wonder if there isn't something else I could take."

At five Dr. Sugita came. Maybe the effect of the medicine had worn off, but I was beginning to have severe pain again.

"He says Dolosin makes him perspire," Miss Sasaki told Dr. Sugita.

"That's too bad," he said sympathetically. "As I've explained before, judging from the X rays most of this pain of yours is neuralgia due to physiological changes in the cervical vertebrae, although part of it seems to come from the nerve centers of the brain. The only way to correct it is to relieve the nerve pressure by traction or by a cast, and that would take three or four months. However, it's not unreasonable for a man of your age to refuse to put up with such a rigorous treatment, and in that case all we can do is give you temporary relief by medication.

There are all sorts of medicines, so if you don't like Dolosin or Nobulon let me try an injection of Parotin. This may hurt a little, but I don't think it will be too bad."

As a result of the injection I am beginning to feel slightly better.

October 1

❀

I keep on having pain in my hand, especially in the last two fingers, and gradually it's extending toward the thumb. The whole palm of my hand aches, up to the ends of the ulnar and radial bones of my forearm; I find it difficult to turn my wrist, as well as extremely painful. The numbness is worst there—it's hard to say which does more to make my wrist stiff, the numbness or the pain. I have injections of Parotin twice a day, afternoon and night.

October 2

❀

The pain continues. Miss Sasaki called Dr. Sugita and gave me an injection of Salsobrocanon.

October 4

❀

Since I don't like the Nobulon injections I tried a suppository, without much effect.

October 9

❀

For the past five days the pain has been so unrelenting that I haven't had enough energy to keep up my diary. All I did was lie in my bedroom, with Miss Sasaki constantly in attendance. Today I feel a little better, a little more like writing. Meanwhile I have tried all kinds of medication, by injection or whatever: Pyrabital, Irgapyrin, Doriden, Noctan—I had Miss Sasaki tell me the names of the drugs I've taken, but I can't possibly remember all of them. Doriden and Noctan are soporifics, not antispasmodics. Lately the pain has kept me awake, something unusual for me, and I've had to resort to various sleeping medicines. Occasionally my wife and Jokichi have come in to see how I feel.

My wife first appeared on the afternoon of the fifth, the day I had the most acute pain.

"Satsuko's been wondering if she ought to come . . ."

I didn't answer.

"So I told her there couldn't be anything wrong with that. Just to look at her would help you forget your pain, I said."

"Idiot!" I shouted, in a sudden blind rage. I knew I would be embarrassed to have Satsuko see me looking so miserable, yet to tell the truth I didn't want her to stay away.

"Oh? You'd rather she didn't?"

"Yes, and I won't have Kugako and the rest coming around here either!"

"I understand that. Only the other day I turned Kugako away, and told her to be patient—no matter how much you say it hurts, it's just your hand. She was crying, too."

"What is there to cry about?"

"And Itsuko kept saying she'd come up, till I put a stop to it. But what's wrong with Satsuko? What do you have against her?"

"You idiot! Who said I had anything against Satsuko? Far from it—I'm too fond of her! That's why I don't want to see her at a time like this."

"Oh, so that's how you feel," she said soothingly, as if she were trying to quiet a baby. "I spoke without thinking, but please don't lose your temper. It's the worst thing you could do." And she scuttled out of the room.

Obviously my wife had touched a sore spot, and I had tried to camouflage my embarrassment by getting angry. As I thought it over quietly after she was gone, I couldn't help worrying about my foolish outburst. How would Satsuko take it, when she heard? Surely she understands me too well to be offended.

"Yes," I told myself, "maybe it *is* best to see her. If I watch for the chance to make some kind of approach . . ."

This afternoon I happened to think of one. My hand was certain to ache for the next few nights—I was almost looking forward to it—and I would call in Satsuko when the pain was at its height. "Satsuko! Satsuko!" I would scream tearfully, like a child. "Help! It hurts!" That would startle her, and she would come in. I wonder if the old man is in earnest, she would think cautiously; you never know what he's scheming. And yet she would come in, pretending to be frightened. "Satsuko's the only one I need!" I would shriek, to chase Miss Sasaki out of the room. "I don't need anybody else!" Then how would I start, once we were alone together?

"All right, Father, tell me what you want. Go ahead— I'll do whatever you say!" Nothing would suit me better, but she isn't likely to fall into that trap. Still, there must be a way to persuade her.

"If you give me a kiss, I'll forget the pain!" . . . "Just on your leg won't do!" . . . "Even plain necking won't do!" . . . "I won't be satisfied without a real kiss!"

Suppose I beg and whimper like that, and then set up a howl. Won't she have to give in? I think I'll try it soon. I said "when the pain was at its height," but I can sham it, I needn't actually be in pain. Only, I'd like to shave first. After almost a week in bed I have quite a growth of whiskers. Perhaps that is more effective in a way, since it makes me look like such an invalid, but a bristly face is no advantage when it comes to kissing. Anyway, I'll take out my false teeth. And I'll keep my mouth as clean and fresh as possible. . . .

Again this evening the pain has stolen up on me. I can't write anymore—I'll lay aside my brush and call Miss Sasaki.

October 10

❁

I had a .5 cc. injection of Irgapyrin. For the first time in days it made me dizzy. The ceiling went round and round, a single beam turned into two or three. It lasted for about five minutes, and left me feeling a heavy pressure at the base of my skull. I took half a grain of Luminal and went to sleep.

October 11

❁

The pain was about the same as yesterday. Today I tried a Nobulon suppository.

October 12

❁

I took three tablets of Dolosin. As usual I was drenched with sweat.

October 13

❀

This morning I am enjoying a little relief, so I'll hurry to set down what happened last night.

At 8 p.m. Jokichi dropped in.

"Feeling any better today?"

"Better? I'm steadily getting worse."

"You're all neat and shaved, aren't you?"

The fact is, my hand hurts so much it's hard to use a razor, though I did manage to shave that morning.

"Shaving isn't easy for me. But if I let my beard get too long I look even more like an invalid."

"Couldn't you have Satsuko give you a shave?"

What made that rascal suggest such a thing? Were his suspicions aroused the moment he noticed I was shaved? From the very beginning he has insisted that Satsuko be treated as "the young mistress" of our house— a natural attempt to compensate for her background— with the result that she is more spoiled than ever. To be sure, I am partly to blame for it, but Jokichi himself, in spite of being her husband, has always seemed deferential to her. I don't know how it is when the two of them are alone, but he makes a point of behaving that way in front of others. Even if I *am* his father, would he really want his precious wife to perform such a menial task for me?

"I'd rather not have a woman touch my face," I told him, at the same time thinking that if I leaned back in a chair to have her shave me I could probably see far up into her nostrils. That delicate transparent flesh would have a lovely coral gleam.

"Satsuko's good with an electric razor! I've had her shave me when I was sick."

"Really? Satsuko will do it for you?"

"Of course! What's strange about that?"

"I didn't think she would be so obedient."

"Have her shave you, or do anything you want. I'll speak to her myself."

"I wonder. That's what you tell me, but would you actually give Satsuko an order like that? To do anything your father says?"

"Don't worry, I'll take care of it!"

I have no idea what he told her, or how, but a little after ten o'clock last night Satsuko unexpectedly appeared.

"You said I shouldn't visit you, but I came because Jokichi asked me to."

"And what happened to Jokichi?"

"He's out somewhere again—just going for a drink, he said."

"I was hoping he'd bring you here and give you the order in front of me."

"He doesn't give *me* orders! It's so awkward for him he's run off—anyway, I listened to what he had to say and sent him out. I told him he'd be in the way."

"That's fine, but there's somebody else who's in the way." Miss Sasaki caught on immediately, and excused herself.

At that moment, as if on signal, the pain in my hand increased. My whole hand from wrist to fingertips got as stiff as a board, and I began to feel tingling pains here and there on both sides. It felt like ants crawling over the skin, except that it was so painful. And my hand was as cold as if I had plunged it into an icy tub of rice-bran mash, so cold it was numb, and still intensely painful. Only the sufferer himself can understand a sensation like this. Even the doctor doesn't seem to, no matter how I explain it to him.

"Satsu!" I screamed. "It hurts!" I wasn't shamming, a scream like that doesn't come out unless you're in real pain. If I had been only pretending, I could never have produced such a realistic effect. Above all, it was the first time I had called her "Satsu," so directly and intimately, and yet it was quite spontaneous. That made me extremely happy. I was happy in spite of the pain.

"Satsu, Satsu! It hurts!" Now I was whining like a spoiled child. I didn't mean to, my voice naturally took on that tone.

"Satsu, Satsu, *Satsu!*" As I called her name over and over, I burst out crying. Tears streamed down my cheeks, the snivel ran from my nose, saliva dribbled from my mouth. I really howled—it wasn't an act, the instant I screamed "Satsu" I had become a naughty, unruly child again. I howled and wept uncontrollably, by that time I couldn't suppress it if I tried. Ah, perhaps I actually had gone mad! Perhaps this was how it felt.

I howled on and on. I don't care if I *am* mad, it doesn't matter what becomes of me—such were my thoughts, but then, worse yet, they gave way to a sudden panicky fear of madness. After that it clearly became an act: I began trying to imitate a spoiled child.

"Satsu, Satsu!"

"Now stop that, Father!"

For some time Satsuko had been silent, staring a little uneasily at me, but when our eyes met she seemed to sense immediately what was going on in my mind. She leaned down and put her mouth close to my ear. "If you keep on pretending to be crazy, you soon will be!" she said in a low, mocking voice. "This ridiculous act proves you're already on the way." Her sarcasm was like a dash of cold water in my face. "Well, tell me what you're after. But I won't do anything for you as long as you're blubbering like that!"

"All right, I'll stop crying." I spoke coolly, as if nothing had happened.

"Of course you will! I'm the stubborn type, and that kind of performance only makes me more so."

I might as well cut this short. She finally got away

without kissing me. She wouldn't let our mouths quite touch—they were only a centimeter apart, and she had me open mine wide, but all she did was let a drop of saliva fall into it.

"There! That ought to satisfy you. If it doesn't you'll just have to make the best of it."

"It hurts, I tell you, it really hurts!"

"You ought to feel better now."

"It hurts!"

"You're screaming again! I'm going to get out of here, so go ahead and cry all you like."

"Listen, Satsuko, from now on let me call you 'Satsu' sometimes!"

"Silly!"

"Satsu."

"You're a spoiled deceitful child—who do you think will fall for that line?" And she left in a huff.

October 15

✿

Tonight I took .3 cc. of barbital and .3 cc. of Bromural. I have to vary my sleeping medicines now and then too, or they soon stop working. Luminal has absolutely no effect on me.

October 17

❀

Dr. Sugita had advised called Dr. Kajiura of the Tokyo University Hospital, who came this afternoon. I'm acquainted with him from his visits some years ago when I had a cerebral hemorrhage. Today he was given a detailed report of my progress since then, and shown X-ray pictures of my cervical and lumbar vertebrae.

Dr. Kajiura said that, not being an orthopedist, he couldn't properly diagnose the pain in my left hand, but was inclined to agree with what they told me at the Tora-nomon Hospital. He would take the pictures to the University and have some of his colleagues look at them, before offering a definite opinion. However, even to a nonspecialist it seemed apparent that a change had occurred in a region affecting the nerves of my left hand. Consequently, if I wouldn't put up with a plaster cast or a sliding bed or traction, nothing could be done to eliminate the pressure from my nerves, I would have to rely on the sort of temporary measures that Dr. Sugita had taken. As for medication, Parotin injections were no doubt best. Irgapyrin had undesirable side effects, and ought to be stopped.

Then he gave me an extremely thorough examination, and left with the X rays.

October 19

Dr. Sugita had a telephone call from Dr. Kajiura, who reported that the University Hospital orthopedic department's diagnosis was identical with that of the Toranomon Hospital.

At about half past eight tonight someone timidly opened my door, without knocking.

"Who is it?" I asked. There was no reply.

"Who is it?" I repeated, and this time Keisuke came stealthily into the room. He was in his night kimono.

"What are you doing up at this hour? Why did you come here?"

"Grandpa, does your hand hurt?"

"That's nothing for a child to worry about. Isn't it your bedtime by now?"

"I was already in bed! I slipped out to come see you!"

"Now, now, go back to bed! It's nothing for a child . . ." Somehow my voice choked and tears began trickling down my cheeks. They were different tears from those I had shed the other day before the child's mother. Then I had howled and wept extravagantly, but this time only a few isolated teardrops welled up in my eyes. To hide them I hastily put on my glasses, but they clouded instantly, making the situation all the worse. Even the child could tell I was weeping.

If my tears the other day had suggested madness, what of today's? This time they were quite unexpected. I have Satsuko's taste for shocking people, and I think crying is shameful for a man; yet in fact I am easily moved to tears—they come at the merest trifle. That is something I have always tried to conceal. Ever since I was young I have enjoyed playing the villain; I am constantly saying spiteful things to my wife, for instance, but as soon as she begins sniffling I lose my nerve. And so I have done my best to keep her from knowing my weakness. In other words, even though I am sentimental and given to tears— as virtuous as that may sound—my true nature is perverse and cold-hearted in the extreme. That is the kind of man I am; and still when an innocent child suddenly shows me such affection I can't keep my glasses dry.

"Cheer up, Grandpa! You'll get well soon!"

To hide my weeping I pulled the covers up over my head. What especially annoyed me was that Miss Sasaki must have noticed.

"Yes, I'll be well soon. . . . Now go upstairs to bed. . . ." That was what I was trying to say, but my voice failed. There in the pitch-black darkness under the covers the tears streamed down my cheeks as if a dam had broken. I wish he'd get out of here! I thought. Is he going to bother me all night?

About thirty minutes later, after my tears had dried, I stuck my head out of the covers. By then Keisuke was gone.

"Master Keisuke says some touching things, doesn't he?" Miss Sasaki remarked. "As little as he is, he really worries about his grandpa."

"He's too forward. I detest such impertinent little rascals."

"Oh, you don't mean that!"

"I left orders for him to be kept out of my room, and he comes sneaking in anyway. A child ought to be more obedient."

I was exasperated to think he could make me cry so easily, at my age. Surely that was unusual even for me. I wonder if it's because I'm near my death. . . .

October 21

❀

Today I had some interesting information from Miss Sasaki. She told me that yesterday afternoon at the dentist's she happened to run into a Dr. Fukushima, an orthopedic surgeon from the hospital where she used to work. They talked about twenty minutes in the waiting room. When Dr. Fukushima asked what she was doing now, she told him she was a private nurse for a certain gentleman; from that the talk led to the pain in my hand. She asked if there wasn't a good treatment other than traction, since I was getting on in years and didn't like anything as troublesome as that; and the doctor told her he thought he could recommend one.

It involves some risk, he said; it's an extremely difficult method and requires so much technical skill that few doctors would even attempt it. But he was sure he could do it safely. Evidently her patient was suffering from a condition called the shoulder-arm-neck syndrome. If the sixth cervical vertebra has been damaged, you inject Xylocaine around its lateral protuberance in order to block the sympathetic nerves at that point; once that is done, the pain in the hand is eliminated. However, since the cervical nerves run behind the main arteries of the neck it is very difficult to insert the needle properly. To injure an artery would be quite serious, and there are also innumerable capillaries running through the neck—if Xylocaine or even a little air gets into any one of them, the patient at once begins to have trouble breathing. That is why most doctors avoid this treatment, but he himself had already used it successfully on a great many patients, without a single failure, and was confident that he could do it again.

When she asked him if the whole process took very long, he said it didn't—the actual injection was over in a minute or two, and even the preliminary X rays wouldn't take more than half an hour. Since it was a matter of blocking a nerve, the pain would die out the moment the injection was complete. In just one afternoon I could be relieved of my suffering and go home cheerful. That was what he had told her—didn't I feel like trying it?

"So Dr. Fukushima is a man you can have confidence in?"

"Indeed he is! There's no question about it, when he's in the orthopedic department of that hospital! And he's a graduate of the Tokyo University medical school. I've known him for years."

"Do you suppose it's really safe? What would happen if he failed?"

"From the way he talks, I don't think there's any danger of that. But if you like I'll go to see him again and find out more about it."

"It sounds almost too good to be true."

I consulted Dr. Sugita immediately, but he seemed to have misgivings.

"Oh? I wonder if he's skillful enough to manage it. That would be quite a feat."

October 22

❁

Miss Sasaki went to ask Dr. Fukushima for more information. I can't understand all the technical details he gave her. Anyway, she said he repeated that he had been very successful with the treatment, he didn't think it was such a remarkable feat. His patients weren't especially uneasy or fearful about it either—they all had their injections willingly, felt better at once, and went home overjoyed. However, there was no harm in having an anesthetist on hand with oxygen, just in case. In other words, if the fluid or air got into the blood vessel, a tube could be immediately inserted into the trachea to provide oxygen. He had never taken this sort of precaution before, nor had anything of the kind been needed; but since the patient was a gentleman of advanced years, he could make special preparations this time. There was no reason for me to worry.

"What do you think you'd like to do, sir?" she asked. "The doctor certainly has no intention of forcing you into it. He says he'd rather you gave up the idea, if it doesn't appeal to you. Well, why don't you think it over . . ."

I keep remembering how I was reduced to tears by little Keisuke the other night, it begins to take on the significance of a bad omen. Surely the reason I cried so much was that I felt a premonition of death. Something must be wrong when a man of my nature, seemingly reckless but in fact timid and cautious, lets his nurse talk him into wanting such a dangerous injection. Perhaps I am doomed to choke to death from it.

Yet haven't I been saying I don't care when I die, haven't I long since been ready to face death? For instance, when I was told last summer that I might have cancer of the cervical vertebrae I remained quite calm, though both my wife and Miss Sasaki turned pale. It astonished me that I could feel so calm—I almost had a sense of relief, to think that my life was finally coming to an end. So isn't this injection a good chance to test my luck? If I lose, what is there to regret? The way my hand tortures me day and night I don't even enjoy looking at Satsuko, and she treats me like a tiresome invalid. Why should I want to drag out this kind of existence? When I think of Satsuko I feel like gambling on the slightest chance to *live* again. Anything else is meaningless.

October 23

❀

The pain continues. I tried Doriden and almost dozed off, but soon found myself as wide awake as ever. Then I had an injection of Salsobrocanon.

I woke up around six o'clock and once more began to think about the risk of dying.

I am not in the least afraid of death, and yet to be confronted with it, to feel it pressing in on me—the very thought is terrifying. I wish I could die as if I were falling asleep, so gently that no one would realize when it happened. And I would like to die in this same room, lying peacefully in my usual bed, surrounded by my family. (No, it might be better not to have them there, especially Satsuko; I'd probably begin to cry again as I said goodbye to her, and Satsuko herself might feel obliged to show a few tears. Somehow that would make dying even harder. When I am dying I hope she will coldly forget about me and rush off to a boxing match, or jump into the pool and practice water ballet—ah, unless I stay alive till next summer I'll never see her swim!)

I don't like the idea of being taken to a bed in a strange hospital, surrounded by strange doctors, however eminent, and treated with exaggerated concern by orthopedic surgeon, anesthetist, radiologist, and the like, while I am on the verge of suffocating to death. That tense atmosphere alone might kill me. How would it feel to breathe with difficulty, begin to gasp and pant, gradually losing consciousness, and have a tube inserted in my windpipe? I'm not afraid of death, but I'd rather be spared the suffering and strain and terror.

No doubt at the last moment my accumulated bad deeds of the past seventy years will appear before me one after another, like the scenes projected on the outer cylinder of one of those old revolving lanterns. I can hear a voice berating me for my sins and exclaiming how impudent I am to want to die peacefully—"It's only natural for you to suffer this way, it serves you right!" I'd better give up that injection after all. . . .

Today is Sunday. It's cloudy and drizzling. Wearily I discussed the matter with Miss Sasaki again.

"Well, suppose I go to see Dr. Kajiura at the University tomorrow," she said. "I'll tell him everything Dr. Fukushima had to say, and ask for his opinion. Then you can have the injection or not, depending on his advice. How would that be?"

And so I have agreed.

October 24

Miss Sasaki returned in the evening. According to her report, Dr. Kajiura said he was not acquainted with Dr. Fukushima, and moreover felt reluctant to offer an opinion on a treatment outside his own field. However, a man with a Tokyo University medical degree and on the staff of that hospital ought to be trustworthy—certainly he wasn't a quack. He would be sure to take every precaution, so why not trust him and let him do it?

I had secretly counted on Dr. Kajiura's disapproval, which would have been a great relief to me. But now there was no way out, clearly I couldn't escape my fate. Yet as such thoughts ran through my mind I still kept trying to find some excuse for giving up the injection. Meanwhile the date was set.

October 25

❀

"I heard about it from Miss Sasaki, but do you think it's safe?" My wife seemed anxious. "I'm sure you'll get well in time, without doing anything like that."

"It won't kill me even if he fails."

"Maybe not, but I couldn't bear to see you faint away as if you'd die any minute!"

"I might as well die as go on suffering like this," I declared tragically.

"When are you having it?"

"The people at the hospital say to come whenever I like. But the sooner I get it over the better, so I'm going tomorrow."

"Oh dear! You're always in such a hurry! Just wait a minute." She went out, and came back immediately with a fortune-telling almanac. "Tomorrow is a bad day, and the day after is even worse. But the twenty-eighth is lucky—make it the twenty-eighth!"

"How can you be so superstitious? The earlier the better, no matter if it's one of the worst days!" Of course I knew she would object.

"No, please make it the twenty-eighth, and I'll come along too."

"You don't have to come."

"But I want to."

Even Miss Sasaki said she would feel relieved if I postponed it.

October 27

This is one of those "worst days." According to the almanac it's unlucky for moving, opening a shop, or whatever. Tomorrow I go to the hospital at 2 p.m., with my wife, Miss Sasaki, and Dr. Sugita, and I'm due to have the injection at 3:00. As it happened, I began to be in severe pain early this morning too, so I've had an injection of Pyrabital. The pain was severe again this evening. I had a Nobulon suppository, and later an injection of Opystan. It's the first time I've used this drug—they say it's a kind of opiate, though not morphine. Fortunately the pain eased and I slept well. During the next few days I won't be able to write, so I'll consult Miss Sasaki's record and make the entries later.

October 28

Woke up at 6 a.m. At last the fateful day. My heart was beating fast, and I felt agitated. Since I was told to remain as quiet as possible, I stayed in bed. I had lunch as well as breakfast here. Miss Sasaki laughed when I told her I wanted Chinese meat cakes.

"If you have that much appetite there's nothing to worry about!" she said. Of course I didn't really mean it, I was only trying to seem in good spirits. For lunch I had a glass of rich milk, a slice of toast, a Spanish omelette, a Delicious apple, a cup of tea. I thought I might see Satsuko if I got up and went to the dining room, but Miss Sasaki said I shouldn't, and I didn't insist on it. Afterward I took a half-hour nap, though naturally I couldn't sleep well.

Dr. Sugita arrived at one-thirty. He gave me a brief examination and took my blood pressure. We left at two.

I sat between the doctor and my wife, with Miss Sasaki next to the chauffeur. Just as our car was ready to leave, Satsuko's Hillman came driving out.

"Father!" Satsuko stopped her car and called to me. "Where are you going?"

"Oh, just to the hospital for an injection. I'll be about an hour."

"Mother's going too?"

"She thinks she may have stomach cancer, so she wants to be examined. It's only her nerves!"

"Of course it is!"

"But Satsu," I began, and then corrected myself. "Satsuko, where are *you* off to?"

"The movies—you'll have to excuse me today." I suddenly recalled that Haruhisa hadn't turned up for some time, now that the shower season was over.

"What are you seeing?"

"Chaplin in *The Great Dictator*."

The Hillman left ahead of us, and was soon out of sight.

Satsuko wasn't supposed to be told my plans for today, but no doubt my wife or Miss Sasaki had informed her. Probably she was playing innocent, and waited to leave at this time so that she could cheer me up. My wife may even have asked her to do that. Anyway, it was nice to get a look at her. She's an expert at putting on an act, and went dashing off in her usual confident way. . . . I feel a lump in my throat, to think that all this may have been due to my wife's concern for me.

We arrived at the hospital on time, and I was taken immediately to a room that had a card on its door bearing my name: "Mr. Utsugi Tokusuke." Apparently I had been formally admitted to the hospital for this one day. Then I was put in a wheelchair and rolled down a long concrete corridor to the X-ray room. Dr. Sugita, Nurse Sasaki, and my wife all came along. My wife is such a slow walker that she was panting from trying to keep up with me.

I had come in Japanese dress, thinking it would be less trouble. With my wife's help they stripped me naked, after which they laid me down on a smooth hard wooden platform and had me assume various postures. Overhead a kind of large box camera descended from the ceiling, and was adjusted precisely to the position of my body. Since they were manipulating a large, complicated apparatus from a distance and had to be accurate within a millimeter, it took a long time to bring the camera down properly on the target. The platform was rather cold, since we are in late October, and my hand was still aching. Perhaps because of the unusual tension neither the cold nor the pain bothered me.

Pictures were taken of my back and neck from all sorts of angles—first as I lay on my left side, then on my right, then prone—and each time the camera had to be readjusted before I was asked to hold my breath again. It was much the same as that day at the Toranomon Hospital.

I was taken back to my room and helped on to the bed. The developed X rays were brought in while the film was still wet. After examining them carefully, Dr. Fukushima announced that he would proceed with the injection. He was already holding an injector filled with Xylocaine.

"Please come over here," he said. "That will make things easier."

"Very well." I got out of bed and walked across the room as firmly and confidently as I could, to stand facing him by the window.

"Now we're ready for the injection. You needn't be afraid, there won't be any special pain."

"I'm not afraid. Please go ahead."

"That's fine."

I could feel the needle being inserted into my neck. So this is all there is to it, I thought. No pain whatever. I'm sure I didn't blanch, I wasn't even trembling. I could tell I had remained calm; although I was ready to face death, it didn't seem as if I was going to die. Dr. Fukushima drew the needle out again to examine it before giving the actual injection, to make sure there was no bleeding. That is standard practice in all kinds of injections, even of vitamins, to guard against inserting the fluid into a blood vessel. A careful doctor always takes that precaution, and of course Dr. Fukushima had done so in a case as serious as this.

But suddenly he seemed disconcerted. "That won't do!" he said. "Something's wrong—I've never touched a blood vessel in all the times I've given this injection, but look here, you see the blood? I must have pierced a capillary."

"Then will you try it again?"

"Not till tomorrow. I'm sorry to ask you to make another trip, but tomorrow there won't be any trouble. This is the first time it's ever happened."

Somehow I felt relieved to have my fate postponed. Saved for today! I thought gratefully. But I also felt like getting it over with right now, whether I lived or died, instead of waiting till tomorrow.

"He's entirely too cautious," Miss Sasaki whispered. "Couldn't he go ahead even if there *was* a little blood?"

"No, that's all to his credit," Dr. Sugita said. "Anybody would want to finish it up, after calling in an anesthetist and making all those other preparations; it isn't easy to stop at the sight of a mere drop of blood. The fact that he did shows he has the spirit of a really fine doctor. All doctors should have that spirit. I've learned a lot from this."

I made another appointment and immediately left for home. Even in the car Dr. Sugita couldn't stop praising Dr. Fukushima's attitude, and Miss Sasaki kept repeating that he ought to have gone ahead. In the end they agreed that overcautiousness was the trouble: he shouldn't have let himself get nervous, worrying so much about the preliminaries.

My wife wanted me to give up the whole idea. "Poking around an artery is too dangerous!" she said. "I've been against it from the beginning."

Apparently we got home before Satsuko. Keisuke was playing with Leslie in front of the kennel.

I had supper in my bedroom too, and was told to rest. My hand began to hurt again.

October 29

Today I left the house at the same time as yesterday, and accompanied by the same people. Unfortunately the results were also the same. Again Dr. Fukushima pierced a blood vessel; there was blood on the needle. He seemed so dismayed, after all his scrupulous preparations, that we felt sorry for him. We discussed the matter together, and decided regretfully that under the circumstances we ought to let it go for the present. Dr. Fukushima himself didn't seem to want to try again, and risk another failure. This time I felt a genuine sense of relief.

I was home at four o'clock. There were new flowers in the alcove of my room: amaranths and chrysanthemums in a basketwork container by Rokansai. Today the Kyoto flower-arrangement teacher must have come. Had Satsuko taken special pains to be kind to her old father-in-law? Had it perhaps occurred to her that these flowers might cheer me up as I recuperated? Even the hanging scroll by Kafu had at last been replaced. Now there was a painting by Suga Tatehiko—an extremely tall, narrow picture, of a lighthouse with its beacon lamp shining. Tatehiko often adds Chinese or Japanese poems to his sketches, and this one had a poem from the Manyoshu written vertically in a single line:

> *Where is my beloved today?*
> *Does he cross distant mountains,*
> *Lonely as seaweed drifting far offshore?*

November 9

❀

It is ten days since my last visit to Dr. Fukushima, and I am finally beginning to get better, just as my wife said I would. I have been relying on Neo-Grelan and Sedes to see me through, but surprisingly enough even patent medicines are effective now. At this rate I think I can go look for a place to be buried, after all. It's been preying on my mind ever since last spring—and isn't this a good chance to make the trip to Kyoto?

November 10

❀

"As soon as you get a little better you want to go off on a trip!" my wife exclaimed. "Do you have to be in such a hurry? What if your hand begins hurting while you're on the train?"

"But it's almost well, and this is already the tenth of November—winter comes early in Kyoto, you know."

"There's no reason why you can't wait till spring, is there?"

"This isn't the kind of thing you can afford to put off! It may be the last time I'll see Kyoto."

"There you go again with such talk! . . . Who do you plan to take along?"

"I'd be lonely with just the nurse, so I think I'll have Satsuko come too." That was actually the principal object of my trip. Looking for a burial place was something of a pretext.

"Aren't you going to stay at Itsuko's house, in Nan-zenji?"

"That would be asking too much of them, since Miss

Sasaki will be along. And Satsuko says she'd rather not, she's had enough of that house."

"Anyway, if Satsuko goes there'll be another quarrel!"

"It would be fun to see them pulling each other's hair!" That made her start off on a different tack.

"Speaking of Nanzenji, the maples at the Eikando Temple must be beautiful now. I wonder how many years it is since I've been there."

"It's too early for the Eikando. This is when they're at their best at Takao, but the way my legs are I don't think I can go around viewing autumn leaves this year."

November 12

Left on the 2:30 p.m. express for Kyoto. My wife and Oshizu and Nomura saw us off. I had planned to sit by the window, with Satsuko beside me and Miss Sasaki across the aisle from her, but they said it would be drafty there once the train started moving, so I had to take the other aisle seat. Unfortunately my hand was aching rather badly. I said I was thirsty, and had the boy bring tea; then I furtively swallowed two tablets of Sedes which I had smuggled along in my pocket for just this purpose. I knew I would be in for a lot of bother if Satsuko or Miss Sasaki saw me take them. My blood pressure was 154 over 93 before leaving, but after boarding the train I could feel myself getting excited. No doubt it was because for the first time in months I had a chance to sit beside Satsuko, even if I had to put up with a third person, and because she was turned out in an odd, provocative way. (She was wearing a fairly plain suit, but her blouse was gaudy and a French-looking five-strand necklace of imitation jewels dangled down to her bosom. Although you often see similar Japanese necklaces, this one had an elaborate jewel-studded clasp, something they can't seem to imitate here.)

When my blood pressure is high I have to urinate frequently, and that makes it go even higher. It's hard to say which causes which. I went to the toilet once before Yokohama, and again before Atami, tottering down the long aisle. Miss Sasaki trembled with fear as she followed after me. I take so much time passing urine that my second visit lasted well beyond the Tanna Tunnel. As I was returning through the car I nearly fell down, and saved myself by clutching a passenger's shoulder.

"Does your blood pressure seem high?" Miss Sasaki asked when we were back in our seats, and leaned over to take my pulse. I brushed her hand aside exasperatedly.

That was repeated again and again, until we reached Kyoto at 8:30 p.m. Itsuko and her two grown sons, Kikutaro and Jeijiro, were waiting for us on the platform.

"It's so kind of you and the boys to come to the station." Satsuko was being unnaturally polite.

"Not at all, it's a pleasure for us!"

The bridge over the tracks at Kyoto Station requires a lot of troublesome climbing, and Kikutaro squatted to offer me his back. "I'll carry you up the stairs, Grandfather," he said.

"Nonsense! I'm not that feeble yet!" But I was glad to have Miss Sasaki pushing from behind. Out of sheer pride I forced myself to keep going all the way, without stopping to rest on the landing; the effort made me painfully short of breath. Everyone was watching me anxiously.

"How long will you stay this time?"

"Oh, I suppose it'll take at least a week. I'd like to spend a night at your house too, but for the present I'll be at the Kyoto Hotel."

Our suite included one room with twin beds and another with a single bed. That was what I had asked for in making reservations.

"Miss Sasaki, will you sleep in the next room? I'll share this one with Satsu." I intentionally called her "Satsu" in front of everyone. Itsuko had a strange look on her face.

"I want the other room," Satsuko objected. "Ask Miss Sasaki to sleep here, Father."

"What's wrong with sleeping in the same room with me? You've done it at home in Tokyo, haven't you?" I said that for Itsuko's benefit. "Miss Sasaki will be near if I need her, there's nothing to worry about. Please, Satsu, sleep here!"

"I wouldn't be able to smoke."

"Of course you could smoke! Go ahead and smoke all you like!"

"If I did I'd get scolded—"

"It's because he has such bad coughing spells," Miss Sasaki put in. "If you smoke around him, he'll never stop coughing and choking."

"Porter, please bring that suitcase in here." Satsuko ignored me and went briskly into the other room.

"Are you all over the trouble with your hand?" Itsuko had seemed intimidated ever since we came, but at last she managed to get in a few words.

"Certainly not! It hurts all the time."

"Really? Mother's letter said you were well."

"That's what I told her! Otherwise she wouldn't have let me come."

Satsuko reappeared after having quickly touched up her face and changed into another blouse, this time with a three-strand pearl necklace. "I'm starved, Father! Let's go to the dining room right away!"

Itsuko said she and her children had already eaten, so only the three of us sat down at the table. I ordered a bottle of Rhine wine for Satsuko. After our meal we all chatted in the lobby for about an hour.

"I can have an after-dinner cigarette, can't I?" Satsuko asked Miss Sasaki, taking her usual Kools out of her handbag. "The smoke won't be so bad here."

To my surprise she also produced a cigarette holder—

a long, slender crimson one. Her nail polish was a matching red, a deeper color than I had seen her wear before, and her lipstick was that color too. Her fingers seemed astonishingly white. Perhaps she meant to show off the contrast to Itsuko.

November 13

❀

At 10 a.m. I went to call on Itsuko and her family, along with Satsuko and Miss Sasaki. I'm told that I've been to this house before, though I find it hard to remember. I often visited them on Yoshidayama while her husband was alive, but I have scarcely seen Itsuko and her children since they moved here to the Nanzenji district.

Today Kikutaro was off at work in a department store, but Keijiro, who studies engineering at Kyoto University, was home. Satsuko said she'd be bored going around looking for a burial site with me, and would like to excuse herself; she was leaving now to go shopping downtown. In the afternoon she wanted to see the autumn leaves at Takao, but hated to do it alone—could anyone take her there? Keijiro volunteered, saying it was better than looking at graveyards. Itsuko, Miss Sasaki, and I decided to have a light lunch at the Hyotei restaurant and then drive around to several temples, beginning with Honenin. The plan was for Satsuko's party and Kikutaro to join us at an inn in Saga that evening, where we could all have dinner together.

In the distant past my ancestors seem to have been merchants in the province of Omi, not far from Kyoto; but since the last four or five generations of my family lived in Edo, and I myself was born there in the old Honjo ward, I am obviously a true Edoite—my roots go deep into the city's past, into the period before its name was changed to Tokyo. Nevertheless, I don't like the Tokyo of today. I feel more nostalgic for Kyoto, which has a kind of charm that reminds me of what Tokyo used to be. Who made Tokyo into such a miserable, chaotic city? Weren't they all boorish, country-bred politicians unaware of the good qualities of the old Tokyo? Weren't those the men who turned our beautiful canals into muddy ditches, men who never knew that whitebait swam in the Sumida River?

I suppose it doesn't matter where they put you once you're dead; still I dislike the thought of being buried in a place as unpleasant as Tokyo, a place that has lost all meaning for me. I even wish I could have the graves of my parents and grandparents moved somewhere else. As it is, they no longer lie where they were originally buried. The bones of my grandfather and grandmother have been disturbed twice: once when their temple was moved from Fukagawa to Asakusa because the whole neighborhood had become industrial, and again, after the temple burned down in the great earthquake, to the Tama Cemetery. So graves in Tokyo have to be constantly shifted to escape destruction. In that respect Kyoto is much the safest place. Anyway, our ancestors must have come from around Kyoto, and my Tokyo relatives will often be here on pleasure trips. "Oh, so this is where the old man was buried!" they will say, stopping in to burn a stick of incense before my grave. Far better than lying in alien territory like that Tama Cemetery.

"Then isn't Honenin best?" said Itsuko as we were going down the steps from Manjuin. "This temple is too out of the way, and even with Kurodani nobody would climb the hill unless they were making a special visit."

"That's what I think too."

"Honenin is right in the city now, close to the streetcar line, and when the cherries are in bloom along the canal it's quite gay; yet the moment you're in the hush of that temple compound you naturally feel calm. I'd say it's just the place for you."

"I don't like the Nichiren sect, so I wouldn't mind changing to the Pure Land. Do you suppose they'd let me have a burial place?"

"I asked the head priest about it the other day—I go there so often I'm fairly well acquainted with him. He told me he'd be glad to arrange it, you didn't have to be a Pure Land believer."

We called off our search at that point and left for the

western outskirts of the city, reaching the Saga inn long before the others. We were given a private room to rest in while we waited. Finally Kikutaro arrived, and then, after half past six, Satsuko and Keijiro.

Satsuko explained that they went back to the Kyoto Hotel in the meantime, and asked if we had been waiting long.

"Certainly we were! Why didn't you come straight here?"

"It seemed to be turning colder, so I wanted to change clothes. You ought to be careful yourself, Father."

No doubt she wanted to try out the things she bought downtown: now she had on a white blouse and a blue sweater trimmed with silver lamé. She had changed her ring too, and for some reason was wearing that notorious cat's-eye.

"Did you pick out a graveyard?"

"I've pretty well decided on the one at Honenin. It seems to be all right with the temple."

"That's fine. Well, when do we go back to Tokyo?"

"Don't be absurd! It isn't that simple—next I've got to have a long talk with the stonecutter and decide on the style of tombstone I want."

"But Father, didn't I see you poring over that book on monuments? You said you wanted a little five-ringed pagoda."

"I'm beginning to change my mind again—I'm not so sure it ought to be a pagoda."

"I haven't the least idea what it ought to be. Anyway, it has nothing to do with me."

"Oh, but it *does*, Satsu—" I hesitated, and then said: "Satsuko, it has a lot to do with you."

"How?"

"You'll soon know!"

"Anyway, I wish you'd settle it, so we can go back to Tokyo."

"Why are you in such a hurry? For a boxing match?"

"Something like that."

All the others—Itsuko, Kikutaro, Keijiro, and Miss Sasaki—were staring at the ring on her left hand. Satsuko seemed as unconcerned as ever. She was sitting with her left hand poised as if to show off the gleaming cat's-eye.

"Aunt Satsuko," Kikutaro spoke up, breaking a strained silence, "is that jewel what they call a cat's-eye?"

"That's right."

"Does a stone like that cost millions?"

"A stone like that, as you put it, costs three million yen!"

"You're pretty good, Aunt Satsuko, getting Grandfather to part with three million yen!"

"Listen, Kikutaro I wish you'd stop calling me 'aunt.' You're not a child yourself any more, and you have no right to treat me as if I were middle-aged, when there's only two or three years' difference between us."

"Then what *will* I call you? No matter how young you are, you're still my aunt, you know."

"Just say 'Satsu'—you and Keijiro both. Otherwise I won't answer you."

"That may be all right with you, Aunt Satsuko—I'm sorry, it came out again—but wouldn't Uncle Jokichi get angry?"

"Why should he? If he did, I'd get angry with *him!*"

"Maybe 'Satsu' will do for Father, but I don't know about letting my children be so familiar," said Itsuko, frowning. "Suppose they call you Satsuko instead. That sounds a little better."

I am strictly forbidden to drink, Itsuko is a poor drinker, and Miss Sasaki refused, though I think she might have liked some, but Satsuko and the two boys made a lively party of it. We didn't finish dinner until almost nine o'clock. Satsuko saw Itsuko and her family home and went back to the hotel; since it was so late, Miss Sasaki and I stayed overnight at the inn.

November 14

Up at 8 a.m. For breakfast I had a local specialty, Saga bean curd. I took some of it along to Itsuko around ten o'clock when I called for her to go visiting the Honenin. Satsuko had telephoned a Gion teahouse to invite out a few geisha friends she met last summer when she was here with Haruhisa; they were having lunch and going to the movies together, and tonight she was taking them off to a cabaret.

Itsuko introduced me to the chief priest of the Honenin, and I was immediately shown the proposed site for my grave. The temple compound was indeed quiet and secluded; even though I had been here several times before, it was astonishing to think we were within a great city. At a glance you knew there was nothing comparable in that overturned rubbish heap of a Tokyo. I am glad I settled on this place. On the way back Itsuko and I stopped for lunch at the Tankuma restaurant; we reached the hotel about two. At three o'clock the master stone-cutter of the temple came to see me, apparently having already heard from the chief priest. I talked to him in the lobby. Itsuko and Miss Sasaki were there too.

I still wasn't sure about the style of tombstone I wanted. After you're dead it hardly matters what kind of stone you're buried under, but I feel concerned all the same. Not just any stone will do. At least, I am far too cranky to be satisfied with the ordinary vulgar kind that almost everyone has nowadays: a flat, smooth rectangular block, suitably inscribed, set on a low pedestal with one hole for burning incense and another for offering water. No doubt I ought to follow the style that has been traditional in our family, but I was determined to have a five-ringed pagoda. It needn't be in a really antique style, I thought; late Kamakura would be fine. I could have one modeled after the five-ringed pagoda at the Anrakuju Temple in Fushimi, for instance, which Kawakatsu Masataro describes as "a typical monument of the transition from mid- to late-Kamakura, with its water-ring narrowing toward the bottom like a jar, the fire-ring thick at its curved edge, and a similarly characteristic shape to the air-ring, the ether-ring, and the finial." And then there was the pagoda at the Zenjoji in Uji, said to be a classic specimen of the Yoshino period, and in a style which seems to have flourished throughout the Yamato cultural region.

However, I had another notion in mind as well. Kawakatsu's book includes photographs of an extraordinarily beautiful stone Amida triad in the Sekijoji Temple in northern Kyoto: the central figure is a seated Amida Buddha, with two standing attendant Bodhisattvas, a Kannon on the right and a Seishi on the left. Although the Kannon statue has been somewhat damaged, the Seishi is in a perfect state of preservation. It has the same ornaments as the Kannon, frontal crown, jeweled streamers, heavenly robe, halo, and so on, all finely carved; a vase of jewels appears at the front of the crown, and the figure stands with its hands clasped in prayer. "One rarely sees a granite Buddhist statue of such beauty.... An inscription on the back of the central figure records that it was dedicated in the second year of the Gennin era (1225). Thus it is a valuable relic both as the oldest dated Buddhist statue in our country to have been carved from a single block of stone, including the pedestal and the halo, and as a work by means of which we can ascertain the early Kamakura Buddhist style." When I saw the illustration a new idea came to me. Might it not be possible to have Satsuko's face and figure carved on my tombstone in the manner of such a Bodhisattva, to use her as the secret model for a Kannon or Seishi? After all, I have no religious beliefs, any sort of faith will do for me; my only conceivable divinity is Satsuko. Nothing could be better than to lie buried under her image.

But the problem was how to fulfill this desire. I could conceal the identity of the model from my wife, from Jokichi, even from Satsuko herself, by seeing that the resemblance wasn't too plain, that the image gave only a vague impression of her. I could use a soft stone instead of granite, and have the figure carved in bas-relief as delicately and indistinctly as possible, so that no one else would be aware of the likeness—no one but I. Surely it could be done. However, what bothered me was that the sculptor would have to be let in on the secret. Whom should I ask? Who would undertake a job so difficult? It wasn't something for an artist of average skill, and unfortunately there isn't a single sculptor among my friends. Supposing that I had such a friend, and that my friend was extremely skillful, I wonder if he would consent willingly, once he knew the purpose of the request. Would he be glad to lend a helping hand to the realization of such a crazy, blasphemous scheme? Wouldn't he be all the more likely, the better he was, to refuse outright? (Not that I have the nerve to make such a shameless request. It would be embarrassing if he thought the old man was going out of his mind.)

After pondering the matter that long, I hit on a possible solution. Only an expert could carve a Bodhisattva in relief, but a shallow line engraving might be within the powers of an ordinary craftsman. Kawakatsu describes a work of this kind too: the "four-sided engraved stone Buddhas" of the Imamiya Shrine in the northwestern section of Kyoto. "The Buddhas of the Four Directions are engraved with a burin on the four faces of a block about two feet square of a fine-textured hard sandstone known as 'Kamo River stone.' . . . Dedicated in the second year of the Tenji era (1125), it is one of the most important early dated monuments of Buddhist sculpture in Japan." The book reproduces rubbings of these four seated Buddhas—Amida, Sakya, Yakushi, and Miroku.

In addition, Kawakatsu shows a rubbing of a Seishi Bodhisattva from an Amida triad engraved on a single stone. "As seen in another illustration, the triad represents an Amida of Salvation with attendant Bodhisattvas and is engraved on three sides of a tall natural block of hard sandstone; this side, which is the best preserved of the three, has a beautiful figure of the Bodhisattva Seishi floating to earth on a cloud. Kneeling with hands clasped in prayer, its heavenly robe fluttering in the wind, the figure creates the atmosphere of the late Heian period when the art of depicting the Amida of Salvation and his attendants was at its most flourishing." The various Buddhas all sit with crossed legs in masculine fashion, but this Seishi kneels demurely like a woman. I was particularly attracted to this Bodhisattva.

November 15

❀

(Continued.)

I don't need images on all four sides, a single Seishi Bodhisattva will be quite enough. Consequently, I don't need a square block of stone, merely one of the right thickness for carving a Bodhisattva on the front; my name and dates, and if necessary my posthumous name, can be on the back. I wish I were familiar with the technique of burin engraving. When I used to go to the temple on festival days during my childhood, I would pass a number of street stalls where amulets were sold, to the squeak of a chisel-like blade carving a child's name, age, and address on the surface of a brass amulet. That tool could produce an extremely fine line—perhaps it was a burin. If so, the work shouldn't be too difficult.

Also, it occurred to me that I could have it done without letting the engraver know the model. The first thing was to find a talented draftsman among the makers of Buddhist articles around Nara, and have him copy the kneeling Seishi Bodhisattva, somewhat after the manner of the engraved Buddhas of the Imamiya Shrine. Next I could show him photographs of Satsuko in various poses, and have him redraw the Bodhisattva so as to hint at Satsuko's face and figure. Then I could take that design to an engraver, and ask him to reproduce it on the stone. In this way I can have the kind of Bodhisattva I want, without worrying about anyone penetrating my secret. I can sleep eternally under the image of my Satsuko Bodhisattva, under the stone image of Satsuko wearing a crown, with jeweled streamers dangling on her breast, with her heavenly robe fluttering in the wind.

From three o'clock till five the stonecutter and I, with Itsuko and Miss Sasaki beside us, talked about tombstones in the hotel lobby. Of course I didn't mention Satsuko, all I did was display learnedly what I had picked up from Kawakatsu's book. Although I dazzled them with my knowledge of Heian and Kamakura pagodas, and of Buddhist sculpture, I kept my plans for a Satsuko Bodhisattva hidden deep in my heart.

"Then what kind of stone would you like, sir? The fact

is, you put even a specialist to shame, I couldn't begin to tell you what to do."

"I still can't quite make up my mind. Just now I've had a slightly different idea, so suppose I think it over two or three days and ask you to come again. I'm sorry to have kept you so long."

Itsuko left soon after the stonecutter. I went back to my room and had a massage.

After dinner I called a taxi, having suddenly decided to go out.

Miss Sasaki was alarmed, and tried to stop me. "Where can you be going at this hour? The evenings are cold now—can't you do it tomorrow?"

"It's only a little way from here. I could even walk."

"The very thought! You know how your wife warned you against getting chilled at night here."

"But I have a few things to buy. You come along too, it'll only take ten minutes or so."

Since I insisted on going, Miss Sasaki followed nervously after me. My destination was a stationer's shop on Nijo east of Kawaramachi, less than five minutes' ride from the hotel. The proprietor, an old friend of mine, was there when we arrived. After exchanging greetings, I bought a small stick of the best Chinese vermilion for two thousand yen. I spent another ten thousand yen on a superb purple-speckled Kwangtung inkstone which was said to have belonged to the late Kuwano Tetsujo, along with twenty large thick sheets of gilt-edged white Chinese paper.

"You seem to be as healthy as ever, after all these years."

"I'm anything but healthy! I've come here to find a burial place before it's too late."

"You must be joking! A man with your vigor is good for a long time yet. . . . Now is there anything else you want? Would you care to see some calligraphy?"

"As a matter of fact, there *is* something I'd like, if you happen to have it."

"What's that?"

"It may sound odd, but I'd like about a two-foot length of red lining silk and a wad of cotton wool."

"Oh? What do you plan to use it for?"

"I have to make some rubbings right away, so I need a dabber."

"I see. For a dabber, is it? Well, there must be something like that around. I'll ask my wife to look."

A few minutes later his wife came out of the living quarters at the back with a piece of red silk and some cotton wadding.

"Will these do?"

"Fine, fine. Now I can go ahead immediately. How much do I owe you?"

"Nothing. You can have all you want."

By this time Miss Sasaki seemed utterly bewildered.

"All right, I'm finished. Let's go back."

I got into the car at once, and we returned to the hotel. Satsuko was still out.

November 16

❀

I was supposed to spend all day today resting at the hotel. Since leaving Tokyo I have been more active than usual, besides taking the trouble to keep up my diary, so it's true that I've needed a rest; furthermore, I had promised Miss Sasaki the day off. This is her first trip to the Kyoto region, a trip she has been looking forward to, and she said she would like a free day to go sightseeing in Nara. For reasons of my own I chose to let her have today, and made a point of sending Itsuko along as her guide.

That is to say, I urged Itsuko to take this chance for an outing, since she hadn't been to Nara in a long time. Itsuko tends to be retiring, and didn't go out much even when her husband was alive. "At least you ought to go see the Nara temples," I told her, "especially now that I'm trying to make my mind up about a new family tomb. You're sure to learn something helpful." I hired a car for the day, and told them to make good use of it. "Stop at the Byodoin in Uji on your way to Nara," I said. "It'll be pretty hard to cover so much ground in one day, but if you leave early in the morning and take along a box lunch—rice cakes with *hamo*, for instance—you can finish the Tōdaiji by noon, eat your lunch at the tea stall in front of the Great Buddha, and after that go around to the Shin-Yakushiji, the Lotus Temple west of the city, and the Yakushiji. The days are short now; you ought to do your sight-seeing while the light holds out, and then have dinner at the Nara Hotel before coming back to Kyoto. I won't expect you till late. You needn't worry about me, Satsuko says she'll stay in all day long."

At 7:00 this morning Itsuko arrived with the car to call for Miss Sasaki.

"Hello, Father," she said. "You always wake up early, don't you?" She untied her cloth parcel and put two packets wrapped in bamboo sheaths on the night table. "I got some rice cakes with *hamo* yesterday, so I brought a few along for you and Satsuko. You can have them for breakfast."

"That's kind of you."

"Isn't there anything you'd like from Nara? How about the local pastry?"

"I don't need any presents, but be sure to look at the Buddha's Footprint Stone when you go to the Yakushiji!"

"The Buddha's Footprint Stone?"

"That's right. It's a stone carved with the imprint of Sakya's feet. One of his miraculous powers was to walk four inches above the ground, and leave behind impressions of the wheel markings that were on his soles. The insects he walked over were spared all harm for seven days. You find these carved stone footprints in China and Korea too; here in Japan we have one at the Yakushiji Temple in Nara. Don't miss it."

"I certainly won't. Well then, we'll be on our way. I'll take good care of Miss Sasaki—and please don't tire yourself, Father."

"Good morning." Satsuko came in from the next room, rubbing her eyes sleepily.

"It's a shame getting you up so early and disturbing your sleep like this," Miss Sasaki apologized. "I'm much obliged to you for today." Still thanking her effusively, she left with Itsuko.

Satsuko had on a quilted blue robe over a negligee, and matching blue satin slippers with a pink floral pattern. She was carrying her pillow; ignoring Miss Sasaki's bed, she dropped down on the sofa, pulled an old tartan lap robe of mine over her legs, and composed herself to go back to sleep. She lay there with her eyes closed, her nose pointed straight at the ceiling, paying no attention at all to me. I'm not sure whether she was still sleepy from being out late at the cabaret last night or just shamming so that I wouldn't bore her with my conversation.

I got out of bed, washed, ordered green tea, and munched away at the rice cakes. Three were enough for breakfast. I ate quietly, trying not to disturb Satsuko's sleep. Even after I finished she was still lying there.

I took out my new inkstone and placed it on the desk;

then I poured in a little water and began slowly rubbing the stick of vermilion back and forth to make ink. I used up about half the stick. Next I tore the cotton wadding into four pieces, two larger and two smaller ones, rolled them into approximately three-inch and one-inch balls, and wrapped them in the red silk to make dabbers.

"Father, do you mind if I leave you for about half an hour? I want to go down to the dining room."

Apparently Satsuko had awakened while I was too busy to notice. She was sitting on the sofa with her legs tucked back, her knees showing between the skirts of the blue robe. I was reminded of the pose of that kneeling Seishi Bodhisattva.

"Why go to the dining room, with all these rice cakes to be eaten? Help yourself."

"All right, I will."

"This is the first *hamo* we've had together since that day after the Kabuki, isn't it?"

"I suppose so. . . . Father, what were you doing?"

"You mean just now?"

"Why were you making vermilion ink?"

"Don't be so inquisitive! Go on, try the *hamo*."

You never know when an odd bit of information will come in handy. When I was young I traveled through China several times, and both there and here in Japan I have seen people making rubbings. The Chinese are remarkably skillful at this craft: even outdoors on a windy day they go about their business calmly, moistening white paper, spreading it over the surface of the monument, tapping on the ink, and they produce splendid work. The Japanese proceed meticulously, nervously, with great caution, saturating dabbers of all sizes with ink or ink paste and painstakingly rubbing each fine line one after another. Sometimes black ink is used, sometimes vermilion. I particularly like vermilion rubbings.

"That *hamo* was delicious, for a change."

As Satsuko drank tea I took the opportunity to begin a casual, leisurely explanation. "These round cotton pads are called dabbers," I said.

"What are they for?"

"You soak them with black or vermilion ink, and tap them over a carved stone surface to make a rubbing. I'm very fond of making vermilion rubbings."

"But you don't have a stone here!"

"Today I won't need a stone, I'll use something else."

"What?"

"I want to ink the soles of your feet, and make a print of them on these square sheets of Chinese paper."

"What on earth for?"

"I intend to have a Buddha's Footprint Stone carved on the model of your feet, Satsu. When I'm dead my ashes will lie under that stone. That will be my nirvana."

November 17

✿

(Continued.)

At first I intended to conceal my purpose from Satsuko. I thought it best not to let even her know my latest plan: to have her footprints carved on stone in the manner of the Buddha's and to have my ashes buried under that stone, my tombstone, the tombstone of Utsugi Tokusuke. However, yesterday I had a sudden change of mind and decided to be frank with her. Why did I do that? Why did I confide in Satsuko?

One reason is that I wanted to see how she would react—the expression on her face, any change of mood. And I wanted to see how she would feel when, realizing my purpose, she gazed at the vermilion imprint of her own feet on a square of Chinese paper. She was so proud of her feet that she would surely be enraptured by the sight of their red seal stamped on white paper, as if they were the Buddha's. I wanted to see her happy face at that moment. Of course she would call it the craziest thing she ever heard of, but how happy she would be at heart!

Then after I die, which won't be long from now, she'll find herself thinking: That crazy old man is lying under these beautiful feet of mine, at this very moment I'm trampling on the buried bones of the poor old fellow. No doubt it will give her a certain pleasurable thrill, though I dare say the feeling of revulsion will be stronger. She will not easily—perhaps never—be able to efface that repulsive memory.

In this life I have been blindly in love with Satsuko, but after death, supposing I bear any malice toward her, I shall have no other means of revenge. Possibly I may not have the least will to revenge once I'm dead. Somehow I can't believe that. Although it stands to reason that the will dies with the body, there may be exceptions. For example, say that part of my will survives within her will. When she treads on my grave and feels as if she's trampling on that doting old's man bones, my spirit will still be alive, feeling the whole weight of her body, feeling pain, feeling the fine-grained velvety smoothness of the soles of her feet. Even after I'm dead I'll be aware of that. I can't believe I won't. In the same way, Satsuko will be aware of the presence of my spirit, joyfully enduring her weight. Perhaps she may even hear my charred bones rattling together, chuckling, moaning, creaking. And that would by no means occur only when she was actually stepping on my grave. At the very thought of those Buddha's Footprints modeled after her own feet she would hear my bones wailing under the stone. Between sobs I would scream: "It hurts! It hurts! ... Even though it hurts, I'm happy—I've never been more happy, I'm much, much happier than when I was alive! ... Trample harder! Harder!"

"Today I won't use a stone," I had told her. "I'll use something else."

If the idea really disgusted her she ought to have had a slightly different expression on her face. But she merely said, "What on earth for?" Even when she learned that I would have a Buddha's Footprint Stone carved on the model of her feet, and that after I died my ashes would lie under that stone, she didn't criticize me. Then I realized that Satsuko, whether or not she had any objection to my plan, at least found it intriguing.

Luckily, our suite includes an eight-mat Japanese-style parlor adjoining my bedroom. I had a boy bring two large sheets, which I spread on the floor one over the other to avoid staining the mats. At one end of the sheets I set down a tray on which I'd put the inkstone and dabbers, and at the other I placed Satsuko's pillow, which I retrieved from the sofa.

"All right, Satsu, this won't be any trouble. Just come and lie down on these sheets. I'll take care of the rest."

"I don't have to change? The ink won't get on my clothes?

"It can't possibly get on your clothes. I'm only going to ink the soles of your feet."

Satsuko did as she was told. She lay face up, her legs stretched out nicely side by side, and bent her feet back a little to give me a better view of the soles.

Now that these preparations were complete I saturated the first dabber with vermilion, after which I patted it against a second dabber to make a lighter shade. Moving her feet a few inches apart, I began carefully patting the sole of her right foot with the second dabber so as to register clearly every fine detail.

The lines between the ball of her foot and the under-arch gave me a good deal of trouble. I was especially clumsy because of the difficulty with my left hand. Although I had said the ink wouldn't get on her clothes, only the soles of her feet, I often bungled and smeared the top of her foot or the skirt of her negligee. But I was also delighted to keep wiping off and re-inking her feet. I felt tense and elated. I started over and over again with undiminished enthusiasm.

At last I finished inking both feet to my satisfaction. Then I lifted each foot up a little, one at a time, and pressed a sheet of the square paper against it from below to make an impression of the sole. But something always went wrong. I couldn't produce the kind of rubbing I wanted. All twenty squares of paper were wasted. I telephoned the stationer's and had him send over another forty squares immediately. This time I changed my method. I washed the ink off her feet completely, even between her toes, and had her sit in a chair while I lay on my back in a cramped position and dabbed the soles of her feet. Then I had her make the impression by stepping down on the paper. . . .

My original plan was to finish the work and remove all trace of it from the room before Itsuko and Miss Sasaki returned. I meant to give the stained sheets to the boy, send the dozens of rubbings to the stationer for safekeeping, and greet them as if nothing had happened. Unfortunately it didn't turn out that way. They were back by nine o'clock, much earlier than I had expected. I heard a knock, but before I could even answer, the door opened and they came in. Satsuko promptly disappeared into the bathroom. Innumerable splotches of red on white were scattered about the Japanese room. Itsuko and Miss Sasaki exchanged bewildered glances. Miss Sasaki silently went about measuring my blood pressure.

"It's 232," she announced gravely. . . .

It was around eleven o'clock this morning that I learned Satsuko had left for Tokyo without a word to me. When I didn't see her in the dining room at breakfast I thought she was still asleep as usual. By then she was already on her way to the airport! Itsuko came to my room to give me the bad news.

"When did you find out?" I asked her.

"Just now. I was going to see if I could take her out anywhere today, but the man at the desk told me Mrs. Utsugi had left by car for the Osaka airport."

"Nonsense! You must have known it before."

"That's absurd! How would I have known?"

"Stop lying, obviously you're in on it."

"Well, you're wrong. The first I heard was from the man at the front desk. It seems she told him she was going back a little early by plane, and he mustn't mention it to her father or anyone until she had time to get to the airport. I was really shocked."

"You liar! I'm sure you made her mad so that she'd leave! You and Kugako have always been good at deceiving people and stirring up trouble. It's too bad I forgot that."

"Oh, you're awful! How can you say such a thing?"

"Miss Sasaki!"

"Yes, sir."

"Don't 'Yes, sir' me! I'll bet you heard about this from Itsuko yourself—the two of you have been deceiving me! You both did your best to annoy Satsuko!"

"If that's the way you feel, I think we'd better excuse Miss Sasaki. Please go and wait in the lobby, Miss Sasaki, this is a good chance for me to tell Father a few things. If he wants to call me a liar, I'll talk just as plainly."

"His blood pressure is high, I'm afraid you'll have to be careful—"

"Yes, yes, I understand."

Then Itsuko began.

"It's absolutely not true that I treated Satsu unkindly. My guess is that she had a special reason for wanting to get back to Tokyo early. I wonder if *you* don't have an inkling of her reason, Father." She was being sarcastic in order to pick a quarrel with me.

"I'm not the only one who knows she and Haruhisa are on good terms," I answered. "She says so openly, and Jokichi knows all about it too. By now it's hardly a secret to anyone. Still, that doesn't prove they're having an affair, and nobody thinks so, either."

"Really?" Itsuko gave me a cynical smile. "I'm not sure whether I ought to mention this," she went on, "but Jokichi's attitude seems a little odd. Suppose there *was* something between Satsu and Haruhisa, wouldn't he simply close his eyes to it? I can't help suspecting he has somebody else himself, somebody besides Satsu. Of course Satsu and Haruhisa would keep quiet about it. In fact the three of them probably have an understanding—"

By then an indescribable rage and hatred had boiled up within me. I managed to restrain myself from roaring at the woman, for fear of bursting a blood vessel; nevertheless I felt a sudden attack of vertigo. Seeing my furious expression, Itsuko turned pale too.

"Stop that kind of talk. Stop it and go home." I kept my voice as low as I could, but I trembled as I spoke. Why did I get so angry? Was it because the old fox surprised me by laying bare a hitherto unsuspected secret—or by revealing something I had long been aware of but had tried to put out of my mind?

Itsuko was gone. Since I was suffering from severe pains in my back, neck, and shoulders, the result of yesterday's overexertion, as well as from lack of sleep last night, I took three tablets of Adalin and three of Atraxin, had Miss Sasaki plaster Salonpas all over the painful area, and went to bed. Still I couldn't sleep. I thought of having an injection of Luminal, but gave it up because I was afraid I might sleep too long. Instead, I decided to catch an afternoon train (I have never been on an airplane), and follow Satsuko home. A friend at the Mainichi newspaper office got a last-minute reservation for me.

Miss Sasaki begged me not to go. "You mustn't think of traveling when your blood pressure is so high!" she objected tearfully. "Please rest for at least three or four days, till we're sure it's back to normal." But I wouldn't listen to her.

Itsuko came to apologize, and said she would accompany me to Tokyo. I told her that if she did she'd have to ride in a different car, the very sight of her provoked me.

November 18

❀

I left Kyoto yesterday by the 3:02 p.m. express. Miss Sasaki and I went first class, and Itsuko second class. We reached Tokyo at nine. Satsuko, Jokichi, Kugako, and my wife were all waiting to meet us on the platform. There was also a wheelchair for me, either because they thought I would have trouble walking or because they decided I shouldn't be allowed to walk. No doubt Itsuko had taken it upon herself to arrange everything by phone.

"That's ridiculous! I'm not paralyzed!"

I fumed and fretted so much they were at their wit's end with me—until I felt a soft hand nestling in mine. The hand was Satsuko's.

"Now, Father, you'd better do as I say!"

I quieted down obediently, and the chair started moving at once. I was taken by elevator to an underground passage and began clattering down a long, dark corridor. Everyone else came trooping after me, but my chair rolled so fast they had a hard time keeping up. Eventually my wife was left so far behind that Jokichi had to go back to look for her. I was amazed at the vastness and complexity of the underground passages in Tokyo Station. We came out on the Marunouchi side, down a special corridor to the court entrance. Two automobiles were waiting. I rode in the first one with Satsuko and Miss Sasaki on either side of me. The others followed in the second car.

"Forgive me, Father. I'm sorry I left without telling you."

"I suppose you had an engagement."

"That wasn't it. Frankly, I was dead tired from humoring you all day yesterday. I simply can't bear having my feet fumbled with like that from morning till night. One day was enough to wear me out completely, so I ran away! I'm sorry." There was something studied, something unlike her usual self in her tone of voice.

"You must be tired, Father. My flight left at 12:20 and arrived here at two o'clock! It makes quite a difference to come by plane, doesn't it?" . . .

Extract from Nurse Sasaki's Report
The patient returned to Tokyo on the night of November 17th and spent the 18th and 19th mostly in bed, probably from accumulated fatigue, although he sometimes got up and went into the study to add to his diary. However, there was a crisis at 10:55 a.m. on the 20th, as described below in my nursing record.

Previously, Mrs. Satsuko Utsugi had returned home alone from Kyoto, arriving at the house about 3 p.m. on the 17th. She immediately telephoned her husband and told him she came back ahead of the old gentleman because she could not put up with his peculiar mental condition, which was going from bad to worse. Mr. and Mrs. Utsugi talked it over, and then went to consult Dr. Inoue, a psychiatrist friend of theirs, without saying anything to the older Mrs. Utsugi. The doctor gave them the opinion that the old gentleman was subject to what might be called abnormal sexual impulses: at present his condition was not serious enough for him to be considered mentally ill; it was just that he constantly needed to feel sexual desire, and in view of the fact that it helped to keep him alive you had to take that into account in your behavior toward him. He suggested that Mrs. Utsugi be especially careful to give her father-in-law gentle, kindly attention, not exciting him unnecessarily but not ignoring his wishes either. That was the only kind of therapy for him.

After the patient's return to Tokyo Mr. and Mrs. Utsugi made every effort to follow the doctor's advice.

Sunday, 20th

Clear.

8:00 a.m. Temperature, 95.9°; pulse, 78; respiration, 15; blood pressure, 132/80. General condition unchanged. Signs of bad humor in speech and behavior.

Patient went into his study after breakfast, probably to write in his diary.

10:55 a.m. Reappeared in his bedroom in a highly excited state. Seemed to be trying to say something. I helped him to his bed and had him rest. Pulse 136, tense, but not intermittent or irregular. Respiration, 23. Blood pressure, 158/92. Gestured to complain of heart palpitations and severe headache, face twisted with fear. I telephoned Dr. Sugita, but received no special instructions from him. This doctor has a habit of disregarding a nurse's observations.

11:15 a.m. Pulse, 143; respiration, 38; blood pressure, 178/100. I called Dr. Sugita for the second time but again received no instructions. Checked room temperature, lighting, and ventilation. The patient's wife is the only member of the family at his beside. Called the Toranomon Hospital and requested an oxygen tank.

11:40 a.m. Dr. Sugita arrived. I gave him a progress report. After making his examination the doctor injected an ampule of vitamin K, Contomin, and Neophylline. While Dr. Sugita was on his way out, the patient suddenly gave a loud cry and lost consciousness. Violent convulsions of the entire body, followed by extreme restlessness, with attempts to overcome restraint. Marked cyanosis of the lips and fingertips. Incontinence of urine and feces. The whole attack lasted around twelve minutes; then the patient fell into a deep sleep.

12:15 p.m. While attending her husband Mrs. Utsugi complained of dizziness, so I had her lie down in another room. She recovered in about ten minutes. Mrs. Itsuko Shiroyama has taken her mother's place at the bedside.

12:50 p.m. Patient sleeping quietly. Pulse, 80; respiration, 16. Mrs. Satsuko Utsugi has come into the sickroom.

1:15 p.m. Dr. Sugita left, after instructing me to refuse visitors.

1:35 p.m. Temperature, 98.6°; pulse, 98; respiration, 18. Occasional coughing, body dripping with cold sweat. Changed the patient's night kimono.

2:10 p.m. Dr. Koizumi, a relative, came to see the patient. I gave him a progress report.

2:40 p.m. Awakened, fully conscious. No speech impairment. Patient complained of stabbing pains extending over his face, head, and back of the neck. The pain in his left arm has disappeared since the attack. Following Dr. Koizumi's instructions, I administered one tablet of Salidone and two of Adalin. Although he recognized young Mrs. Utsugi, he closed his eyes and remained calm.

2:55 p.m. Natural urination, 110 cc., no turbidity.

8:45 p.m. Complained of extreme thirst. Mrs. Utsugi gave him 150 cc. of milk and 250 cc. of vegetable soup.

11:05 p.m. Light sleep. Patient seems to be out of danger. However, because of possible relapse I advised asking Dr. Kajiura of Tokyo University to look at him, and young Mr. Utsugi went to fetch the doctor right away, in spite of the hour.

After making his examination Dr. Kajiura said that this stroke was caused by spasms of the blood vessels of the brain, not by a cerebral hemorrhage, so there was no special need for concern. I was told to administer a 20 cc. injection of 20% glucose, with 100 mg. of vitamin B_1 and 500 mg. of vitamin C, twice a day, morning and evening, as well as two tablets of Adalin and a quarter tablet of Solven half an hour before bedtime. Dr. Kajiura gave me very detailed instructions: the main thing was for the patient to have about two weeks of rest; we should continue to refuse visitors; bathing should be put off until he was feeling fine; even after he could get out of bed he should be limited to his room at first; once his condition seemed to warrant it he could take little walks in the garden on sunny days, but he was strictly forbidden to leave home; he should avoid worrying or brooding, and keep his mind as relaxed as possible; writing his diary was absolutely prohibited.

Extract from Dr. Katsumi's Clinical Record

15 December

Clear, followed by thick haze, later clear.

Chief complaint. Attacks of angina pectoris.

History. High blood pressure for thirty years: systolic 150/200, diastolic 70/95, sometimes as high as 240. Ten years ago suffered an apoplectic stroke, resulting in minor difficulty in walking. For several years has had neuralgic pain in the left arm and especially the left hand; cold increases the pain. Had venereal disease in youth; drank heavily, but now only takes a cup or two of sake. Quit smoking in 1936.

Current case history. Almost a year ago a drop in the ST and flattening of the T wave in the cardiogram indicated possible myocardial lesion, but until recently the patient had no complaints about his heart. On 20 November an attack of severe headache, convulsions, and clouding of consciousness, diagnosed as spasms of the cerebral blood vessels by Dr. Kajiura; progress normal under prescribed treatment. On 30 November, quarelled with a daughter he dislikes, and felt mild anginal pains on the left side of his chest for about fifteen minutes; frequent similar attacks since then. A new EKG showed no significant change from last year's. On night of 2 December, after straining at stool, had violent strangulating pains in cardiac region for almost an hour; a neighborhood doctor was called in, and an EKG the next day indicated possible anteroseptal infarction of precordial leads. On night of 5 December another severe attack of about fifteen minutes, followed by frequent slight attacks daily, especially after bowel movements. Treatments have included various oral medicines, oxygen inhalation, injections of Papaverine, sedatives, etc.

On 15 December the patient was admitted to Tokyo University Hospital, Dept. of Internal Medicine, and assigned to Room A. I heard a report on the illness from Dr. Sugita, the attending physician, and from Mrs. Satsuko Utsugi, and performed a brief examination. The patient is rather corpulent; no signs of anemia or jaundice; slight edema in lower legs. Blood pressure 150/75; pulse 90, regular. No visible distention in veins of neck. Chest: faint moist rales in lower lobes of both lungs; heart not enlarged; slight systolic murmur in aortic valve. Abdomen: no palpation of the liver or spleen. Some motor disturbance said to occur in right arm and leg, but no weakening of general strength, and no evidence of abnormal reflexes. Knee-jerk reflexes weakened on both sides to the same degree.

No signs of abnormality in the cranial nerves; family members say his speech is unchanged, although the patient himself considers it somewhat impaired since his stroke. Dr. Sugita warned against his unusual sensitivity to drugs—a third or half the standard dose being highly effective, and the normal amount too strong. Mrs. Utsugi said intravenous injections should be avoided, since they had caused spasms.

16 December

Clear, occasional cloudiness.

Perhaps due to relieved anxiety after hospitalization, the patient slept well last night. Toward morning he felt several mild anginal upper chest pains of a few seconds' duration, possibly neurotic. I recommended a laxative to avoid constipation, but he was already using Bayer Istizin, which he had ordered from Germany. As a long-time sufferer from high blood pressure and neuralgia, he is very well informed about drugs—enough to give a young doctor stiff competition. He brought along so many medicines that I had only to choose among them. In case of another attack, he is to take his nitroglycerin tablets sublingually. Oxygen equipment has been placed at his bedside, as well as supplies for an immediate injection. Blood pressure 142/78; EKG about the same as on 3 December, indicating ST, T abnormality and possible anteroseptal infarction; a chest X ray showed only slight enlargement of the heart but signs of arteriosclerosis. No perceptible acceleration of blood precipitation, increase in white blood count, or elevation of SGOT value. The patient has had prostatic hypertrophy for some years, and says urination is often difficult and urine cloudy; but today's was clear, with no albumen and a trace of sugar.

18 December

Clear, later cloudy.

No severe attacks since hospitalization. Chiefly mild anginal pains in upper or left side of the chest, seldom lasting more than a few minutes. An electric heater and a propane gas stove have been provided to augment the unreliable radiator, since the cold is conducive to heart attacks, besides neuralgic pain.

20 December

Thin clouds, later clearing.

From about 8:00 to 8:30 last night suffered anginal pains from solar plexus to dorsal sternum. Soon relieved by nitroglycerin tablets and injections of a sedative and a vasodilator administered by the doctor on duty. No change in EKG. Blood pressure 156/78.

23 December

Clear, later partly cloudy.

Light attacks daily. Because of sugar in urine the patient was given a rich breakfast this morning, to check blood sugar value for diabetes.

Sunday, 25 December

Clear, with some cloudiness.

Call from hospital around 6:15 p.m., reporting attack of severe anginal pains in left side of chest lasting over ten minutes. Gave emergency instructions to the doctor on duty, and arrived at hospital by 7:00. Blood pressure 185/97, pulse 92, regular. Patient calmed down soon after sedation. Often has attacks on Sunday, perhaps from anxiety because of absence of his physician. Blood pressure tends to rise during attacks.

29 December

Clear, followed by hail and thick haze, later clear.

No severe attacks recently. Vector cardiogram confirms suspicion of anteroseptal infarction. Blood serum Wassermann negative. Tomorrow will begin use of a new vasodilator from America.

3 January 1961

Clear, then cloudy, followed by rain.

Seems to be progressing favorably, perhaps effect of new medicine. Urine now turbid, full of white blood cells.

8 January

Clear, followed by thick haze, later clear.

Patient examined by Dr. K of the Urology Department. Reported hypertrophy of the prostate and microbial infection from anuria, and advised prostatic massage and antibiotics. Slight improvement in EKG. Blood pressure 143/65.

11 January

Partly cloudy.

Increasingly severe lumbar pains for several days; and this afternoon a strangulating pain in both sides of the chest lasting about fifteen minutes. His worst attack recently. Blood pressure 176/91, pulse 87. Soon relieved by nitroglycerin tablets, vasodilator, and sedative. No change in EKG.

15 January

Fair.

Spondylosis deformans diagnosed from yesterday's X-ray. Back should be kept straight, will use a bedboard.
[omission]

3 February

Fine weather.

EKG also much improved, even slight attacks are rare. Probably soon ready for discharge.

7 February

Partly cloudy.

Left hospital in good spirits. Exceptionally warm for February. Since cold is harmful to him, we sent him home in a heated car at midafternoon. It seems there is a large stove to warm his room.

Extract from Notes by Mrs. Itsuko Shiroyama
Soon after his stroke of November 20th, Father began to suffer from angina pectoris; on December 15th he was admitted to Tokyo University Hospital. Luckily he managed to pull through, thanks to Doctor Katsumi, and was able to return home on the seventh of February. But he still isn't over his angina—even now he's occasionally bothered by a light attack and has to resort to nitroglycerin. From February through March he never set foot outside his bedroom. Miss Sasaki had stayed on to look after Mother, and with Oshizu's help has taken care of Father ever since he came home. She feeds him all his meals, helps him to the lavatory, and so on.

Since I'm not too busy in Kyoto these days I spend half the month here looking after Mother for Miss Sasaki. As soon as Father sees me it puts him in a bad temper, so I do my best to stay out of his sight. Kugako has the same problem with him. Satsuko is in a particularly delicate and difficult position. She's been trying to show him affection, as Dr. Inoue suggested, but if she is *too* affectionate, or stays at his bedside too long, he gets overexcited. Sometimes it brings on an attack. Yet unless she comes in to see him often he's sure to be disturbed about it, which makes his condition worse.

Father seems to be as much in a dilemma as Satsuko. An attack of angina can be intensely painful, and although he claims he isn't afraid of death he *is* afraid of physical agony. You can tell he is inwardly struggling to avoid being treated too intimately by Satsuko, even though he can't bear to be entirely apart from her.

I have never been upstairs to Jokichi and Satsuko's part of the house. According to Miss Sasaki, they don't share the same bedroom any more— apparently Satsuko has moved into the guest room. And I also hear that Haruhisa steals upstairs now and then.

One day when I was back in Kyoto I had an unexpected telephone call from Father, asking me to get some rubbings of Satsuko's feet he'd left with a stationer, and have the stonecutter we talked to earlier carve them on a tombstone in the manner of the Buddha's Footprint Stone. He said that Chinese records describe the footprints of the Buddha as twenty-one inches long and seven inches wide, with wheel markings on both feet. The wheels needn't be inscribed, but he wanted the design from Satsuko's feet expanded, without distorting it, to the same length. He told me to be sure it was done exactly that way.

I couldn't possibly make such a ridiculous request, so I called back and said the master stonecutter was away on a trip to Kyushu, and would reply later. After a few more days I had another call from Father, telling me to send all the rubbings to Tokyo. I did as he said.

Finally I heard from Miss Sasaki that the rubbings had arrived. She said Father pored over the dozen-odd rubbings and picked out several of the better ones, which he spent hours gazing at, one by one, as if completely enthralled. She was afraid he might get excited again, but couldn't very well forbid him that little pleasure. At least it wasn't as bad as being with Satsuko.

Around mid-April he began to go for half-hour walks in the garden, weather permitting. Usually the nurse accompanies him, but once in a while Satsuko leads him by the hand.

That was also when the garden lawn was dug up to begin construction of the pool he promised.

"Why go to all the expense?" Satsuko asked her husband. "Once it's summer, Father won't be able to come out in the sun anyway."

But Jokichi disagreed. "The old man's head is full of daydreams, just watching them work on that pool. And the children are looking forward to it too."

NAOMI

Na-o-mi. The three syllables of this name, unusual in 1920s Japan, captivate a 28-year-old engineer, who becomes infatuated with the girl so named, a teenage waitress. Drawn to her innocent demeanor, Joji is eager to whisk young Naomi away from the underbelly of postwar Tokyo and to mold her into his ideal wife. But when the two come together to indulge their shared passion for Western culture, Joji discovers that Naomi is far from being the naïve girl of his fantasies, and his passion descends into a comically helpless masochism. A literary masterpiece that helped to establish its author as Japan's greatest novelist, *Naomi* is both a hilarious story of one man's torment and a brilliant evocation of a nation's cultural confusion.

Fiction/Literature/0-375-72474-5

QUICKSAND

At once savagely funny and timorously exact in its portrayal of sexual enthrallment, *Quicksand* is a novel of erotic gamesmanship and obsession. Cultured, ingenuous, and with a touch of coquetterie, the voice is that of Sonoko Kakiuchi, an Osaka lady of good family married to a dully respectable lawyer. Sonoko has become infatuated with the beautiful art student Mitsuko—a femme fatale as seductive and corrupt as any in the history of fiction, and a deceiver so accomplished she can turn even Sonoko's husband into her accomplice.

Fiction/Literature/0-679-76022-9

THE REED CUTTER *and* CAPTAIN SHIGEMOTO'S MOTHER

In these two novellas, Tanizaki probes the translucent screen that separates idealized yearning from humiliating desire in a society of impenetrable decorum. In *The Reed Cutter*, the narrator encounters a reed cutter who tells him of going with his father to spy on the beautiful Lady Oyu, his father's secret love. In *Captain Shigemoto's Mother*, a nobleman's wife is given as a gift to her husband's rival at a drunken party, leaving behind a young son who longs intensely for his mother. Rich with literary allusion, these stories offer the experience of love as both an aesthetic pursuit and a devastating affliction.

Fiction/Literature/0-679-75791-0

SEVEN JAPANESE TALES

A beautiful blind musician exacts the ultimate sacrifice from the man who is both her disciple and her lover. A tattoo artist turns the body of an exquisite girl into a canvas of her predatory inner nature. A young man is erotically imprisoned by memories of his absent mother. In these seven stories, Tanizaki explores the territory where love becomes self-annihilation, where the contemplation of beauty gives way to fetishism, and where tradition becomes an instrument of refined cruelty.

Fiction/Short Stories/0-679-76107-1

THE MAKIOKA SISTERS

In Osaka in the years immediately before World War II, four aristocratic women try to preserve a way of life that is vanishing. Tsuruko, the eldest sister, clings obstinately to the prestige of her family name even as her husband prepares to move to Tokyo, where her name means nothing. Sachiko compromises valiantly to secure the future of her younger sisters. The unmarried Yukiko is hostage to her family's exacting standards, while the spirited Taeko rebels by flinging herself into scandalous romantic alliances. The story of the Makioka sisters is a poignant yet unsparing portrait of a family—and an entire society—sliding into the abyss of modernity.

Fiction/Literature/0-679-76164-0

SOME PREFER NETTLES

In Tokyo in the 1920s, Kaname and his wife, Misako, share a parody of a progressive Western marriage. They have long since stopped sleeping together, and Kaname sanctions his wife's liaison with another man. But at the heart of their arrangement lies a sadness that impels Kaname to take refuge in the past, in the serene rituals of the classical puppet theater—and in a growing fixation with the coquettish, doll-like O-hisa, his father-in-law's mistress. Ethereally suggestive, psychologically complex, *Some Prefer Nettles* addresses the crisis of every culture as it hurtles into modernity.

Fiction/Literature/0-679-75269-2